D0555995

ATLANTIS, series book one

ISBN: 978-0-9842575-8-4

Who Dares Wins Publishing

www.whodareswinspublishing.com

Bob Mayer is the best-selling author of 40 books. He is a West Point graduate, served in the Infantry and Special Forces (Green Berets): leading an Infantry platoon and then Battalion and then Brigade level Reconnaissance platoons; commanding an A-Team and as a Special Forces battalion operations officer; commanded a training company, and was an instructor at the JFK Special Warfare Center & School at Fort Bragg. He also served in Special Operations Western Command on a variety of classified assignments. He has been studying, practicing and teaching change, team building, leadership and communication for over thirty years.

WHO DARES WINS: THE GREEN BERET WAY TO CONQUER FEAR AND SUCCEED was just published by Pocket Books. A draft of WHO DARES WINS: THE GREEN BERET WAY TO BUILD THE WINNING A-TEAM has been completed. In the pipeline are WDW books on Leadership and Communication, Who Dares Wins is also an excellent program for small businesses and sports teams to learn how to become elite like the Green Beret A-Team.

He uses Who Dares Wins to help writers become successful authors with his Warrior Writer Program. The program is designed to help authors overcome the fears that have been holding them back in the world of publishing and succeed where others have failed. He brings a unique blend of practical Special Operations Strategies and Tactics mixed with the vision of an artist.

His books have hit the NY Times, Wall Street Journal, Publishers Weekly, USA Today and other best-seller lists. He has been published in many genres, including thriller, science fiction, suspense, romance and non-fiction. He has appeared on PBS, NPR and the Discovery Military Channel and in USA Today, The Wall Street Journal, Sports Illustrated and Army Times among other publications as an expert consultant. He has sold over 3 million books.

He is an honor graduate of the Special Forces Qualification Course, the Special Warfare Center Instructor Training Course and the Danish Royal Navy Fromandkorpset School. He is Master Parachutist/Jumpmaster Qualified and earned a Black Belt while living in the Orient and also taught martial arts. Bob earned an MA in Education. He also graduated the International Mountain Climbing School and completed 14 marathons including qualifying for the Boston Marathon.

He's spoken before over 500 groups and organizations, ranging from SWAT teams, the University of Georgia; IT teams in Silicon Valley, the CIA, Fortune 500 Company, Romance Writers of America and the Maui Writers Conference. He has written a Staff Walk for the Gettysburg Battle for the Special Warfare Center; a Special Forces Forward Operating Base Standing Operating Procedure; a Special Forces A-team Standing Operating Procedure and contributed the Maritime Operations Standing Operating Procedure.

To learn more about Bob Mayer please visit his website at www.bobmayer.org.

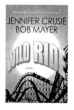

ASSAULT	15-May-10
BATTLE FOR ATLANTIS	01-June-10

Praise for ATLANTIS
"Spellbinding! Will keep you on the edge of your seat. Call it techno thriller, call it science fiction, call it just terrific storytelling." Terry Brooks

THE GREEN BERETS SERIES:

EYES OF THE HAMMER	15-June-10
DRAGON SIM-13	01-July-10
SYNBAT	15-July-10
CUT OUT	01-Aug-10
ETERNITY BASE	15-Aug-10
Z	01-Sept-10

Praise for EYES OF THE HAMMER
"A minor masterpiece of technology and suspense...a thriller that delivers in all areas—plot, suspense, authenticity and pace. Not to be missed by fans of the genre." Library Journal

Praise for SYNBAT
"Action packed entertainment...An atavistic milieu plausibly conjured up by Mayer in the latest of what now promises to be a durable series."

Praise for DRAGON SIM-13
"Fascinating, imaginative and nerve-wracking." Kirkus

Praise for CUT OUT
"An adrenaline cocktail from start to finish." Kirkus

THE NOVEL WRITERS TOOLKIT: A GUIDE TO WRITING GREAT FICTION AND GETTING IT PUBLISHED

"Something for every writer. From neophyte to old hand. My hat is off to Bob." Elizabeth George.

"An invaluable resource for beginning and seasoned writers alike. Don't miss out." Terry Brooks.

WHO DARES WINS: THE GREEN BERET WAY TO CONQUER FEAR AND SUCCEED

"Bob Mayer gives us a unique and valuable window into the shadowy world of our country's elite fighting forces and [demonstrates] how you can apply many of the concepts and strategies they use for success in your own life and organization." -Jack Canfield, creator of the Chicken Soup book series

DON'T LOOK DOWN (co-written with Jennifer Crusie)

"This first collaboration between best-selling romance writer Crusie and adventure-thriller writer Mayer is a rare delight. Mayer's delectably dry sense of humor perfectly complements Crusie's brand of sharp wit, and together the two have cooked up a sexy, sassy, and smart combination of romance and suspense that is simply irresistible." *John Charles*

ANGES AND THE HITMAN (co-written with Jennifer Crusie)

"A comic caper and raucous romance…laugh-out-loud funny…a fun ride." Kirkus Reviews

"A bubbly novel with amusing banter and surprising moments of poignancy." Publishers Weekly

Books currently available under the pen name of Robert Doherty

THE ROCK
AREA 51 (over one million copies of the Area 51 series sold)
AREA 51: THE REPLY
AREA 51: THE MISSION
AREA 51: THE SPHINX
AREA 51: THE GRAIL
AREA 51: EXCAIBUR
AREA 51: THE TRUTH
AREA 51: NOSFEERATU
AREA 51: LEGEND

PSYCHIC WARRIOR
PSYCHIC WARRIOR PROJECT AURA

SECTION 8
THE CITADEL

BODYGUARD OF LIES

Praise for Bodyguard of Lies: "Thelma and Louise go clandestine." Kirkus Reviews
"Heart-racing non-stop action that is difficult to put down." Mystery News

LOST GIRLS

Praise for Lost Girls: " . . .delivers top-notch action and adventure, creating a full cast of lethal operatives armed with all the latest weaponry. Excellent writing and well-drawn, appealing characters help make this another taut, crackling read." Publishers Weekly

ALTANTIS
series book ONE

by

Robert Doherty

PART I: THE PAST

THE DROUGHT AD 800

ANGKOR KOL KER

It was well into the first month of the wet season but not a drop of rain had fallen. Concern in the first week had turned to fear by the fourth week. As the water level of the deep moat fell, so did the will of the occupants of the capitol city. Anxiety was spreading like a sickness from person to person and mother to babe.

The city had taken the people over five hundred years to build. Within its watery protection lay all their wealth, memories and the graves of ten generations of their ancestors. It was the most advanced and beautiful city on the face of the planet.

Thousands of miles to the west, Charlemagne was being crowned Emperor of the Holy Roman Empire in the Eternal City, but this place deep in the jungles of Southeast Asia dwarfed even Rome in comparison. It was the center of kingdom extending south to abut the Srivijayan Empire of Sumatra and the Shailandra Empire of Java. To the northeast, the Tang Dynasty of China ruled, while to the west, in the Middle East, the tide of Islam was rising. The capitol city of Angkor Kol Ker, the heart of the Khmer empire, held architecture the likes of which Europe would not see for half a century. But within the empire lay a Shadow--a dark place which closed off all travel toward India and the world beyond.

The ancestors of the Khmer people had traveled halfway around the globe to avoid the shadow and for many generations they had seemingly foiled the force that had destroyed their original homeland. That place had birthed the Ones Before; the ones who knew the secrets of the Shadow. Secrets that their descendants had forgotten or remembered only as myth. But two generations ago, myth and legend reappeared in the lives of the Khmer. The Shadow had appeared in the

1

mountainous jungle to the northwest, sometimes coming close, sometimes almost disappearing, but always stopping at the water. Now the water was disappearing.

The Emperor and his advisers gazed toward the mist covered jungle beyond the evaporating moat knowing the Shadow had removed their choices as quickly as the sun took away the water. They spotted a fire from the guard tower on top of a northern mountain that poked above the mist. The fire burned for two nights, then went out and never came back.

The Emperor knew it was time. The Ones Before had written thousands of years ago of abandoning their home. He knew the cost of quitting the city. The Ones Before had chosen a hard thing to save the people. The next morning, the Emperor issued the order to evacuate the city.

Wagons were piled high, packs were placed on backs, and en masse, almost the entire population of the city crossed the lone causeway and trekked away to the south.

Fifty strong men remained. Warriors, standing tall, spears, swords and bows in hand, they had chosen to represent all the people of the Khmer. The would face the Shadow, so the city would not die alone. They destroyed the causeway and waited on the northern edge of the city, staring across at the dark mist that approached. It grew ever closer despite their prayers that the clouds would come overhead and rain would fall, filling the moats.

The men had been tested in battle numerous times. Against the Tang people to the northeast, and the people of the sea along the coast to the south, they had fought many battles and won most, expanding the kingdom of the Khmer. But the warriors of the Khmer had never invaded the jungle covered mountains to the northwest. They had never within living memory gone in that direction, nor had any intrepid traveler from the lands on the other side come through.

The warriors were brave men but even the bravest's heart quavered each morning as the mist grew closer, and the water still lower. One morning they could see the stone bottom of the moat and only puddles were left, drying under the fierce sun. The moat was over four hundred meters wide and surrounded the entire rectangle of buildings and temples, stretching four miles north and south and eight miles east and west.

Inside the moat, a high stone wall enclosed the city. Over 200,000 people had called Angkor Kol Ker home, and their absence reverberated through the city, a heavy weight on the souls of the last men. The tread of the warriors' sandals on the stone walkways echoed against the walls of the temples. Gone were the happy cries of children playing, the chants of priests, the yells of merchants in their stalls. And now even the jungle sounds were disappearing as every animal that could flee did so.

In the center of the city was the central temple, Angkor Ker. The center Prang of the temple was over five hundred feet of vertical, massive stone, a hundred feet taller than the Great Pyramid of Giza. It had taken two generations to construct and its shadow lay long over the city as the sun rose in the east, merging with the Shadow that crept closer from the west.

As the last puddle dried, tendrils of the thick mist crossed the moat. The warriors said their prayers loudly, so their voices would prove to the gathering Shadow that this was a city well loved. Angkor Kol Ker and the fifty men waited. They did not wait long.

FLIGHT 19 AD 1945
FORT LAUDERDALE AIR STATION

"Sir, I request stand-down from this afternoon's training flight."

Captain Henderson looked up from the papers on his desk. The young man standing in front of him wore starched khakis, the insignia of a corporal in the Marine Corps sewn onto the short sleeves. On his chest were campaign ribbons dating to Guadalcanal.

"You have a reason, Corporal Foreman?" Henderson asked. He didn't add that Lieutenant Presson, the leader of Training Flight 19 had just been in his office making the same request. Henderson had denied the officer's immediately, but Foreman was a different matter.

"Sir, I've got enough service points to be mustered out in the next week or so." Foreman was a large man, broad shouldered. His dark hair was swept back in thick waves, flirting with regulations, but with the war just a few months over, some rules had waned in the euphoria of victory.

"What does that have to do with the flight?" Henderson asked.

Foreman paused and his stance broke slightly from the parade rest he had assumed after saluting. "Sir, I--"

"Yes?"

"Sir, I just don't feel good. I think I might be sick."

Henderson frowned. Foreman didn't look sick. In fact his tan skin radiated health. Henderson had heard this sort of thing before, but only before combat missions, not a training flight. He looked at the ribbons on Foreman's chest, noted the Navy Cross and bit back the hasty reply that had formed on his lips.

"I need more than that," Henderson said, softening his tone.

"Sir, I have a bad feeling about this flight."

"A bad feeling?"

"Yes, sir."

Henderson let the silence stretch out.

Foreman finally went on. "I had a feeling like this before. In combat." He stopped, as if no further words were required.

Henderson leaned back in his seat, his fingers rolling his pencil end over end.

"What happened then, corporal?"

"I was on the *Enterprise*, sir. Back in February. We were scheduled to do an attack run off the coast of Japan. Destroy everything that was floating. I went on that mission."

"And?"

"My entire squadron was lost."

"Lost?"

"Yes, sir. They all disappeared."

"Disappeared?"

"Yes, sir."

"No survivors?"

"Just my plane's crew, sir."

"How did you get back?"

"My plane had engine trouble. The pilot and I had to bail out early. We were picked up by a destroyer. The rest of the squadron never came back. Not a plane. Not a man."

Henderson felt a chill tickle the bare skin below his own regulation haircut. Foreman's flat voice, and the lack of detail, bothered the captain.

"My brother was in my squadron," Foreman continued. "He never came back. I felt bad before that flight, Captain. As bad as I feel right now."

Henderson looked at the pencil in his hand. First, Lieutenant Presson with his feelings of unease and now this. Henderson's instinct was to give Foreman the same order he'd given the young aviator. But he looked at the ribbons one more time. Foreman had done his duty many times. Presson had never been under fire. Foreman was a gunner, so his presence would make no difference one way or the other. "All right, corporal, you can sit the flight out. But I want you to be in the tower and work the monitoring shift. Are you healthy enough to do that?"

Foreman snapped to attention. There was no look of relief on his face, just the same stoic Marine Corps stare. "Yes, sir."

"You're dismissed."

Lieutenant Presson tapped his compass, then pressed the intercom switch. "Give me a bearing," he asked his radio operator, seated behind him.

"This thing's going nuts, sir. Spinning in circles."

"Damn," Presson muttered. He keyed his radio. "Any of you guys have a bearing?"

The pilots of the four other TBM Avengers reported a similar problem with their compasses. Presson could sense the irritation and underlying fear in some of the voices. Flight 19 had been experiencing difficulties from take off and the other crews were in training with little flight experience.

Presson looked out of his cockpit and saw only ocean. It was a clear day with unlimited visibility.

They should have been back at the airfield by now. Two hours ago they had passed a small string of islands that he assumed had been the Florida Keys. He wasn't as sure of that assumption now. This was his first training mission out of Fort Lauderdale Air Station. He had been recently transferred from Texas, and, as he stared at his wildly

5

spinning compass, he wished he had paid more attention to their flight route.

He hadn't wanted this flight. He'd asked the Squadron Commander to replace him, but the request had been denied because Presson could give no good reason for his request. He hadn't voiced the real reason: to fly today would be a bad idea.

Well, it had been a bad idea, Presson thought to himself. And now he was beginning to question his judgment. Believing they had flown over the Keys, he'd ordered the flight to turn northeast toward the Florida Peninsula. But for the last 90 minutes, they had seen nothing but empty ocean below them. Could he have been mistaken? Could they have flown over some other islands and were they now well over the Atlantic, rather than the Gulf of Mexico like he had assumed? Where was Florida?

They had barely more than two hours of fuel left. He had to make an immediate decision whether to turn back, but now he couldn't depend on his compass for a westerly heading. He glanced at the setting sun over his shoulder and knew that west was roughly behind them, but a few degrees off either way, and *if* Florida was behind them, they could pass south of the Keys and really end up in the Gulf. But if his original assumption had been right, then Florida should be just over the horizon ahead.

Presson bit the inside of his mouth, drawing blood but the pain was unnoticed as he struggled with the problem, knowing the wrong decision would put them all in the sea. Presson ordered his radio operator to try and make contact with someone, anyone, to get a fix on their position. As he waited, Presson checked his fuel gauge, the needle now on the negative downslope toward empty, the sound of the plane's engine droning loud in his ears. He could almost sense the high octane fuel getting sucked into the carburetors and being burned, the fuel tanks growing emptier by the second.

"I've got someone," the radio operator finally reported. "Sounds like Fort Lauderdale. Coming in broken and distorted."

"Can they fix us?" Presson demanded.

"I'm asking them but I'm not sure they're receiving us clear, sir."

Thirteen lives in addition to his own weighed on Presson's mind. It should have been 14, but Corporal Foreman had been excused from the flight. Presson wondered how the corporal had managed that.

6

Presson tried to concentrate on the present. "Come on. Get me a fix!" he yelled into the intercom.

"I'm trying, sir, but I'm not receiving anything now."

Presson cursed. He once more looked out at the sea hoping to see something other than the endless water. And he did see something. A swirl of mist that had not been there seconds earlier. It was boiling out of the sky above the surface of the ocean several miles directly ahead, strangely bright in a sky that was turning dark with night. It was as if there was a glow deep within it. It was a yellowish white color with dark streaks running through, highlighted by the internal glow. It was several hundred yards across, billowing outward at a rapid rate.

At first Presson thought it might be a ship making smoke, but he had never seen such strange colored smoke produced by a ship before, nor had he ever seen smoke that was brighter than the surrounding sea. As the mist rapidly grew in size, Presson knew it was no ship. Whatever it was, it was directly across their flight path.

His instinct was to turn and fly around it, but with their compasses out, he feared he would lose the heading they were on. Of course he wasn't sure if their heading was taking them closer to land and safety or further away.

Those seconds Presson wasted on mental debate brought Flight 19 within a mile of the rapidly growing fog bank. It was now a wall in front of them, reaching their current flight altitude, growing at a rate that defied any man-made or natural phenomenon Presson had ever experienced.

Presson stared hard. The fog was swirling around its center. Inside of the glow, he could now make out a pitch black circle, darker than anything he had ever seen. It was like the center of a whirlpool, the mist spinning around, getting sucked in.

"Let's go over," Presson called out over his radio, but he got no response. He looked around. The other four planes were in formation. He pulled back on his yoke, gaining altitude, hoping they would follow his lead, but a glance to the front told him it was too late.

He hit the edge of the mist, and then he was in.

At Fort Lauderdale, Corporal Foreman had watched Flight 19 on the radar since it had taken off. After crossing some of the western islands of the Bahamas near Bimini, the flight had inexplicably turned to the northeast, heading toward open ocean. The planes had threaded a needle, passing to the south of Grand Bahama and north of Nassau with nothing but open ocean ahead, the only land within flight range being the Bahamas to the far northeast.

At first, following the flight, Foreman had not considered that overly unusual. Perhaps Lieutenant Presson had wanted to give the other new pilots some more open ocean flying time. Flight leaders had a lot of latitude in how they trained the crews under their command.

But as the flight had strayed farther from land, neither turning back or heading directly for Bahama, Foreman had finally reacted, trying to contact them by radio. Occasionally he had picked up worried calls from the pilots but he couldn't establish contact. Foreman had radioed the Flight's location to orient them but the planes had continued heading northeast, away from land, indicating the aircraft were not receiving him.

"Flight 19, this is Fort Lauderdale Air Station," Foreman said for the thirtieth time. "You are heading northeast. You must turn around now. Your location grid is--"

Foreman stopped in mid-sentence as the radar image of the flight simply disappeared. Foreman blinked, staring at his screen. They were too high to have crashed. He watched his screen while he kept calling out on the radio. With his free hand he picked up the phone and called Captain Henderson's office.

Within ten minutes Henderson and other officers were in the control tower, listening to silence play out the unknown fate of Flight 19. Foreman quickly brought them up to speed on what had transpired.

"What's their last location?" Henderson asked.

Foreman pointed at a point on the chart. "Here. Due east of the Bahamas."

Henderson picked up a phone and ordered two planes into the air to search for the missing flight. Within minutes, Foreman could see the large blips representing the two Martin Mariner searchplanes.

"What's their weather, corporal?" Henderson demanded.

"Clear and fair, sir," Foreman reported.

"No local thunderstorms?"

"Clear, sir," Foreman repeated. The men gathered in the control tower lapsed into silence, each trying to imagine what could have happened to the five planes. By now they knew the planes were down, having run out of fuel. Each man also knew that even in a calm sea, surviving a ditched TBM was a dicey proposition at best.

Less than thirty minutes into the rescue flight, the blip representing the northernmost Martin, the one closest to Flight 19's last position, abruptly disappeared off the screen.

"Sir!" Foreman called out, but Henderson had been watching over his shoulder.

"Get them on the radio!" Henderson ordered.

Foreman tried, but like Flight 19, there was no reply, although the other search plane reported in.

That was enough for Henderson. "Order the last plane back."

"Yes, sir."

Many hours later, after the mystified officers had left the control tower worried about inquest panels and careers, Foreman leaned over the chart and stared at it. He put a dot on the last location he'd had for Flight 19. Then he put a dot where the Mariner had gone down. He drew a line

between the two. Then he drew a line from each dot to Bermuda, where Flight 19's troubles had begun. He stared at the triangle he had drawn, raising his head to look toward the dark and ocean.

After being rescued eight months ago he had tried to discover what had happened to his brother and squadron mates. He'd learned that the area of ocean his squadron had gone down in was known to local Japanese fisherman as the Devil's Sea, an area of many strange disappearances. He'd even gone ashore after the surrender and traveled to one of the villages that faced that area. He'd learned from one old fisherman that they fished in the Devil's Sea, but only when their village Shaman told them it was safe to do so. How the Shaman knew that, the fisherman could not say. Today, staring out at the sea, Foreman wondered if the village shaman just got a bad feeling.

Foreman reached into his breast pocket and pulled out a photograph. It showed a family, two boys who were obviously twins and in their teens, standing in front of a large man who had a big, bushy beard, and a small woman with a bright smile, her head turned slightly, half-looking up at her husband. Foreman closed his eyes for several long minutes, then he opened them.

Foreman pulled the chart off the table and folded it up. He stuffed it into the pocket of his shirt. He walked out of the control tower and down to the beach. He stared at the water, hearing the rhythm of the ocean, his eyes trying to penetrate over the horizon, into the triangle he feared. His head was cocked, as if he were listening, as if he could hear the voices of Flight 19 and something more, something deeper and darker and older, much older.

There was danger out there, Foreman knew. More than the loss of Flight 19. He looked at the picture of his family once more, staring at his parents who had ignored the warnings of danger six years ago and had been swallowed in the inferno of Europe during the dark reign of Hitler.

He was still standing there when the light of dawn began to touch that same horizon.

WATER AND JUNGLE
1968

On one side of the world a secret aircraft capable of several times the speed of sound was leveling off at very high altitude; on the other, a nuclear submarine, the pride of the fleet and equipped with the latest technology and weapons, was letting seawater into ballast tanks as it began its descent. They were linked electronically to a point in the Middle East.

The listening station had been placed in the rugged mountains of northern Iran to monitor the southern belly of the Soviet Union, Today it had a different mission: coordinate the SR-71 Blackbird spyplane flying out of Okinawa and the USS *Scorpion*, a fast attack submarine that had been detached from normal operations in the Atlantic for this classified mission.

The man in charge of this operation wore a specially wired headset. In his left ear he could hear the relayed reports from the *Scorpion* coming up a shielded line being unreeled out of a rigging on the rear deck of the submarine, to a transmitter buoy that bounced on the waves above the sub. In his right ear, he could hear the pilot of the SR71, call sign Blackbird, directly. He used his own name, Foreman, not concerned about concealing his identity with a code name because he had no other life than his work. In the Central Intelligence Agency he had become not a legend, but more an anachronism, whispered about not in awe but as if he didn't really exist.

In front of him were three pieces of paper. One was a chart of the ocean northwest of Bermuda where the *Scorpion* was currently operating, one a map showing Southeast Asia, where the SR-71 was flying, the other a chart off the east coast of Japan. Three triangles, one highlighted in blue marker on the Atlantic chart, one in red on the Pacific chart, the last one highlighted in green on the map, were prominently outlined.

The Bermuda Triangle Gate, as Foreman preferred to call it, covered an area from Bermuda, down to Key West and across through the Bahamas to San Juan, Puerto Rico. It had not had the name

'Bermuda Triangle' when Foreman had listened to Flight 19 disappear, but with the publicity over that incident the legend had grown and some reporter had come up with the moniker for lack of a better label. Foreman wasn't interested in legends; he was interested in facts.

He called these places 'Gates' because they were doorways, of that he was convinced, but the perimeters were never stable, growing and shrinking at various rates. At times, they almost completely disappeared, at other times they reached a triangular shaped limit. While the center of each was fixed geographically, the size was more determined by time, sometimes swinging open, sometimes apparently completely shut.

The Angkor Gate's legends were more distant and faint, lying off the beaten path of modern civilization and in the midst of a country known as the world's largest minefield; the result of decades of civil and international war. It had taken Foreman many years to even begin to hear rumors of the place and many years more to determine that indeed there was another place on the planet that warranted his attention. Of more significance to Foreman was that the Angkor Gate lay on land, not hidden in the ocean. He called it Angkor Gate because of the legends surrounding that area which mentioned an ancient city in the area, Angkor Kol Ker.

As near as he had been able to determine, the Angkor Gate was in northwestern Cambodia, bounded on the north by the Dangkret Escarpment separating Cambodia from Thailand, and on the south by the floodplain of Lake Tonle Sap, the largest freshwater lake in Southwest Asia. The maximum apexes of the Angkor Gate that Foreman had so laboriously worked out over the years from various sources were all positioned so that the land inside held no roads, no cities and were roughly bounded by streams and rivers along all sides. At maximum it was considerably smaller than the largest opening of the Bermuda Triangle Gate, but held much more potential as far as Foreman was concerned not only because it was on land but also because it was more consistently "active".

The Devil's Sea Gate was named thusly because it marked the boundaries of the Devil's Sea. Since it encompassed water like the Bermuda Triangle, Foreman preferred to focus his attention on the Bermuda Triangle. There were also the reports he occasionally received of intense, covert Japanese interest in the Devil's Sea Gate area.

Somehow they were all connected and Foreman lived only to discover the true nature of what these Gates were, what was causing them and what was on the other side of the Gates.

"Clearing one thousand feet depth," the commander of the *Scorpion*, Captain Bateman, reported. "Heading nine-zero degrees. Estimated crossing of line of departure in five mikes. Status all good."

"Level at sixty thousand," the pilot of the SR-71 called in. "ETA five mikes."

Foreman didn't say anything. He had personally briefed the pilot and the captain of the *Scorpion* the previous week. He had made it abundantly clear that timing and positioning had to be exact. He looked at the large clock in the front of the listening room, watching the second hand make another circle. Then another.

"Three minutes," *Scorpion* called. "All go."

"Three minutes," Blackbird echoed in his other ear at the same time. "All clear."

Foreman looked down. A penciled-in line on the chart represented the *Scorpion's* course. He knew that three minutes out meant that the submarine was less than a half-mile from the current edge of the Bermuda Triangle Gate along the western line drawn from Bermuda to Puerto Rico. A line on the map of southeast Asia had the SR-71's flight route, and Foreman knew it was ninety miles from the green line, heading in from the south, currently passing over Lake Tonle Sap. He had waited years to do this, watching, until both Angkor and Bermuda Triangle were active to this extent at the same time.

Another circle of the second hand. "Transmitting via HF," *Scorpion* reported, indicating that the special high frequency transmitter that had been attached to the sub's

front deck the previous week was now active.

"Ah, Foreman, this is Blackbird."

Foreman sat straighter. He could sense a change in the normally laconic voice of the SR-71 pilot.

"I've got something ahead and below."

Foreman spoke for the first time. "Clarify."

"A yellow-white cloud. Maybe some kind of fog but it's growing fast."

13

"Can you go above it?" Foreman asked.

"Oh, yeah. No sweat. I've got plenty of clear sky. Entering Angkor Gate airspace now."

"We're in," Captain Bateman reported. "Still transmitting. We're getting some electric anomalies in our systems, but nothing major. Sonar reports the ocean is clear out to limits."

"How about HF?" Foreman asked, wanting to know if the SR-71 was picking up the signal from the submarine or vice versa. There was normally no way the HF signal could reach the SR-71 on the other side of the Earth. But the operative word in that sentence, as Foreman knew, was normally. There was nothing normal about either of the locations the two craft were closing on and the whole point of this exercise was to prove a link between the two Gates.

"Ah, I have a positive on the high frequency. I'm picking up *Scorpion's* HF signal."

Foreman tapped a fist against the desktop in triumph. The two Gates were most definitely connected, and in a way that was not possible using known physics.

He keyed the radio. "Captain Bateman, can you read the SR-71 HF transponder?"

"Roger. I don't know how we can, but we are. Loud and clear."

There was brief silence, then a startled yell from the pilot. "What the hell?"

Foreman was leaning forward, his eyes closed. The feeling of triumph faded.

"Blackbird," Foreman said. "What is going on?"

"Uh, this fog. I'm over it now but it's growing fast. It doesn't look right. I'm getting some electronic problems."

"Will you be clear before it reaches your altitude?" Foreman asked.

"Uh, yeah." There was a long pause. "I think so."

"What about HF from *Scorpion*?" Foreman prodded.

"Still have HF. That's strange. Yeah, it's--hey!"

There was a garble of static in Foreman's right ear. "Blackbird? Report!"

"Shit. I've got major failures here," The pilot's voice sounded distracted. "Compass out. On-board computer is going nuts. I'm--shit! There's light coming out of the cloud. Lines of light. Jesus! What the

14

hell is that? That was close. There's something dark in the very center. Shit! I'm kicking it to--" the voice broke into unintelligible static. Then silence.

Foreman pressed the transmit button. "Blackbird? Blackbird?" He didn't waste any more time, hitting his other transmit. "*Scorpion*, this is Foreman. Evacuate the area. Immediately."

"Turning," Bateman acknowledged. "But we're getting a lot of electronic interference. Some system failures. Really strange."

Foreman knew the sub would have to complete a wide turn to clear the Bermuda Triangle Gate. He also knew how long that would take. He checked the clock.

"There's something weird coming in over sonar," Bateman suddenly announced.

"Clarify!" Foreman ordered.

"Sounds almost like someone's trying to contact us via sonar," the captain of the *Scorpion* reported. "Pinging us. We're copying. Oh no!" he suddenly exclaimed. "We've got problems in the reactor."

Foreman could hear Bateman yelling orders, his hand still keeping the channel open but the mike away from his lips. Then Bateman came back. "We've got a major reactor failure. Coolant lines down. We've also got something coming this way on sonar. Something big! It wasn't there before."

Foreman leaned forward listening to the faint voices as the captain again addressed his men in the conning tower. "Jones, what the hell is it? You told me we were clear. That thing's going to be up our ass in a couple of seconds!"

"I don't know, sir! It's huge, sir. I've never seen anything that big and moving."

"Evasive action!" the captain yelled.

"Sir, the reactor's off-line," another voice was shouting in the background. "We don't--"

"Goddamnit," the captain cut the other man off. "Get us out of here, number one! Blow all tanks. Now!"

The voice of the sonar man Jones, echoed tinnily in Foreman's ear. "Sir, it's right next to us. Good God! It's huge. It's real--"

There was a crackling sound and a few more faint unintelligible yells then the sound abruptly cut off in Foreman's left ear.

Foreman leaned back in the seat. He reached into a pocket and pulled out some peanuts. He slowly cracked the shell on the first one and paused before throwing the contents into his mouth. He looked his hand. It was shaking. His stomach was shooting sharp pains. He threw the shell and peanut to the floor.

He waited one hour as agreed. Not another sound had come through either side of his headset. Finally he took it off and walked over to the radio that connected him to a man who sat on the National Security Council. He had a link between the Bermuda Triangle and Angkor Gates, but it looked like a high price had been paid to gain that information.

THE TEAM
SOUTHEAST ASIA, 1968

The jungle pressed up against the edges of the camp, a dark wall of shivering sounds and shadowy menace in the early evening light. Clear fields of fire had been cut for a hundred meters from the outer perimeter, but beyond that neither eye nor bullet could penetrate far.

"I'm so short I could play handball on the curb," the team leader told the other three men in the small hootch that served as their home. The team leader kissed his fingers, then tenderly touched the photo of a young woman that was tacked to the wall on the right side of the door. "See you soon, babe." With his other hand he pulled a CAR-15 off its peg and tucked it into his side as he strode out into the setting sun. A miniaturized version of the M-16, the metal parts of the automatic weapon had a sheen that spoke of numerous cleanings and hard use.

"I imagine Linda knows how short you really are," the second man out of the hootch said in a rumbling, deep voice to the laughter of the other two men.

"Don't be talking about my fiancee that way," the first man rejoined, but there was no threat in his voice. He paused, letting the rest of the team catch up. The team leader and oldest of the four, Sergeant First Class Ed Flaherty was twenty-eight, but a stranger would have

16

thought them all older. The war had aged their faces and their hearts, etching lines that were the physical memories of the fear, fatigue and stress. The men wore tiger stripe fatigues with no patches or nametags. Each one had a different weapon, but they all had the same look in their eyes: the haunted look of men intimate with death and violence.

This morning, Flaherty's face was creased with worry lines, befitting his position as team leader. He was tall and skinny with red hair cut tight against his skull and a green drive-on rag tied around his neck. Given the short hair, the large, flaming red mustache on his upper lip seemed incongruous. His hands were cradled around the CAR-15. Hooked by a snap link to his load bearing equipment was an M-79 grenade launcher. Flaherty liked keeping it loaded with a flechette round rather than the normal 40 mm high explosive round, in effect making the launcher a large shotgun. He had inherited it from his own team leader after his first tour of duty and he'd carried it ever since. He called the M-79 his ambush buster.

On Flaherty's back was his rucksack, a battered green pack loaded with water, ammunition, mines and food. The pack had gone with him on sixteen cross-border operations since he'd joined this specialized outfit. It was as much a part of him as the weapon in his hands.

The next senior man, Staff Sergeant James Thomas, had been on fourteen of those trips which allowed him to joke about Flaherty's fiancee with impunity. Thomas was the radioman and his ruck was larger than Flaherty's, holding the same essential supplies as well as the team radio and spare batteries. The ruck, large as it was, looked small when placed on Thomas's back. He was over six and a half feet tall and heavily muscled. His black skin was covered in sweat, even here at four thousand feet with the cool evening air swirling in. It was a running joke on Recon Team Kansas that Thomas would sweat even at the north pole. In Thomas's hands his weapon, the M-203, combination M-16 rifle and 40 mm grenade launcher, looked like a toy.

The third senior member of RT Kansas was Sergeant Eric Dane and both Flaherty and Thomas were damn glad to have him along. Dane was the team's weapon's man and carried an M-60 machine-gun, capable of spewing out over a thousand rounds of 7.62 mm ammunition per second. But it wasn't the firepower he carried that endeared Dane to his teammates' hearts; it was his ability to move stealthily on the ground in the point position and keep the rest of them from walking into ambushes. In three tours in Vietnam, Flaherty had never seen anyone as good. Already, Dane had walked them around four different ambushes, any one of which Flaherty knew would have been the end of RT Kansas.

Dane was of average height and had thick black hair. He wore army-issue glasses, the thick plastic frames marring an otherwise handsome face. He was lean and well-muscled, able to handle the twenty-two pounds of machine-gun without trouble.

Carrying the machine-gun, by conventional tactics, Dane wasn't supposed to be on point, but the firepower was outweighed by his uncanny ability. And Dane never complained, never felt it was someone else's turn to take the most dangerous place in the patrol. Since the second time 'over the fence' when he'd rotated into the position, he'd stayed there. One night when they were alone, Flaherty had talked to Dane about it, telling him they could continue rotating the dangerous position but Dane had said it was where he belonged and for that Flaherty was silently grateful. Dane was a quiet man who kept to himself, but the other two senior members of RT Kansas were as close to him as anyone had ever been.

The fourth man, Specialist Four Tormey, was new. The others didn't even know his first name. He'd been assigned to the team two days ago and the intervening time had been spent on more important things than becoming asshole buddies, such as teaching Tormey their immediate action drills. Tormey also wasn't Special Forces and that was another line between him and the older men. Tormey was an indicator of things to come. Special Forces had lost too many men in the meatgrinder of Vietnam. The people factory at Fort Bragg was only turning out a limited number of trained replacements every year. 5th Group had begun picking up volunteers like Tormey from regular infantry units in-country to replace dead or rotating members.

Tormey had seen combat but he'd never been on a mission over the fence. Tormey carried an AK-47, a weapon he must have acquired somewhere in his previous unit. Flaherty didn't mind Tormey carrying it as it's report might confuse the bad guys with their own AK-47s. Tormey was only twenty-one and his eyes were darting about,

18

searching for behavioral clues. The three older men knew how he felt, getting ready to go on his first cross-border mission, but they didn't say anything about it because they still felt that same way, no matter how many missions they had under their belt. More missions meant they were better at what they did, not less afraid.

The four men strode through knee high grass toward the landing zone where their chopper was due. They were halfway when Dane suddenly whistled and held up a fist. Flaherty and Thomas froze in place, and, after a slight hesitation, Tormey did the same.

Dane reached over his shoulder and quietly pulled a machete out of the sheath on the right side of his backpack. He edged forward, past Flaherty and Thomas, his feet moving smoothly through the grass.

The blade flashed in the setting sun as Dane swung it. Then he reached down and pulled up the four foot long body of a King Cobra snake. The head was cleanly severed.

"Jesus," Thomas said, relaxing. "How the hell did you know it was there?"

Dane just shrugged, wiping the blade on the grass, then sheathing it. "Just knew." That had been Dane's answer about sensing the ambushes. He grinned at Flaherty and offered him the snake. "Want to take it home to Linda? Make a nice belt."

Flaherty took the body and flung it away. His stomach hurt. He'd have stepped on the thing if Dane hadn't stopped him. "I'm getting too old for this shit," he muttered.

Dane cocked his head. "Chopper inbound."

"Let's go," Flaherty ordered, even though he couldn't hear the helicopter.

The terrain below was unlike any the men of RT Kansas had ever seen. It was much more rugged and emanated a sense of the primeval, of a land that didn't acknowledge time or man's preeminence in other parts of the globe. Jagged mountains thrust up from the thick green carpet of jungle, their peaks outlined against the setting sun. Rivers wound through the low ground, surrounded on either side by towering limestone cliffs or fertile riverbanks. There was little sign of mankind's intrusions below and one could well imagine the land having existed like this for millennium.

The chopper was heading northwest, and each of the four men in the cargo bay knew they had crossed the "fence," the border between Vietnam and Laos long ago.

"Any idea where we're going?" Tormey yelled, straining to be heard above the sound of the blades overheard and the turbine engines just behind the firewall their backs were resting against.

Flaherty kept his eyes oriented toward the ground, keeping track of their progress. Thomas appeared to be asleep, his head lolling on his large shoulders. Dane looked at Tormey and a half-smile creased his lips. "I don't know where we're going but I do know we're not in Kansas anymore."

It was an inside joke. Every recon team operating out of CCN, Combat Control North, MACV-SOG, Military Assistance Command Vietnam, Studies and Observation Group, was named after a state. The team leader before Flaherty had been from Kansas, and had so christened the team. Since RT Kansas had not lost a man since that name was assigned, the name stuck, everyone considering it to be good luck. Soldiers were a strangely superstitious lot; the green rag around Flaherty's throat had gone on every mission with him and he considered it his good luck talisman. Lately, though, he and Thomas had been considering Dane their good luck charm.

Flaherty glanced at Dane who returned his troubled look. Tormey had asked a good question. None of them had ever been on a mission like this. They'd simply been told to gear up and get on board the chopper. No target information, no mission briefing, nothing other than their commander bidding them farewell at the helipad at their base in Vietnam and instructing them to take orders from whoever met them at the other end. And where could the other end be now that they were over the border?

And there were no "little people," the affectionate term the American Green Berets used for the Montagnard natives who made up the other half of RT Kansas, on board. Their commander had been no more able to explain why the orders from Saigon said Americans only, as he could explain anything else about this mission. Flaherty and the other men weren't happy about leaving half their team at the forward operating base. They'd never gone on a mission before without their indigenous personnel.

The second indication of trouble had been the chopper as it came in to the landing zone at the CCN launch site. The aircraft wasn't army, that was for sure. Painted all black with no markings, Flaherty knew that it was part of Air America, the CIA's private airline. The pilots hadn't said a word to their cargo, simply taking off and heading northwest. The pilots' long hair flowing out from under their wildly painted helmets and their large mustaches indicated they were CIA or perhaps part of the Ravens, a group of Air Force officers secretly loaned to the Agency for the air war in Laos.

Dane leaned close to Flaherty. "Long Tiem," he yelled in Flaherty's ear.

The team leader nodded in agreement at Dane's guess as to their immediate destination. He'd heard of the small town and airstrip in northern Laos where the Ravens were headquartered and the CIA was coordinating its secret war. RT Kansas had been in Laos before, but much closer to the border, checking out the Ho Chi Minh Trail and calling in air strikes. They'd never been this deep nor had any other CCN team to their knowledge. He wondered why the CIA would want an American Special Forces recon team. The Agency normally hired Nungs or other oriental mercenaries for any onthe-ground work this far in, putting one of their own paramilitary personnel in charge of the indigs.

Change was in the air though, and maybe that was the reason for this strange mission. Flaherty and the other two senior men knew that the secret cross-border war into Cambodia was going to become above-board sooner or later. The word was that the NVA and VC sanctuaries in Cambodia were going to get hit, and hit hard by the US regular army and air force. Nixon was going to allow the military to cross the border and destroy the bases from which the NVA and Viet Cong had been launching their attacks all these years. This trip they assumed, might have something to do with that.

"What's your feel?" Flaherty asked Dane. Next to them, Thomas's head moved ever so slightly, his ear closer to hear the answer, belying the impression that he was sleeping.

"Not good." Dane shook his head. "Not good."

A grimace crossed Thomas's face and Flaherty felt his stomach tighten. If Dane said it wasn't good, then it wasn't.

The chopper cleared a large mountain and then swiftly descended. Flaherty could make out a landing strip next to a small town. There were numerous black painted OV-1, OV-2 and OV-10 spotter aircraft and various helicopters parked on the landing strip along with propeller driven fighter aircraft. Air America. Long Tiem as Dane had predicted.

The chopper touched down and a man on the steel grating waved for them to get off. The man wore tiger stripe pants, a black t-shirt and dark sunglasses. A pistol was strapped to his waist and a knife to his right calf. He had long, shiny blond hair and looked like he belonged on a college football field rather than in the middle of a secret war.

"This way!" he yelled, then turned his back and headed off. RT Kansas shouldered their packs and followed him into a building with walls of plywood and a corrugated tin roof.

"My name's Castle," the man said, sitting on a small field table while the team dropped its rucks and settled down into folding chairs. "I'll be leading this mission."

"And I'm Foreman," a voice came from the shadows to the left front. An older man, somewhere in his late forties, stepped forward. The most distinguishing feature that caught everyone's attention was his hair. It was pure white and combed straight back in thick waves. His face was like a hatchet, with two steely eyes set on either side of the blade of his nose. "I'm in charge of this operation."

Flaherty introduced the team but Foreman didn't seem to care what their names were. He turned to the maps mounted on the wall behind him. "Your mission is to accompany Mister Castle on a recovery mission to this location." A thin finger touched the map in northeast Cambodia, along the Mekong River. "You will take all orders from Mister Castle. Infiltration and exfiltration will be handled by air assets from this location. All communications will be to me."

Flaherty and the other men were still staring at the map. "That's Cambodia, sir," Flaherty said.

Foreman didn't answer. He reached into his pocket and pulled out several peanuts and began cracking the shells, throwing the contents in his mouth as soon as he had one open. He dropped the empty shells to the floor.

Castle cleared his throat. "I have all call signs and frequencies. It will be a simple mission. Straight in to a landing zone, move a couple of klicks to our objective and do the recovery, then a few more klicks to a pick up zone."

"What about air cover?" Flaherty asked.

"None," Foreman said, cracking another shell. "As you've noticed," he said without a trace of sarcasm, "you are going into Cambodia. Although that theater of operations will be legalized before long, it isn't legal now." Foreman shrugged. "Closer to the border, yes, we could bring in some fast-movers and claim they misread their maps, but you're going in somewhat deeper."

"What are we supposed to be recovering?" Dane asked. Flaherty was surprised as Dane rarely spoke or asked questions during mission briefings.

"An SR-71 spy plane went down over Cambodia last week," Foreman said. "Mister Castle's job is to go in and retrieve certain pieces of classified equipment from the wreckage. Castle's been fully briefed. You are simply to provide him security."

"How did the plane go down?" Flaherty asked.

"You don't have a need to know that," Foreman said.

"What about the pilot and recon officer?" Thomas asked.

"The crew is assumed to be dead," Foreman answered.

"Did they make any radio contact prior to going down?" Flaherty wanted to know.

Foreman's answer was abrupt. "No."

"How did it go down?"

"We don't know," Foreman said. "That's why you're going there. To get its black box."

"You say it went down last week. Why have we waited this long?" Flaherty asked.

"Because that's the way it worked out," Foreman said. His dead stare indicated he wanted no further questions.

"How accurate is the plot of the wreckage?" Flaherty asked.

"It's accurate," Foreman said.

"Who's the enemy?" Flaherty asked. "Do we fire up anyone we come across or do we run and hide? What are our rules of engagement?"

Cambodia was a nightmare of warring parties with shifting alliances. There were the Khmer Rouge, the Royal Cambodian Army, and of course, the North Vietnamese and Viet Cong.

"You won't make contact," Foreman said.

Flaherty stared at the CIA officer in surprise. "That's the stupidest thing I've ever heard." The team leader stood. "These men are my responsibility and I'm not about to send them out on a half-assed operation like this."

Foreman pointed at Flaherty. His voice was level and cold. "Sit down, sergeant. You will go wherever I want you to. Those are your orders and you will follow them. Clear?"

"Not clear," Flaherty said, forcing himself to calm down. "I report to CCN, MACV-SOG, not to the CIA."

Foreman reached into his breast pocket and pulled out a piece of paper. He negligently threw it at Flaherty. "No, you report to me for this mission. It's been authorized at the highest levels."

Flaherty unfolded the orders and read. Then he refolded it and started to put it in his pocket.

Foreman snapped his fingers. "Give it back."

"I'll keep this copy," Flaherty said.

Foreman's hand slid down to the pistol on his right hip. Dane was up, his pistol pointing at the CIA man's forehead.

"Whoa!" Flaherty yelled, more shocked by Dane's action than Foreman's.

"Tell your man to back off," Foreman said, his voice under tight control.

"Dane," Flaherty said, his tone indicating what he wanted.

Dane reluctantly holstered his pistol.

Foreman tapped Flaherty in the chest where he had put the copy of the orders. "You are mine for the duration of this mission. There will be no more questions. Your chopper leaves in ten minutes. Get to the landing zone."

Castle had remained still throughout the confrontation. Now he pointed to the door. "Let's go." The CIA man picked up his own rucksack and threw it over his shoulder.

Flaherty jerked his thumb and the team walked out. Flaherty felt the straps of his pack cut into his shoulders as he got close to Dane. "What's with you?"

"This is screwed," Dane said. "Foreman's lying about something and Castle is scared."

"Hell, *I'm* scared," Flaherty said.

"Castle's more scared than just going on a deep mission over the fence," Dane said.

"Maybe he's a cherry," Flaherty said.

Dane just shook his head.

Flaherty knew Foreman was full of crap but the part about Castle being scared was news.

Dane stopped and pointed. Two Nung mercenaries, powerful looking Chinese men armed to the teeth, were watching them from the edge of the landing zone, their hands moving in certain gestures toward the recon team.

"What's with them?" Flaherty asked.

"Do you wonder why they had to get us when the CIA usually uses people like them?" Dane asked.

"Yeah, I been thinking about it," Flaherty said. "But I figure now it's cause of the SR-71. Maybe they don't want anyone to know they lost one and they're keeping this American only. That's why we had to leave our little people behind."

"I've never seen Nungs afraid of anything," Dane said, "but those guys are scared. Those symbols are to ward off evil spirits."

"Oh, Christ," Flaherty muttered as they continued to the chopper. "Just what we need. Evil spirits."

"And they're not even going with us," Dane noted.

The refueled black Huey was waiting for them, its blades slowly turning. RT Kansas, along with Castle, got on board and the chopper immediately lifted, heading southwest.

Flaherty looked at his map, noting the location that Foreman had indicated the plane had gone down. It was near the Mekong river, about a hundred klicks from where the river crossed from Laos into Cambodia. The map was mass of dark green and contour lines in the area. No sign of civilization.

Flaherty glanced over at Dane. The younger man was tense, his hands holding his M-60 tightly. Flaherty didn't know how Dane knew what he did about Foreman and Castle and the Nungs, but he didn't doubt that it was the truth. Dane just knew things, like he had known about the cobra at the base camp.

Flaherty knew little about Dane, only what had been in his thin personnel folder he'd had with him when he'd signed in to CCN six months ago. Dane never got any mail and he kept mostly to himself, not joining the others when they unwound by getting shit-faced at the CCN bar in their compound. But Flaherty had instinctively liked the younger man when he'd first met him and over the months that feeling had deepened into mutual respect.

Flaherty shifted his gaze from Dane to the terrain below. They were flying high, over six thousand feet and the landscape below was bathed in bright moonlight. Flaherty oriented himself, but it was hard as fast as the chopper was flying. He had no doubt though, when they came over the Mekong. The wide river reflected the moon and he could see occasional rapids. They flew above the river for an hour, then the chopper suddenly banked and headed west.

Flaherty felt a hand on his arm. It was Castle. "No maps now," Castle said, his hand on the edge of Flaherty's map.

"Where the hell are we going?" Flaherty demanded as the Mekong disappeared to the east. "The crash site you indicated is south."

"Just do what you're told," Castle said. "We'll be in and out in twenty-four hours."

Flaherty gave up the map. He had hoped to leave this behind when he went into Special Forces: following stupid orders that could get you killed for reasons you would never know. Flaherty now knew that Castle and the CIA were playing secret games. They didn't want the team to know exactly where the SR-71 had gone down. For all Flaherty knew they might be going into China, but that would require another right turn and a long flight north.

They flew west for an hour. Flaherty had to shrug when Dane and Thomas wanted to know why they had left the Mekong so far behind. There was nothing he could do. They were under orders and they were on board a CIA bird.

Finally, Castle turned to them, holding up a finger. "One minute out. Lock and load."

Flaherty looked out. The land below was triple canopy jungle with mountains poking through here and there. There was no sign of humanity. No roads, no villages, nothing. He took a magazine of 5.56 mm ammunition out of his ammunition pouch and placed it in the well on the bottom of his CAR-15. He slapped it to make sure it was seated, then pulled the charging handle on the weapon to the rear and let it slam forward. Then he placed the weapon between his knees, muzzle pointing down. He also took a 40 mm flechette round and loaded his M-79. He watched as Dane carefully fed a 100 round belt of 7.62 mm into the M-60 machine-gun, making sure the first round was locked in place, then attaching the canvas bag holding the rest of the belt on the side of the gun, making sure it could freely feed, yet be covered. Flaherty had seen plenty of grunts carrying the belts of ammunition across their chests or over their shoulders; he'd also seen plenty of those guns jam up as the dirty rounds fed into the machine-gun. The other three members of RT Kansas all gave Flaherty a thumbs up.

The chopper slowed and then descended rapidly. Flaherty glanced forward. The pilots seemed to be arguing about something, pointing at the instrument panel. Still they went down. A small clearing on the side of a ridge line loomed ahead and below. The chopper slowed further and the pilot maneuvered them in close, touching the right skid against the side of the hill while the other one hung in the air. Castle gestured and Flaherty jumped off, the rest of the team and Castle following.

The chopper was gone just as quickly, heading back east. Flaherty knelt behind his rucksack, weapon at the ready as the sound of the aircraft slowly faded. Finally, the noise of the jungle returned. Flaherty felt what he always felt on infiltration after the friendly noise of the chopper disappeared into the distance: abandoned in Indian Country. He took comfort from the presence of Dane and Thomas. Tormey he didn't feel much about either way. The man would have to earn his place.

They were all clustered together on the steep hillside, under the cover of trees just off the clearing. Castle made a low whistle and the men gathered closer.

"We go over this ridge, then down to a river on the other side. The crash site is just across it. Then we follow the river for four klicks north, recross, and move back east about six klicks to our pick up zone."

Flaherty pulled out his compass and looked at the glowing needle. His eyes widened. The needle was spinning.

"Your compasses won't work," Castle said, noticing what the team leader was doing.

"Why not?" Flaherty asked.

"Let's get out of here," Dane said in a low voice. "This is real bad."

Flaherty reached out and grabbed the collar of Castle's t-shirt. "What's going on?"

"You were told," Castle said. "We're here to recover pieces of the SR-71." He peeled Flaherty's hands off his shirt.

"How do you know the compasses won't work?" Flaherty asked, trying to get back under control.

Castle shrugged, but he didn't quite pull off his attempt at nonchalance. "That's what the pilots were saying as we came in. Their instruments were going nuts. Maybe there's a large ore deposit nearby. I don't know."

"Call a Prairie Fire," Dane said. He hadn't even heard what Castle said. Dane was looking about, his expression extremely worried.

Flaherty rubbed his hand along the green rag tied around his neck as he considered Dane's words. Prairie Fire was the code for an emergency exfiltration to CCN headquarters. The CIA bird might have brought them here, but Flaherty's ace in the hole was that CCN took care of its own. He knew if he called in a Prairie Fire, a CCN chopper would be inbound, weather permitting. Or should be inbound. They might be so far over the fence now that CCN couldn't give authorization to fly. Hell, Flaherty cursed to himself; he didn't even know exactly where they were.

Flaherty looked at the circle of faces. Dane's fear was evident. Thomas was Thomas, his face inscrutable, but Dane's words were having an effect as the large black man was nodding in agreement to Dane's suggestion. Tormey also looked scared, but this was his first time across the fence. The issue for Flaherty was Dane. The man was solid. They'd been in firefights together and the weapons sergeant had always done his share and more.

Flaherty tapped Thomas on the arm. "Get up on the radio and call in a Prairie Fire. I want exfiltration ASAP. We can guide them in using radio direction off our set."

Castle was shocked. "You can't do that. We have to recover the black box off that SR-71."

Flaherty ignored him. "Let's get a perimeter here. Dane, there. Tormey, you cover downslope."

Castle leveled his CAR-15. "We have to go over into the valley and get to the plane."

Dane was looking at the ridge line as if he could see the valley on the other side. "You go over there and you'll never come back."

"What the hell is he talking about?" Castle demanded.

"I don't know, but I trust him," Flaherty said. He was trying to ignore the CAR15, but Castle looked ready to lose his cool.

"You're just security and pack mules to bring back the equipment," Castle said. "We've got imagery of the area. There's no sign of VC or NVA."

"Put the weapon down," Flaherty said. Dane had his M-60 trained roughly in the direction of the CIA man's stomach.

Castle reluctantly lowered the muzzle. "Foreman will have your asses," he said.

"He can have our asses," Flaherty said. Hell, he was going home in less than a week and trading in his uniform for civilian clothes. He didn't need this shit. What was Foreman going to do? Give him a dishonorable discharge?

Thomas had the team's radio out. He talked quietly into the handset for a little while, then he worked on the radio, turning dials and maneuvering the antenna.

"Damn," Thomas finally said, throwing down the handset. "I can't get diddly on FM."

"Interference?" Flaherty asked.

"Nothing I've ever seen. Like we're on the dark side of the moon. I can't even pick up Armed Forces radio and they blanket this part of the world from Vietnam to Thailand."

"Is the radio busted?" Flaherty asked.

"It's working," Thomas said with conviction. "Something's interfering, but I couldn't tell you what."

"FM Radios don't work here either," Castle said.

"The chopper pilots told you that too?" Flaherty asked.

"Yes."

"Any other piece of information you could dribble over to us?" Flaherty demanded.

Castle pointed to the west. "Our exfil bird is laid on for the PZ," Castle said. "We have to go into the valley to get there anyway. I suggest we get moving if we're going to make it on time. Since radios don't work, there's no other way out of here unless you want to walk through five hundred kilometers of unfriendly territory."

Flaherty cursed. He had no options. "Let's move. Everyone stay alert. Dane, take point."

RT Kansas moved upslope, weapons at the ready. Once they were clear of the small opening, they were under the triple canopy of the rain forest. It was pitch black with even the faint light of the moon blocked out. Dane picked his way with care, moving uphill by feel. The other men followed, keeping their eyes on the small glowing dot on the back of the man in front's field hat.

Flaherty checked the glowing face of his watch. At least dawn wasn't far off.

Then he shook the timepiece. For all he knew, it wasn't working either.

They made slow progress up the ridge. It took two hours before they reached the crest and the eastern sky was just beginning to lighten as they broke out of the jungle onto the rocky knife edge that overlooked the river valley. In that time, Flaherty confirmed that his watch had stopped working.

Flaherty looked down. He couldn't see the river, it was too dark. On the far side the land sloped up but less steeply. As near as he could tell in the moonlight, there was a broken plateau stretching as far as they could determine on the western side of the river. Dane tapped Flaherty on the shoulder, pointing to the right, where the ridge went even higher. There was something large and blocky there.

"Ruins," Dane said.

"Take ten," Flaherty said and the team slid down to their stomachs, rucks in front, weapons pointing out. It was getting light fast. Flaherty could see that Castle was doing something with his ruck, his hands hidden from sight.

"Never seen anything like that," Dane whispered, still looking at the ruin. Large stone blocks were built up into a three story structure, with apertures for guards along the top. The tower overlooked the valley. It was about thirty feet high and each side was almost forty feet long. The jungle had encroached on the stone, creepers climbing the side, but it was still an imposing structure.

"Let's check it out," Castle said.

Flaherty looked at him. "This part of the mission? Checking ruins?"

"It gives a good view of the valley," Castle said. He got to his feet and headed toward the stones, a hundred meters away.

Flaherty signaled for Thomas and Tormey to remain in place. Taking Dane with him, he followed Castle. The closer they got to the structure, the more impressive it was. The stone blocks were each about six feet high and wide. The stone was cut very smoothly. The joints were so well done that Flaherty doubted he could slide a knife edge between them. Flaherty thought of the staggering weight each stone represented and the effort required to get them to this place.

There was an entrance on the side, and Castle disappeared. Flaherty followed. Dane paused, then slowly entered. The inside was small with stone stairs wrapping around the outside wall, leading up to what had once been a wood roof but was now open. The three men took the stairs until they were at the top landing where a small, four foot wide stone ledge was built inside the outer wall, making a parapet for watchers to stand on. They view was unobstructed for many miles in all directions.

Nothing but jungle and mountains as far as the eye could see. Early morning fog was rolling down the valley below, covering the river and its banks. Castle had his rucksack out and was looking inside.

"What are you doing?" Flaherty asked.

"Repacking my load," Castle said.

ATLANTIS

Flaherty figured the CIA man had some sort of transponder locator in the ruck that told him where the SR-71 was. Why Castle wouldn't check it openly was beyond Flaherty.

Dane was staring down into the valley and at the land beyond, hidden in the early morning mist. Then he stepped back and looked at the ruins they were standing on. "This is old," he said to Flaherty, his hand resting on the parapet. "Very, very old."

"What do you think it is? A guard outpost?" Flaherty asked. He'd never seen anything like it in Vietnam or in Laos. He'd heard there were massive ruins in Cambodia, and if this lone building was any indication, that rumor was true.

Dane nodded. "A guard post. But the question is, what did it guard against?" He pointed to a large cairn in the southwest corner of the top. "Looks like that was for a signal fire. Maybe this was an early warning post against invaders." He lowered his voice, so Castle couldn't hear. "We shouldn't go down there, Ed."

"VC?" Flaherty asked. "NVA?" He could see no sign of life, but maybe Dane did.

Dane shook his head. "I don't think it's either. Just something bad, real bad." He pointed at the walls of the ruin. There were very old, faded drawings of warriors on them. The figures had spears and bows in their hands. Several were mounted on elephants. There were elongated circles in the air about them, perhaps representing the sun or moon, Flaherty guessed, except there were more than one. There were also lines drawn through every picture, some of the lines intersecting with the warriors. There were also some sort of symbols scattered about the pictures, writing, although Flaherty had never seen anything like it before. On each corner of the rampart, there was a stone sculpture of a seven headed snake, a figure Flaherty had seen at other sites in southeast Asia. He knew it had something to do with the religion in the area. The carvings bothered Flaherty and he involuntarily jerked his shoulders and stepped back.

"Weird stuff," Flaherty muttered.

"They all died," Dane said.

"Who did?" Flaherty asked.

Dane spread his hands. "The warriors who manned this post. And those they guarded. All dead. They were great once. The greatest of their time."

"Yo, Dane," Flaherty slapped his teammate on the back. "Come back to me, man."

Dane shivered. "I'm here, Ed." He tried to smile. "I don't want to be, but I'm here."

Between Castle and his mysterious rucksack, the compass and radio not working, and Dane's warnings, Flaherty was anxious to get moving to the pickup zone.

"We'll get out OK," Flaherty said to Dane, but he could tell the words were finding no purchase. Castle had finished doing whatever it was he was up to, but continued to stare toward the jungle.

"Let's go," Flaherty said to Castle.

The CIA man sealed his pack and threw it back on his shoulder.

"Can't we just move along the high ground?" Flaherty asked. "We can see everything from up here."

"We have to go down to the river," Castle said. "The crash site is on the other side. Down there."

It was lighter now, but fog still blanketed the ground below, hiding whatever was down there. It looked like the fog was lifting on this side of the river but it was just as thick on the other side.

"That's strange," Flaherty commented. He didn't like the look of the fog. It was yellowish-gray with streaks of something darker in it. He'd never seen anything like it in all his years in the field. He turned back to Castle.

"My man here," Flaherty said, pointing at Dane, "thinks we're going to get blown away if we go down there. So far he's four for four on calling ambushes. I suggest you listen to him."

"There's no VC down there," Castle said.

"I don't know what's down there," Flaherty said, "but if Dane says there's something bad, then something bad is there."

A shadow came over Castle's face. As if he were resigned, Flaherty thought with surprise. "We have to go," Castle simply said. "The quicker we get this over with, the better. This isn't negotiable. It's too late for all that. We all signed on, we do what we're paid to. There's no other way."

The three of them stood on the ancient stone rampart, each lost in their own thoughts, each realizing the truth of Castle's words. They had all taken different roads to get here, but they were here together, cogs in a machine that was not overly concerned with the quality or length of their lives.

"Let's get going then," Flaherty said, accepting that words had no real meaning here.

They rejoined the other two men and began the descent, Dane in the lead. As they left the craggy rocks behind, they again went under the blanket of green. It was dim now, despite the sun. Flaherty was used to that. No light penetrated the triple canopy unblocked. Halfway down the ridge toward the river, tendrils of fog began snaking their way through the trees until visibility was down to less than forty feet.

They pressed on. It was like walking in place, the trees and other fauna the same, the ground sloping down, the fog crowding around. Then they could hear water running, getting closer, until Dane, walking point, saw the ground drop off in front of him.

Dane halted, looking out onto the river. It was shallow and fast moving. The swirling fog occasionally parted to show the far side, a dark green line of jungle forty meters away but his vision couldn't penetrate beyond that. The fog was much thicker across there, a smear of grayish white overlaid on top of the green vegetation. But even the trees looked strange, sickly almost. It was chilly and the sweat on the men's skin met the damp air, producing goose-bumps and shivers.

Castle moved past Dane and slithered down the bank until he was knee deep in the water. He pulled a jar out of his ruck and filled it with the water, resealing the lid and putting it back in his pack.

"We have to cross," Castle said, looking up at the four men who were kneeling on the bank, the muzzles of their weapons pointing in the direction Castle wanted to go.

"What are you doing?" Flaherty demanded. The water sample bothered him.

"I'm not authorized to tell you that," Castle said.

"No, you're only authorized to get us killed," Flaherty muttered. He gestured. "Thomas and Tormey, cross with Castle. Dane and I will provide far security, then you cover us."

Thomas climbed down without a word or a look back. Tormey looked at Flaherty, then across the river and back at his team leader before he followed. Flaherty thought he had never felt the responsibility of command as sharply as the moment Tormey's face shifted to utter resignation.

Dane extended the bipod legs of the M-60 and lay down on the bank behind a log. He flipped up the butt plate and put his shoulder under it. Flaherty joined him. The other three men were moving in a triangle, Castle in the lead, Thomas on the left and Tormey on the right, ten meters between each man.

"Call them back," Dane suddenly said as the men reached the halfway point.

"What?"

"Call them back. It's an ambush!" Dane's voice was low but insistent.

Flaherty whistled and Thomas stopped, ten meters from the bank. He looked back and Flaherty gestured, indicating for him to return. Thomas hissed, catching Tormey's attention. The new man halted. Castle looked over his shoulder, irritated, then continued, reaching the far bank.

Thomas was backing up now, retracing his steps, his M-203 swinging in arcs, aimed over Castle's head. Tormey was frozen, uncertain what to do. Flaherty gritted his teeth, waiting for the explosion of firing to come out of the tree cover of the far bank and the bodies to be riddled. Castle climbed up, but nothing happened as the CIA man disappeared. He seemed to just fade from view and be swallowed up by the fog and jungle.

Flaherty blinked, but Castle was gone. If there was going to be an ambush it would have been sprung while the men were in the kill zone of the river.

"No ambush," Flaherty said.

"There's something over there," Dane insisted.

Castle suddenly reappeared on the far bank in a brief opening in the fog, angrily gesturing for them to follow.

Flaherty stood and indicated for Thomas to hold. "We have to cover Castle," Flaherty put his hand on Danes arm. "Plus he's the only one who knows where the pickup zone is."

Dane reluctantly stood and followed his team leader down the bank and into the river. They hurried through the water, linking up with Thomas and Tormey.

As they clambered up the bank, Dane suddenly grabbed Flaherty's arm. "Listen!" he insisted.

Flaherty paused and strained his ears as Thomas and Tormey got to the top of the bank. "I don't hear anything."

"The voice," Dane said.

"What voice?" Flaherty cocked his head but heard nothing.

"A warning," Dane whispered, as if he didn't want to be heard. "I've been hearing it for a while, but it's clear now. I can hear the words. We have to get out of here."

Flaherty looked ahead. Castle was nowhere to be seen. Flaherty heard nothing, the silence in the midst of the jungle as disconcerting as Dane saying he heard a voice. "Let's get Castle," Flaherty ordered, not wanting to let the CIA man further out of sight.

They climbed up. All four paused as they reached the top. Dane staggered and went to his knees, vomiting his meager breakfast. It felt as if his stomach had been turned inside out. His brain was pounding, spikes of pain crisscrossing in every direction. And still the voice was there, inside his head, telling him to turn around, to go back.

Flaherty shivered. The fog was different here. Colder and there was a smell in the air that he'd never experienced before. The air seemed to crawl across his skin and he couldn't seem to get an adequate breathful.

"You all right?" he asked Dane.

Dane shook his head. "You feel it?" he asked.

Flaherty slowly nodded. "Yeah, I feel it. What is it?"

"I don't know," Dane said, "but I've never felt anything like it before. This place is different from anywhere I've ever been. And there *is* a voice, Ed. I can hear it. It's warning me not to go forward."

Flaherty looked around. Even the jungle itself was strange. The trees and flora weren't quite right, although he couldn't put his finger on the exact differences. Dane

struggled to his feet.

"Can you move?" Flaherty asked. "Let's get Castle and get the hell out of here."

Dane nodded, but didn't say anything.

The team went into the jungle about fifty meters, the eerie quietness making each member of RT Kansas jumpy. Flaherty shivered, not so much from the cold but the feeling of the fog against his skin. It felt clammy, and he could swear he felt the molecules of moisture ripple against his skin like oil.

Then there was a sound, one that pierced through each man like an ice pick. A long, shivering scream of agony from directly ahead. The four men paused, weapons pointing in the direction of the scream. Something was crashing through the undergrowth coming toward them, hidden by the vegetation and fog. Fingers twitched on triggers and then suddenly Castle was there, staggering toward them, his left hand clamped onto his right shoulder, blood pouring between his fingers. He fell to his knees ten feet from them. He reached out, bloody hand toward the team. Four inches below his shoulder, his right arm was gone, blood pulsing out of the artery with each beat of his heart.

Then something came out of the fog behind him, freezing every member of RT Kansas in his tracks. It was a green, elliptical sphere about three feet long by two in diameter. It was moving two feet above the ground, with no apparent support. There were two, strange dark bands crisscrossing it's surface, diagonally from front to rear. The bands seemed to pulse but the men couldn't make sense of it until it reached Castle. The front tip, where the bands met, edged down toward the CIA man, who scrambled away. The tip touched Castle's left arm, held up in front of his face, and the arm exploded in a burst of muscle, blood and bone. For lack of any better comprehension, the men could now see the bands were like rows of black, sharp teeth moving at high speed on a belt. From the widest part of the elongated sphere, the thing suddenly expanded a thin sheet of green like a sail and the object slid forward, catching the remnants of Castle's left arm in the sail. Then the green folded back down, taking the flesh and blood with it.

RT Kansas finally reacted. Dane's M-60 machine-gun spewed out a line of rounds right above Castle's body into the sphere, which promptly floated back into the fog. Dane raised the muzzle and cut a swath through the undergrowth into the unseen distance. Tormey spewed an entire magazine of his AK-47 on automatic. Thomas fired off a magazine, quickly switched it out, then fired three rounds of 40 mm high explosive in three slightly different directions to their front as quickly as he could reload. Flaherty contributed his own thirty rounds of 5.56 mm from his CAR-15. Silence reigned as their weapons fell silent. There was the stench of cordite in the air and smoke from the weapons mingled with the fog.

Remarkably, Castle was still alive, crawling across the jungle floor toward the team, using his legs to push himself, leaving a thick trail of blood behind.

"What in God's name was that?" Thomas demanded, his eyes darting about, searching the jungle.

"Let's get him," Flaherty ordered. He and Dane ran forward and grabbed the CIA man by the straps of his ruck and dragged him back to where Thomas and Tormey waited.

Flaherty ripped open the aid kit. Castle was in shock. Flaherty had seen many wounded men in his tours of duty and he knew the signs. Castle's face was pale from loss of blood and he didn't have much time. Even if they had a medevac flight on standby there was no way the man would make it.

Flaherty leaned forward, putting his face just inches from Castle's. "What was that?"

Castle ever so slightly shook his head. "Angkor Kol Ker," he whispered, his eyes unfocused, the life in the them fading. "The Angkor Gate."

"What?" Flaherty looked up at Dane. "What the hell did he say?" When he turned back to Castle, he was dead.

"Angkor Kol Ker," Dane repeated. "That's what the voice said," Dane stared at the dead man in surprise.

"Let's move to--" Flaherty began, but then he paused.

There was a noise, something moving in the jungle.

"What is that?" Thomas hissed as the noise grew louder. It was closer now and whatever it was, it was big, bigger than the thing that had gotten Castle. From the sound, it was knocking trees out of the way as it moved, the sound of timber snapping like gunshots was followed by the crash of the trees to the ground.

And now there were more sounds, many objects moving unseen in the fog and jungle. Noise was all around them, but not the natural noise of the jungle; strange noises, some of them sounding almost mechanical. All the while somewhere to their left front was that incredibly large thing moving.

"We'll be sitting ducks in the river," Flaherty said, glancing over his shoulder.

"We'll be dead if we stay here," Dane said. "We have to get out of this fog. Now! Safety from these things is across the river. I know it."

Tormey screamed and the three men turned right. The newcomer's body was off the ground, quickly moving up into the first level of canopy. His body was surrounded by a golden glow that emanated from a foot wide beam extending into the fog.

Even as they brought their weapons to bear, Tormey's body was drawn back into the fog and disappeared.

"Oh fuck!" Thomas said. Then he staggered back, a look of surprise on his face as some unseen force hit him in the chest. The big man dropped his weapon, his hands to his chest, blood flowing through them. There was a neat circular hole about the size of a dime cut through the uniform into his chest.

"What's wrong?" Flaherty asked, stepping toward the radioman, then freezing as a half-dozen unbelievably long red ropes flickered out of the fog and wrapped around Thomas, dragging him toward their invisible source.

Dane fired, the M-60 rolling on his hip, the tracers disappearing in the direction of whatever was controlling the ropes. The firing jerked Flaherty out of his shock. He moved forward toward Thomas when movement to his left caught his eye. Something on four legs was bounding toward him. The image seared into his consciousness: a large serpent head with a mouth opened wide, three rows of glistening teeth, a body like that of a lion, long legs with clawed feet and at the end a tail with a scorpion's stinger.

Flaherty fired his CAR-15, the rounds slamming into the chest of the creature, slowing it, stopping it, knocking it down, black fluid flowing out of the wounds. He emptied his magazine even though the creature had stopped moving.

A beam of gold light came out of the jungle to the right of where the red ropes were dragging Thomas and hit Flaherty on his shoulder. He felt instant pain and could smell his own skin burning. He rolled forward and to his right, putting a tree between himself and the beam. The tree trunk glowed bright gold for a second, then exploded, scattering splinters across the jungle floor, peppering Flaherty's side. Flaherty rolled onto his other side and looked around.

Thomas was still screaming, feet kicking in the ground. Thomas had his knife in his hand and was hacking at one of the ropes that held him.

The muzzle of Dane's M-60 was glowing red when the weapon suddenly seized up and jammed. He threw it down and drew his pistol and fired, emptying the clip. Flaherty started again for Thomas, who had now dropped his knife and had both large hands wrapped around a tree. Flaherty tossed his CAR-15 to Dane and ran forward, unhooking the M-79 from his LBE.

Something scarlet-hued dropped down from above and Flaherty dodged it as it curled forward, reaching for him. It missed. He came to the tree, stepped to the side and fired the M-79 down the line of ropes. The flechette round spewed its deadly load, but the round seemed to have no effect. Flaherty drew a 40 mm high explosive round out of his ammo pouch and slammed it into the breach.

"Don't let it get me," Thomas pleaded

Dane was there now, firing short sustained bursts into the ropes with Flaherty's CAR-15. Flaherty fired the HE round into the fog and heard the dull thump of an explosion, muffled as if it were under sandbags.

Then the fog suddenly changed, coalescing, becoming darker, forms coming out of nothingness. Several spheres like the one that had gotten Castle floated in the darkness, rows of black teeth whirling around their forms. Flaherty and Dane went from trying to help Thomas to self-preservation, stepping back, dodging the wildly shifting and probing objects.

Thomas's hands were ripped from the tree, leaving a layer of skin and blood.

Then he was gone into the fog, his scream echoing through the jungle. The scream was cut off in mid-yell as if a dungeon door had slammed shut.

A flash of blue light came out of the mist and hit Flaherty in the chest. It expanded around his body until he was encased in a glowing, second skin. He looked at Dane who seemed to be immune for the moment from the attacking forms.

"Run!" Flaherty yelled, his voice muted. "Run, Dane."

Dane rolled left, under one of the figures, and came up to his knees. He fired the rest of the magazine in the CAR-15 along the line of the light, until it was empty. Then he drew his knife.

"No!" Flaherty screamed as he was lifted into the air. "Save yourself!" Then the team leader was being pulled rapidly through the air, toward the source of the blue light beam.

The last Dane saw of Flaherty was his face open and contorted, yelling for Dane to run, the words already distant and muted. There was a flash of bright, blue light around Flaherty and then he was gone in the mist.

A beam of gold light slashed out of the fog and touched Dane on his right arm, slashing up his forearm, leaving charred flesh in its wake, and causing him to drop the knife. Another beam of blue light came, wrapped around the knife, lifted it, then dropped it, continuing its search.

The voice was louder now, more insistent, screaming inside of Dane's head, telling him to leave, to get away.

Dane turned and ran for the river.

PART II: THE PRESENT

CHAPTER ONE

The plane was eight miles out of Bangkok and climbing rapidly, heading due east, the four Pratt & Whitney TF33-P-100A turbofan engines at full thrust. Dawn was touching the eastern sky, coming out of the Sea of China and reaching over Vietnam toward Cambodia and Thailand.

The aircraft was a modified Boeing 707 that had been specially built over twenty years ago for the US military. Since its sale, the US Air Force insignia had been painted over and the entire fuselage was now a flat black, except for the plane's name, scripted in red on the nose: *The Lady Gayle.* The most notable change on the outside from the standard 707 was the large 30 foot diameter rotodome on top of the plane, just aft of the wings. There were also no side windows, hiding the interior from prying eyes.

After buying the used plane from the government for twenty million dollars, Michelet Technologies, the company that now owned it, had spent two years renovating it. The interior of the modified 707 had cost Michelet an additional forty million dollars to refurbish to its own specs. The company had recouped their investment and much more in the first three years the plane had been in service. Most recently, there was the mission over northern Canada where the plane had helped Michelet's special earth survey crew target eight sites as potential diamond fields. So far, two sites had turned up diamonds, three had been busts and the other two still had field teams on the ground. The two good fields had already yielded over eighty million dollars profit in product, with three times as much projected to be mined over the next two years. It would have taken ground survey crews years to find the sites and do the initial scans, something the plane had done in one day with one pass over the area.

The *Lady Gayle* was the latest and most unique wrinkle in geologic exploration, able to accomplish missions from looking for diamond fields to searching for deep buried oil. Of course, it wasn't the plane itself, but the forty million dollars of high tech surveillance and imaging equipment which produced the finds. The plane was the platform for the sophisticated equipment and the scientists. Their information was data-linked to Michelet Corporate headquarters in Glendale, California.

At both locations there was a member of the Michelet family, third richest in America according to those in the know. In Glendale it was the senior man himself, Paul Michelet, sixty-four years old and not looking a day over fifty. He ran the entire Michelet multi-national empire, but the Imaging Interpretation Center, IIC, buried four stories underground beneath the chrome and black glass Michelet Building, was his favorite place. He also had a personal tie to the crew of the *Lady Gayle*, named after his late wife, a woman with some distant connections to the English monarchy. On board the 707, his daughter and only child, Ariana Michelet was in charge.

This was no case of unfounded nepotism and every person on board the *Lady Gayle* knew that. Ariana Michelet had a PhD in earth sciences and a masters degree in computers. She not only understood the machines, she understood what the machines were coming up with. And she had spent the last ten years working in the field for Michelet Technologies before being promoted the previous year to head of field surveys. Besides her technical expertise, she also had an uncanny way with people, something her father could appreciate.

At the present moment she was having each person in her crew run through a diagnostics check to make sure that their equipment was working properly and that each data link with Glendale IIC was full integrated. All of it was tied to a master computer, named Argus, on board the plane and a similar computer at the IIC.

From front to rear, the plane's interior was designed for a specific job. There were no rows of seats and no windows. Directly behind the door leading to the cockpit was a separate compartment with two seats facing the rear on a raised platform. This area was the communications console. Banks of radio gear filled the plane beyond with a small passageway leading further back to a single seat surrounded by computer and imaging screens which was the office where Ariana oversaw all. A wall separated her from the next room in line, the console center where there were six seats facing two rows of equipment. There was a lot of space around the consoles, even a conference table where the crew could hold meetings while airborne.

Each operator sat in a specially contoured crash seat that was mounted on tracks, allowing it to be moved to any console if need be. The seats could be locked down to the track itself at any location. Lighting was turned low, a mellow glow that allowed the people to concentrate on their computer screens.

The space behind the console center, above the wings and slightly to the rear was filled with racks holding computer mainframes and other high-tech gear. Behind the computers, the tail of the plane held eight bunks, a small galley, shower and restrooms. When on deployment, the crew of the *Lady Gayle* stayed on board because security was vital.

The pilot had over ten thousand hours in 707s, his co-pilot not much less. Their instrumentation was state of the art, as good as anything currently coming off of Boeing's assembly line.

The crew that manned the cabin of the plane consisted of eight specially trained personnel. With the aid of Argus, the imaging crew was able to do the job of many more. In fact, Argus was so sophisticated that Ariana could practically fly the plane from her rear position, using the master computer in conjunction with the autopilot and automatic tracking system. The Michelet personnel at the IIC in Glendale could also fly the plane from the other side of the world using their own master computer, sending commands via satellite link to the autopilot.

Ariana oversaw all operations from her small office using video cameras and sensors. More importantly, she had a dozen small computer screens arrayed around her, each one showing multiple feeds from the screens behind her in the console area. To her immediate rear, her systems analyst and chief aide, Mark Ingram, oversaw the imaging consoles. He knew as much about the systems as any of the operators. Between Ariana and the cockpit sat her chief communications man, Mitch Hudson, surrounded by his radios.

Ariana was thirty-four years old and the gods had not subtracted from her looks to bestow the gift of brains. She was tall and slender, her coloring a mixture of olive and dark. And though she looked lovely in bright colors, she tended toward khaki and denim slacks and shirts that were loose and comfortable and effectively hid her hard flared hips and full bosom. Ariana was extremely appreciative of her abilities as a scientist. Her looks, while important to some, were of little importance to the woman herself.

She had deep brown eyes and when the smile left her face, those eyes would flash with displeasure. Right now, those eyes were flashing at Hudson, who was standing in the door to her office, having just reported to her that their trailing radio/imaging wire was having problems unreeling. The wire was in a pod under the tail of the plane and as the *Lady Gayle* gained altitude it spooled out until over two miles of it trailed behind the plane, a most effective antenna. Except at the moment, it wasn't working properly, having stuck with only a quarter mile unreeled.

"Can you fix it?" Ariana asked.

"I'm going to reel it back in," Mitch said. "Maybe there's a kink and that will knock it out."

"Get it working. We only have one run and I have to give the final go at the Cambodian border which," she looked at a numeric display, "is only six minutes away."

Hudson ducked into the passageway leading to his station. "I'm on it."

Ariana leaned back in her seat and scanned the computer screens. No other problems had been reported. She knew her crew would report trouble to her right away. It was the environment she fostered. She believed in honesty both ways, telling her crew everything she could and expecting them to keep her abreast of the latest developments. Unlike many managers, she also didn't eviscerate the bearers of bad tidings, unless, of course, the bad tidings were the result of the bearers' incompetence. In that case, the worker was quickly removed from Michelet Technologies. With billions of dollars and a corporate empire at stake, there was little room for incompetence.

"We can do the run without the wire if we have to," Ingram said, suddenly appearing in the passageway that led to the rear. He was in his mid-forties and showed the stress of having worked for her father since leaving MIT over twenty years ago. His hair was prematurely gray and his body in poor physical condition, about thirty pounds overweight on his six foot frame, but his mind was as sharp as ever.

In the beginning he had always been looking over her shoulder, checking everything, but over the past year he had accepted that she knew what she was doing and he had gone back to concentrating on his own responsibilities. It had relieved a lot of pressure for both of them, but there was still residual tension in Ingram having been de facto demoted when Ariana took over his job. His pay had in fact been increased, but she knew there were times he missed being in charge.

"I know we can do without the wire," Ariana replied.

Ingram nodded and went back. Ariana could sense some frustration on his part. For years this had been his place and he was uncomfortable working in the main console area. There had been no need for him to check on Hudson's systems. On one hand she could appreciate Ingram's thoroughness, on the other she could resent his intrusion. She decided to go with the former and focused her mind on the upcoming mission.

Ariana picked up a small, cordless headset and put it on. She clipped a frequency changer onto the belt of her khaki pants. She flipped the channel on the changer without having to look, then spoke. "Glendale, this is *Lady Gayle*. How do you read me?"

"We read you loud and clear," a voice instantly responded. "Mister Michelet wishes to speak with you, Miss Ariana."

She leaned back in her seat as her father came on. "Ariana, how do things look?"

She didn't hesitate. "A little problem with the trailing wire, but other than that all systems are go."

"Can you go without the trailing wire?"

"Yes."

"Good."

"I'll call you when we get on station," she said, a dozen tasks awaiting her attention. Her father understood and signed off.

At the IIC in Glendale, Paul Michelet tried to stay out of the way of his subordinates. Unlike his daughter, he didn't understand what all the machines in the room below him were doing. That's why he paid top dollar for those who did. His success over the years was based on his ability to understand people and the big picture and making the hard decisions. The details he left to others.

Paul Michelet was currently standing in a small conference room that looked out over the imaging and interpretation center. A one-way glass wall separated him from the technicians below. He could see and hear everything that happened and they never knew if anyone was in the conference room. Michelet had long ago discovered that such a set up increased efficiency. If people never knew whether the boss was looking, they had to assume he was and work accordingly.

There were two men in the room with Michelet. One stood so perfectly still that he might have been missed by a person casually glancing in. He was Lawrence Freed, Michelet's chief of security and all around trouble-shooter. Freed was a slender black man, less than five feet ten inches tall and looked like a strong wind might easily sway him. Michelet had had difficulty believing the man's dossier when he'd interviewed him three years ago for the position. The man described on paper was an ex-Delta Force commando, a black belt in five martial arts, and a brilliant operations officer. Not only was Freed's physical appearance deceiving, the man was so quiet and soft of voice that one had great difficulty imagining him capable of violence. Michelet had had his doubts, but Freed came highly recommended from some of Michelet's contacts in Washington so he'd taken a chance. He hadn't regretted it yet in the past three years. Freed got results.

The other man in the room was Freed's polar opposite. Roland Beasley had not stayed still from the moment he entered the room. Beasley was a large bear of a man, with a pale white forehead and a large bushy gray beard. Michelet had recently hired Beasley. He too came highly recommended. Beasley had yet to prove his worth.

Michelet turned from the IIC. There was a map spread on the teak wood table in the center of the room. "It's taken me seven months to pay off the right officials in Cambodia to allow this overflight." He wanted Beasley to know that this wasn't some academic lark but a serious business venture with much at stake. Michelet had dealt with "academic" experts before and he knew it was important to make them realize they were no longer in the ivory halls.

"It should be most interesting," Beasley said. He spoke with a slight British accent, but his dossier indicated no significant time in England and a birth place of Brooklyn. Michelet assumed Beasley had acquired the accent in his academic circles. Beasley was an archeologist/historian, with a specific area of expertise in Southeast Asia.

Freed didn't indicate that he had heard either comment. Of course, as Michelet knew, Freed had been in charge of organizing all those payoffs through their intermediary in Cambodia. He'd also gathered the material in Beasley's dossier.

Michelet continued. "Michelet Technologies, and everyone else in the geologic business, know that there are vast mineral resources in Southeast Asia. Bangkok is the center of the world's gem business and Thailand is the largest exporter of uncut stones on the planet. But we think Cambodia holds even more than Thailand."

"You're talking about spending so much money, though," Beasley said. "Can it be worth that?"

Michelet stared at Beasley as if the man had just uttered a string of profanities. "Rubies and sapphires are different colors of an element called corundum, which is the crystalline form of aluminum oxide. Trace elements inside the corundum give the gems their color. For rubies the trace element is chronium. For sapphires it is titanium. Rubies are perhaps the rarest of gems, commanding four times the price of diamonds weighing the same amount."

Beasley frowned. "I know that some Thai businessmen have been running a blackmarket mining operation in southwestern Cambodia, extracting some precious gems under the protection of the Khmer Rouge whom they pay off, but I didn't think it was that lucrative."

"It isn't if you consider forty millions dollars a year gross on the black market not lucrative," Michelet said, reevaluating Beasley. Obviously the man hadn't stuck his head in the textbooks all his life. "We think they are working a weak field area." He tapped the map of Cambodia on the conference table. "The area the *Lady Gayle* is overflying is one that we believe, based on imaging from satellites and the space shuttle, holds very strong gem and crystal fields, estimated to be ten times as dense as the best field in Thailand. The Cambodian highlands, north of Tonle Sap. No one has ever gone into that area and looked.

"The problem has always been two-fold. One is penetrating the harsh mountainous jungle region to survey for those gems. The other is surviving the various fighting factions and the over ten million landmines laid in Cambodia. Both those factors have effectively stopped any ground surveys. The lack of a stable government in Cambodia for decades has also been a problem."

Beasley nodded. "The closest I've been to the area is the ancient city of Angkor Thom which contains the temple Angkor Wat, just north of Tonle Sap Lake. I never attempted to go further north nor do I know anyone who has. It would have been most unhealthy. If the Khmer Rouge or bandits didn't get you, as you said, the mines would or the triple canopy jungle in very rough terrain, or the wild beasts of the region. There are no roads, no villages, nothing. A most dangerous area."

Michelet pulled out a binder and flipped it open. There were various photos inside, all taken from high altitude. "Last year, the Space Shuttle *Atlantis* did some imaging on Cambodia as it flew over. I had contacts at the Jet Propulsion Lab forward me some of the basic data."

Beasley was looking at the photos with interest. "Amazing!" he said. His fingers traced over one of them. "Look at the Angkor Thom complex in this one. You can see the moats most clearly. I know archeologists who would give quite a bit for these."

Not enough, Michelet thought. It had cost him six hundred thousand dollars to get the imagery. Michelet more than most knew that everything had a price, and loyalty was usually the lowest.

"The data from these photos told my interpreters that the area deserves a more detailed look. The initial readouts indicate a high likelihood of the type of geological formations that hold precious stones present in quantities worthy of exploitation."

Beasley nodded. "Cambodia has vast resources that have gone untapped in the midst of all the turmoil. There are parts of that country that no white man has ever seen. There were rumors of a great city in Cambodia for many years but the first explorer to reach Angkor Thom didn't get there until 1860. And it's my personal opinion that Angkor Thom wasn't the city of the legend, but a later, smaller city."

Michelet had done some checking with other sources and knew the specific area he wanted the *Lady Gayle* to survey was even more remote. He narrowed down the area he had indicated, tracing it on the map. "This area, the highland region of the Banteay Meanchey region, is practically unmapped and uninhabited."

Beasley looked at it. "There's a reason for that besides the roughness of the terrain, the mines and the Khmer Rouge."

"Excuse me?" Michelet was surprised. This was news to him. "And what is that reason?"

"Angkor Kol Ker," Beasley said.

"And that is?" Freed took a step closer.

"As I was saying. There was a legend of a great city in Cambodia for many years. When the French naturalist Henri Mouhot discovered Angkor Thom in 1860 everyone thought he had solved the mystery of the legend. But there have always been, and still are, rumors of ruins, to the north and east of this area. Of a city even more ancient and more magnificent than Angkor Thom and its temple Angkor Wat. It's called Angkor Kol Ker. Many legends surround those ruins, but very little fact is known. A French expedition tried to get there in the 1950's but it disappeared. It was assumed that they ran into unfriendly guerrillas, the forerunners of the Khmer Rouge. Since then, no one else has tried. It is not even certain that the city ever existed. It might just be a myth. Sort of a jungle Shangri-la. Some of the legends that are associated with it are rather fantastic."

Beasley's hand twirled an edge of his mustache. "The legends, if they are to be believed, promise dire consequences to anyone entering Angkor Kol Ker or the area surrounding it. So in mythical terms, this area is cursed."

Michelet turned his back to Beasley at the last sentence. Freed had quietly moved over and he was also looking at the map. "Let's hope *Lady Gayle* gives us some pinpoint data. That region is over forty-thousand square kilometers. That's a lot of jungle to survey."

Michelet smiled. "With the imagery from the *Lady Gayle*, the interpreters will pinpoint possible sites down to within a half a kilometer."

"That good?" Beasley was impressed.

"That good."

Beasley was excited. "I wonder if we might be able to find Angkor Kol Ker using the data." He squinted at the space shuttle imagery. "Hell, I bet no one's even looked at these pictures for ruins, have they?"

"Ruins don't make money," Michelet said.

"Schliemann made out pretty well after he found the ruins of Troy," Beasley commented. "And remember, people thought Troy was as much a legend as Angkor Kol Ker."

"What about the curse?" Freed asked. "Doesn't that concern you?"

"I didn't say I believed in the legends," Beasley said. "I just believe it's worth looking into. Some of them are legends based on legends, including one that the people who settled this area over ten thousand years ago were refugees from Atlantis. In the same manner there are those who believe the early Egyptians, the ones who built the Sphinx and the Great Pyramids were also refugees from a greater kingdom."

Michelet was focused on the large electronic map in front of the IIC where the small dot represented the *Lady Gayle* had crossed the Cambodian Border and was approaching the target area which was outlined in blue light.

Freed glanced over at Beasley. "Do you think Angkor Kol Ker was real?"

Beasley spread his fat hands. "It is a personal belief of mine that there is always much more truth to legend that most scientists believe. But, to convince those others, I must hold a stone from a ruin of the city in my hand and smash it over their forehead. Then they might believe it is real. Until then, it is only a myth to them and thus for me."

"The stones we are looking for are more valuable than any that could come out of an old city," Michelet said.

Beasley picked up the imagery and looked at it more closely. "I would not be so sure of that."

At fifteen thousand feet, the *Lady Gayle* was cruising at three hundred knots and beginning to loop north toward the target area. Ariana had their location pinpointed to within ten meters, updated every one-thousandth of a second by use of the global positioning receiver mounted in the rotodome. The GPR worked off the band of global positioning satellites, GPS, the United States had blanketing the world, picking up a signal emitted by the three closest and then a computer in the GPR immediately determined location through triangulation. They were getting close to the target area and the interior of the 707 was a bustle of activity as controllers prepared their equipment.

"Slow to imaging speed," Ariana ordered and the pilots reduced thrust until the 707 was flying only 20 knots above the aircraft's stall speed.

Ariana knew the routine by heart but she used the checklist taped to an open space on her console anyway. "Open viewing doors."

Along what had been the luggage compartment of the aircraft, hydraulic arms slid open doors on the right side of the plane. Inside were mounted the eyes of the *Lady Gayle*. There were regular video and still cameras with various degrees of telephotic lenses thermal sensors, and imagers that could view throughout the spectrum from infrared to ultraviolet. Although they couldn't directly see the outside world from the enclosed space of the plane, the analysts could now see the world below through the magic of their machines.

Verbal reports came back to Ariana through her headset, confirming what her console told her; they were ready.

"Mark," she said to Ingram, "let Argus take over and give us the planned racetrack over the area."

Ingram coordinated with the pilots and soon the plane was being flown by the master computer along a pre-determined path. The 707 banked to the right, aligning all the sensors with the ground and began a long, slow turn.

"We're getting some interference on FM," Mitch Hudson announced in her ear.

"Switch frequencies," Ariana ordered.

"We've got nav problems," Ingram was looking at the relay he had from the cockpit.

"Specify," Ariana ordered as she leaned forward and her fingers flew across the keyboard of the closest computer, drawing up the navigational information.

"Our compasses are going nuts," Ingram said.

"GPR still working?" she asked.

Ingram's hands were flying over his control panel. "Roger. We still have GPR and satellite communications, but our FM and UHF are down."

"High frequency radio?"

"Still working."

Her father's voice crackled in her headset. "Ariana, what is going on? They're going crazy down in the IIC."

"We're getting some interference, dad," Ariana said. She glanced at Ingram's data, then spoke to him over the intercom. "Can we make the run, Mark?"

"Imaging is fine. I've switched from normal data link to putting everything through satellite. So far so good. But if we lose satellite and HF we have no back-up. Standard operating procedure for this situation is we abort."

"This is our only window of opportunity," Ariana said. "Syn-Tech will be here, if they aren't already, and get a jump on us if we don't do it now."

Ingram's voice was impassive. "I'm telling you the rules we wrote, Ariana."

Ariana thought for a second, then keyed the radio. "Dad, I think we should abort."

"What's that?" her father's voice was now distant and scratchy. "I . . . hear . . . . said. Repeat . . ."

"We're over target area," Ingram cut in on intercom. "Everything's rolling, but we're scattered on the satellite link."

Ariana slapped a palm onto her chair arm. "All right. We--" She froze as the plane dipped hard right and alarms began going off.

"I've got controls!" the pilot's voice was calm and controlled. "Auto pilot is down. Nav link and GPR are down. Argus is off-line to flight controls."

"Can you handle it?" Ariana demanded. She felt her stomach tighten and her breakfast threaten to come up.

"We're trying," the pilot responded.

"Abort and return to Bangkok," Ariana ordered. She was forced to swallow down a trace of acidic vomit that came up her throat.

"Oh hell!" the pilot yelled in the intercom. "We're losing control. There's some sort of strange mist outside."

Ingram's voice came from the console area. "The wings, the tails, they're controlled by radio. If we're losing all spectrums, then the pilots are losing their ability to control the plane using normal controls."

"Carpenter!" Ariana called out the name of the woman who was responsible for the master computer. "What's with Argus?"

"I don't know," Carpenter's voice came back through the intercom. "He's going nuts, spewing garbage!"

"Take Argus off-line on all systems!" Ariana ordered. "Get the back-up going."

Ariana felt her stomach lurch as the nose tipped over. Mugs and papers crashed to the floor. She couldn't help it now as she leaned over and threw up on the floor to her left. She sat back up. She rapidly typed into her keyboard, bringing up the same view the pilots had, via the front looking video camera. All she saw was a yellowish mist with streaks of black in it, swirling. Visibility was less than fifty feet. If the pilots had lost instruments--the thought chilled Ariana.

"We're working the controls manually," the pilot announced, as if reading her mind. "Trying to keep it level and steady but all our instruments are lousy."

Ariana knew that meant the pilots were trying to manhandle the large plane with muscle power, the pilot and co-pilot gripping the yoke with both hands, muscles bulging as they tried to force their commands through the back-up hydraulic system.

Hudson's voice suddenly came over the intercom. "I'm getting a weak FM transmission from the ground!"

"Record and forward to IIC," Ariana automatically ordered.

"Roger," Hudson said. The plane rolled left. In the back, one of the controllers had not locked his seat down and he went spinning down the rails toward the rear of the plane.

"We can't keep it up!" the pilot yelled. "I don't have altimeter. I don't know how low we are. I have no instruments and no visual. Controls are not responding. Prepare for crash landing!"

Hudson yelled to Ariana. "Your father is calling."

A weak voice came over the radio. "Ariana . . . going . . . "

Ariana had no time to respond to her father, even if she could. She tore off her headset and yelled into the corridor, so that everyone in the bay could hear her. "Lock your seats in! Prepare for crash landing!"

Ariana looked at the video displays that showed the pilots' view. Nothing but the strange mist. There was a flash of gold light on the right side of the display.

"What the hell?" the pilot exclaimed.

Another flash of gold, this time to the left, then the screen went dark.

"I don't believe it," the pilot's voice was almost a whisper in Ariana's ears. "Sweet Jesus, save us."

"What's happening?" Ariana demanded. She felt herself press against her seatbelt. She knew the feeling: zero g. That meant they were in a terminal dive.

"We've lost both our--" the pilot began, but suddenly the intercom went dead.

Then all went black as the plane seemed to come to a sudden halt and Ariana was thrown hard against her shoulder straps, her head slamming back against the headrest in recoil.

In Glendale, Paul Michelet threw open the door to the conference room and took the stairs to the IIC two at a time, Freed just behind him. Michelet burst into the control room. "What's going on?"

"We're losing contact with the *Lady Gayle*," the senior tech told him.

"That's impossible," Michelet sputtered.

"What about the plane's transponder?" Freed asked.

"We're getting the HF transponder intermittently," the tech said. He pointed at the board. "We've got location but it's losing altitude fast." He checked his computer screen. "Eight thousand and descending." He stared. "That's strange."

"What?" Michelet demanded.

"It's just going straight down, no forward velocity. Like it just came to a halt in mid-air. That's not possible. And the descent--" the man paused, not believing what his instruments were telling him.

"Go on!" Michelet ordered.

"The descent is not terminal now. It's like it's being controlled but that's physically impossible given the rate and speed of the plane."

"Put the *Lady Gayle* on the speaker," Michelet said.

There was a burst of static, then they could hear the pilot's voice. "*Lady Gayle* .. . . attitude . . . two . . . four . . . power . . . . Mayday . . . . there's . . . . God . . . . strange . . . . Jesus!" then suddenly the static was gone.

"She's down," the tech said.

175 miles above the southwest Pacific, a KH-12 spy satellite began receiving electronic orders from the National Security Agency at Fort Meade, Maryland. At that location, all Patricia Conners, the imagery operator knew, was that the person ordering the new mission had a sufficient CIA clearance and went by the code name Foreman. What Conners found strange about the request was that Foreman only wanted a large scale shot covering a section of north-central Cambodia.

Conners thought such a request a waste of the advanced equipment. The KH-12 she was tasking was one of six in orbit. They were the cutting edge of satellite technology, carrying an array of sensors. To keep them in orbit and available for taskings such as this, each one was refuelable, a classified operation which space shuttle crews accomplished every few missions.

She had a model of the KH-12 on top of a bookcase along one wall of her office. It looked like the Hubble Space Telescope with a large engine attached to provide maneuverability. The body of the satellite was 15 feet in diameter and almost 50 feet long. It was a tight fit in the cargo bay of the Space Shuttle. Two solar panels were extended out of the body once the satellite was in orbit to provide power, each over 45 feet long and 13 feet wide.

Inside her office two floors underground, beneath the main NSA building at Fort Meade, Conners could not only change the KH-12's orbit, she could down-load real time images from the satellite and forward them to any location on the planet. She did this through the large screen computer that sat in the center of her desk.

On the left side of the computer she had a large framed picture of her grandchildren gathered together at the last family reunion, all six of them, two via her daughter and four from two sons. On the right side of the computer was a pewter model of the Starship Enterprise, the one from the original TV series. Stuck on the side of her monitor were various bumper stickers from the science fiction conventions she religiously traveled to every year, ranging from one indicating the bearer was a graduate of Star Fleet Academy to another warning that the driver braked for alien landings.

Conners' attention was fixated on the computer screen. She watched her display as, with the burst of a booster engine, the particular KH-12 she had commanded shifted its orbital path and moved northwest. The satellites were positioned so that any spot on earth could be looked at within 20 minutes of getting a mission tasking. Conners estimated a time on target of twelve minutes.

She got a thrill every time she did this, knowing that she was one of the few people on the planet who actually "drove" a spacecraft, even if from the safety of her chair and office. She actually had a set of astronaut pilot wings that her late husband had made for her. They were pinned to the front of a baseball cap, the one her husband had always worn when he went fishing. The cap rested on top of her computer monitor.

Conners spent the intervening minutes double-checking all systems. As the KH12 swooped across Cambodia, infrared cameras took a series of pictures with other imagers recording their own spectral data. The satellite's telescope had an electrooptical resolution of less than three inches but they wouldn't even come close to needing that on this shot.

Conners quickly typed in new commands, getting a new screen. She looked at the map of the target area. With the regular spectrum camera she knew that great resolution wouldn't help much with the triple canopy jungle. The best effect would come from the infrared and thermal imaging. Of course, she didn't know the objective of the search.

She believed that knowing what she was looking for would greatly increase her efficiency. She was the expert on the KH-12 and the other satellite systems the NSA controlled and she knew that she was the best-qualified to judge how the systems should be used. But she usually had no need to know, therefore she didn't. One of her favorite pastimes was looking over the imagery requested and trying to figure out exactly what the requester was looking for.

Conners downloaded the data the KH-12 transmitted to her, making a copy for NSA's computer bank--every piece of downloaded data ever picked up by a satellite was somewhere in the NSA system-- and bounced a copy to the designated MILSTARS address for Foreman indicated in the original tasking.

So out of curiosity Conners pulled up the downloaded data and ran it through her computer to the printer. She wasn't supposed to do that, since she certainly didn't have a "need to know" but Conners thought it was a stupid regulation. She was a human being after all, not part of some machine with no curiosity. Besides, she rationalized, the more she knew, the better she could do her job.

She made a cup of tea while the machine gently hummed, spewing out three pages. Taking a sip, she looked at the first one. Her initial impression was that the printer must be broken. It was a thermal image and the center of the shot was a fuzzy, white haze in the shape of a triangle.

"What the heck?" Conners muttered as she fanned through the optic and infrared shots. All showed the same triangle in north-central Cambodia.

"But that can't be," Conners spoke the words aloud. There were no atmospheric conditions which could block all three types of imaging.

She quickly sat down at her desk and checked the printer, running a test. It was working fine. She bit the inside of her lip. The next possible problem was the computer on board the KH-12. She checked--the satellite was now heading south toward Malaysia. She gave the commands for the imagers to take some shots. As the data appeared on her screen, there was no triangular blur on it. She sent it to the printer. The paper showed clear images.

Conners sat back at her desk and looked at the three images Foreman had requested. There was no type of man-made interference that could do that as far as she knew. Conners stared at the three pictures once more. But something had.

CHAPTER TWO

The golden retriever watched the frisbee fly just over her head, then followed it, waiting until it landed before reluctantly retrieving the disk via a very slow walk.

"Lazy dog," Dane laughed. "I remember when you used to jump for it."

The dog gave him a look, its golden eyes and white snout telling him that she was too old for such youthful maneuvers, but her wagging tail indicated she did enjoy the sport.

The two were standing on a grassy lawn which had been disfigured by the treads of heavy equipment. To the right, smoke still wafted from the ruins of the factory complex. Firetrucks, bulldozers, backhoes and cranes all crowded around the rubble. There was an air of desperation in the air and the sound of jackhammers punctuated the steady rumble of the other heavy gear as they tore at the twisted steel and shattered concrete. It was morning and Dane was glad to see the sun after working most of the night under the blaze of the large Klieg lights that had been hastily rigged around the area.

Dane knelt and took the dog's head in his callused hands, rubbing her behind the ears. "Good dog, Chelsea, good dog." He wearily sat down next to her and they both looked at the destroyed factory with sad eyes. Chelsea leaned her head against his shoulder.

"How can you do that?" A woman's high-pitched voice shrieked to his left. The owner of the voice came into view, a woman in her fifties, her eyes red from crying. She was hastily dressed and her hair was in disarray. "My husband's trapped in there and you're out here playing with your dog! Have you no decency?"

Dane slowly stood. He spoke slowly, as if he'd said it before but was repeating it with respect for the woman's grief and anger. "Ma'am, Chelsea," he patted the golden retriever on the head, "has been working all night long. You might not believe it, but she gets very depressed doing this. I have to keep her spirits up so that she can keep searching.

"Right now the fire department is clearing out another section for us to get into and search. I'm sorry about your husband and I hope we'll find him alive in there, but there's nothing I can do right now except keep Chelsea ready to go."

The woman had been staring at him, hearing the words but not really registering it. Dane had seen and heard it before. In Oklahoma City, after the Federal Building had been bombed, he'd had a grief-stricken FBI man from the local office threaten him with a gun to get back in the building and look for his colleagues after catching Dane and Chelsea playing close to the building. That had been the worst ever, with so few survivors and so many dead. Dane had refused any more calls for eight months afterward.

A police officer came and took the woman by the arm. "Ma'am, you have to wait behind the lines. They're doing the best they can."

The cop led the woman away and Dane sat back down. He could sense Chelsea's unhappiness. In Oklahoma, not only had he and the other handlers had to play with their dogs to keep their spirits up; some had staged mock rescues. They'd go into a cleared section and "find" a rescuer who pretended to be a victim. The dogs reacted positively and it kept them going. Dane was content tossing the frisbee to Chelsea; she was too smart to fall for the mock rescue technique.

Dane was bone-tired. They'd been here for ten hours now, searching in the rubble, without anything longer than a thirty minute break to gulp down some coffee. Dane hadn't eaten; he never ate during a search.

"Mister Eric Dane?" a low voice came from behind.

Dane turned his head without getting up. He saw a slender black man in an expensive suit walking toward them.

The man halted, looking at the dust and sweat encrusted coveralls Dane wore, searching for a nametag, but there was none. "Are you Eric Dane?"

"Yes."

"My name is Lawrence Freed. I work for Michelet Technologies."

Freed looked past him to the ruins. It had been a paint factory until last night; now it was a graveyard. Something had gone wrong with a batch of the chemicals used and there had been a massive explosion. The three story structure, poorly built during the thirties and

60

poorly maintained, had pancaked until now there was only a ten foot mound of rubble. As part of his job, Dane had studied building structure and he knew that unexpected forces applied in an unforeseen direction could have devastating consequences on any structure.

"Never heard of it or you." Dane said. He had turned his attention back to the ruins. A crane was lifting a large piece of steel reinforced concrete up into the air. There was a bustle of excitement.

"I would like to talk to you about acquiring your assistance."

"My assistance in what?" Dane asked. A pair of firefighters in long yellow coats and helmets were coming toward them.

"A rescue."

"As you can see, I'm already occupied," Dane said.

"This is a different sort of--" Freed paused as two firefighters arrived and Dane stood.

"Dane, we're in to the southeast side," the first of the firefighters said.

Dane nodded. He walked away from Freed without further acknowledging the other man's presence and headed in to the ruin. Freed began to follow but the firemen stopped him. "It's not safe in there. Authorized personnel only. Whole thing could shift and then we'd have to dig you out too," one of them said.

Dane climbed over what had been the outer wall of the factory, carefully picking his way through shattered brick. At least there wasn't much glass in the building. He always had to be concerned for Chelsea's paws getting cut. Chelsea nimbly followed him, surprisingly agile for her weight.

Dane passed areas they'd already searched as he went farther into the building. Over his head was open to the sky, the path that the heavy equipment operators had forged, torn between the rush to get into the building and the fear of shifting some of the rubble and possibly killing someone who was trapped inside some void area.

The woman's confrontation outside showed the paradoxes of Dane's and Chelsea's work, yet everyone here worked under dual pressures that conflicted. Dane paused and put his hands to his head. He felt a driving pain over his left eye and the eyelid flickered uncontrollably. It was always like this. He'd taken some pain killers on the second job, but he'd found they interfered too much. Since then he'd accepted the pain as the price to be paid.

A group of firemen were gathered around a dark opening. They turned as Dane and Chelsea came up. The leader had a steel cable in his hand and he pointed into the hole. "I've been down. You get to the first floor, then move horizontal. Goes about thirty feet. There's void areas all along what used to be a corridor. One interior wall is holding good and appears solid. I couldn't see too well."

From long experience, Dane knew that void areas were what rescuers prayed for. Open spaces in the rubble where a person might have survived. Dane had seen many destroyed structures over the years, but all of them had had some spaces in them.

"What's on the plans?" Dane asked as he knelt and looked in, shining a flashlight that one of the firemen handed him.

"Down there is the first floor, admin section." A fireman laid a set of blueprints on a piece of shattered concrete. "It's the last place we have to get to, but it's also where there were the most employees who were at work at the time. Best we could find out was that there were seven, maybe eight people in there."

Dane closed his eyes as the pain in his head picked up the beat. Seven, maybe eight. Throughout the rest of the factory they'd found eight bodies, spaced among the machinery. This would be different. Seven or eight all together. He's seen that, and worse, before.

"Did you run a mike down?"

The fireman nodded. "No noise. We yelled and got nothing back. Ran fiber optic as far as it will go and nothing either."

Dane glanced at Chelsea who had settled down on the dusty remains of a heating duct, her head between her paws. She looked reluctant to go in. Dane wasn't exactly keen on it either, but there was always the chance someone was unconscious down there.

"Let's go," Dane said, standing. He switched on the light he wore on his hard-hat and pulled the chin strap down.

The fireman hooked the steel cable to the harness that Dane wore then to Chelsea's harness. Dane hooked a leash from his harness onto the Chelsea as an extra safety. Then he looked down once more into the hole. He closed his eyes for a second and concentrated, then he slid his legs in. Chelsea was on her feet, her muzzle next to his face as he lowered himself down. "Good girl," Dane said.

He felt with his toes, getting support, then he reached up. The firefighters handed her to him and he grunted from the weight. "Big fat dog," he whispered affectionately. "I'm going to have to put you on a diet."

Chelsea growled and nuzzled her head into his armpit. Awkwardly and with great difficulty, Dane made his way down until he reached the ground level, then he put Chelsea down. He shone his flashlight around. To his right was a cinder block, load bearing wall, the reason this void space existed. The opening extended about thirty feet straight ahead, at one point narrowing to a two foot opening.

Dane turned the flashlight and the light on his helmet off. He slowed his breathing and ignored the pain over his left eye. He stayed perfectly still for a minute, then he turned the lights back on and looked at Chelsea. "Search," he whispered in her ear.

Chelsea moved forward, her head down, sweeping back and forth, her tail straight up and erect. Dane watched her, his face resigned. She stopped after six feet and turned her head to the left. She raised a paw. Dane pulled a small red flag out of his backpack and marked the spot. Another body lay somewhere underneath.

They continued down the corridor, leaving three more red flags. As he was placing the last one, Dane suddenly lifted his head. He looked to his right. The cinder block wall was solid on that side. He pressed up against the wall as Chelsea watched him curiously, until as much of his body as possible was touching it. He stayed like that for thirty seconds, then he suddenly pushed away.

"Stay!" he ordered Chelsea. She obediently sat down as Dane made his way back until he was at the bottom of the shaft.

"I need a jack-hammer!" he called up.

"Right away." Ten seconds later the equipment was lowered on a rope. Dane dragged it behind him back up the corridor, making sure the air pressure hose didn't get snagged on rubble. He returned to where Chelsea waited.

He placed the tip of the hammer against the cinder block and went to work.

Chips of cinder flew, but his steel rimmed glasses protected him. He carefully took out eight blocks, one at a time, making sure that those surrounding the hole remained intact, a technique he had learned from a rescue expert in Houston during a job there.

As he removed the last block, Chelsea suddenly lunged forward and pressed against, him, her nose in the hole, barking furiously, her tail wagging, thumping Dane on the leg. "Yeah, yeah, yeah," Dane said, patting her head. "Good dog."

He pushed the jackhammer aside and slithered into the hole. The beam of light from his helmet caught the suspended dust and raked over the edge of a desk that had taken the impact of the concrete floor from above. Dane could see a tiny space where the metal front of the desk didn't touch the tiled floor. He slid his hand through, fingers probing into the space under the desk.

His entire focus was on the ends of his fingers, feeling tile, dust, the outline of the desk well, the splintered leg of a chair. Then he felt something warm and yielding: skin. Living skin, he knew as soon as he touched it.

Dane turned on the small FM radio for the first time. "I've got a live one," he whispered into the mike.

"We're coming down!" was the immediate reply from the firemen waiting above.

Dane kept his fingers pressed against the flesh. He knew whoever it was, was unconscious, but he also knew the importance of human contact, even to an unconscious mind.

Soon the small space on the other side of the cinder block wall was filled with men and equipment. Dane remained where he was as they carefully widened the hole in the wall and then came through. The firefighters shored up the collapsed ceiling so they could rip the desk out of their way and not have everything tumble in on them.

Finally they went to work on the desk with the jaws of life, carefully tearing sections of it away until they exposed the person on the other side. A fireman shone his light in, illuminating a young woman, her features covered with dust and blood. They carefully scooped her out and Dane finally let go. He rolled onto his back as the woman was strapped to a stretcher and hustled down the corridor and out to the surface.

"Want to come up?" the head rescue man asked him.

Dane slowly shook his head. He wanted to just lie where he was and for everyone to leave him alone. "There's three or four more missing. Maybe somebody else made it." But he knew there weren't any more survivors, even an unconscious one. The building was dead and everyone who had been in it were dead. He knew it, but he had to go through the paces.

Dane got to his feet, hunched over under the collapsed ceiling. "Come on, Chelsea. Just a little further."

Chelsea whimpered disapprovingly but she moved. Dane knew she knew what he did, but they could at least locate the other bodies. They slowly went down the remains of the corridor and by the time they reached the end of the void space, they'd planted three more flags where Chelsea had tapped her paw.

Dane finally turned her around and led her out, handing her up to rescuers who helped them out of the shaft.

"The woman's going to be all right," one of them told Dane, slapping him on the back. "Couple of broken bones and a knock on the head, but otherwise she's going to be fine."

Dane nodded. There was a lighter mood in the air. Fifteen bodies and one survivor, but that one was what everyone here had worked for. The reality of the dead would come home to all later, when they were in bed and their mind played back the crushed and mutilated bodies.

Dane shook hands and walked out of the wreckage. He gratefully accepted a cup of coffee from a Red Cross worker, but only after getting a bowl of water for Chelsea and watching her loudly slurp it up.

Dane removed his glasses and ran a dirty hand across his face. The headache wasn't as bad now.

"Mister Dane."

Dane didn't even turn his head. "Mister Freed," he said.

"I wasn't sure you heard me before you went into the building," Freed began.

"You want me to help you with a rescue," Dane said.

"Yes."

"You don't seem very concerned," Dane said, finally looking at the other man. "Or in much of a rush."

"Time is of the essence," Freed said, somewhat taken aback by Dane's comments.

"Isn't it always?" Chelsea pressed her head against Dane's leg and his hand automatically began scratching behind her ears. "I work through FEMA," Dane said, referring to the Federal Emergency Management Agency. "They contact me, fly me to the site, and then we get to work."

"This doesn't fall under FEMA's jurisdiction," Freed said.

"Everything in the States' falls--" Dane paused. "All right, why don't you just tell me what the situation is and why you want my help?"

"A plane has crashed and we need your help in finding survivors."

Dane frowned. "I haven't heard of any plane crash on the news. And besides, Chelsea's a search dog, not a tracking dog."

"The plane went down in Southeast Asia," Freed said, "and it's not Chelsea we want. It's you."

Dane slowly went to one knee and ran his hand through Chelsea's coat, from the nape of her neck to the root of her tail. It comforted him as much as it did her and right now he needed the comfort.

"The plane went down yesterday," Freed continued. "We don't have much time."

"Surely you have people closer," Dane said.

Freed ignored that statement. "I have a limousine waiting and a private jet at the airfield. All I ask is that you go with me to California and listen to an offer. You say no, I'll fly you back wherever you like. Plus you get ten thousand dollars just for going to California."

After a few moments, Dane finally spoke. "I don't understand. Why do you want me?"

"I think you do understand, Mister Dane. Because you're the only person we know of who ever came out of there alive."

"Where--" Dane began, but Freed answered the question before it was asked.

"Cambodia. North-central Cambodia."

The Lear Jet was two hours out of Washington. Only one man was in the

passenger compartment, lounging in a deep leather chair. A single overhead light glowed over his head, otherwise it was dark in the

66

cabin. He had long wavy hair that had turned completely white. His face was well-tanned, the lines hard, as if cut from stone. Much had happened but one could still recognize the young marine gunner who had looked out over the ocean after Flight 19 had disappeared fifty-four years ago, listened to the disappearance of the *USS Scorpion* and the SR-71 and sent a special forces reconnaissance team deep into Cambodia thirty years ago.

A fax machine was next to Foreman, hooked to the plane's satellite dish. The green light on top began blinking, then it gently puffed out a piece of paper. Foreman picked up the paper and looked at it as a second sheet came out, followed by a third.

Unlike Patricia Conners, Foreman was not surprised at the hazy triangle in the center that blocked the view, nor did he suspect there was anything wrong with the equipment.

He reached into a briefcase and pulled out several similar images. He placed a new one on top of an old one and held the paper up to the overhead light.

A frown creased his aged forehead at what he saw. He reached down and picked up the satellite phone resting on the arm of the chair. He punched in auto-dial. A voice answered on the second ring.

"Yes?" the woman's accent was strange, hard to place.

"Sin Fen, it's me. I will be landing in twelve hours."

"I will be waiting."

"Any activity?"

"It is as you predicted. I am watching."

"Cambodia?"

"Nothing yet."

Foreman glanced at the paper once more. "Sin Fen, it is changing."

"Smaller or larger?"

"Larger this time and the fluctuations are severe. More than I've ever seen."

There was no reply, not that he had expected one.

"Sin Fen, I am going to try the orbital laser. Also I am going to check the other Gates."

"It is as we discussed," Sin Fen said, which was all the agreement he was going to get.

"Do you--" Foreman paused, then continued--"sense anything?"

"No."

Foreman glanced at another piece of paper. A surveillance report. "Michelet has contacted Dane."

"That is also as we discussed," Sin Fen said.

"I'll see you shortly," Foreman said.

The phone went dead. Foreman opened up his briefcase and pulled out a slim laptop computer. He hooked the line from the satellite phone into the computer. Then he accessed the NSA and typed in the commands for what he wanted.

Finished with that, he then punched the number for his superior in Washington. He always believed in acting first, then getting permission, especially when dealing with small minds. The phone was picked up on the second ring.

"National Security Council."

"This is Foreman," Foreman said. "I need to speak to Mister Bancroft."

"Hold."

Foreman listened to the static. He hated talking to anyone else about his project. He was considered an anachronism in the Black Budget Society of Washington, a man with much power dealing with an unknown entity. As such he engendered much animosity. With over sixty billion dollars a year pumped into it, the Black Budget had many strange little cells, searching into different areas, from Star Wars defense systems, to the Air Force's classified UFO watchdog group, to Foreman's Gate program.

A new voice came on. "Go."

"Mister Bancroft, this is Foreman. I'm going to use Bright Eye to take a look into Cambodia."

The President's National Security Adviser sounded irritated. "Is that necessary?"

"The fluctuations are severe. Over forty percent. Another twenty percent bigger and the Angkor Gate will touch several populated areas."

"So? It's Cambodia for Christ's sake. No one gives a shit."

"Remember the connection to what's off our coast," Foreman said.

"The only connection to what you think is off our coast is in your head," Bancroft rejoined. "You tried making that connection a long time ago and a lot of men died and a lot of careers were ruined trying to cover up for it."

"Those men made the connection," Foreman said.

"One high frequency radio transmission," Bancroft said. "That isn't exactly conclusive."

"Something's happening," Foreman insisted.

"Yes, something is happening," Bancroft's voice was sharp. "Paul Michelet lost his plane and his daughter overflying that Goddamn place. Forget to fill me in on that little detail?"

"It was his decision," Foreman said, not surprised that Bancroft already knew about the *Lady Gayle* going down.

"But he wasn't playing with all the facts when he made that decision," Bancroft said. "You don't want someone like Michelet to be angry with you. He has a lot of power. The President is not going to be pleased."

Foreman cared as much about Paul Michelet as Bancroft did about the Cambodian villagers near the Angkor Gate.

"Using Bright Eye might allow us to help Michelet," Foreman said. "If we can pinpoint his plane, we can forward that information to him."

Bancroft snorted. "And? What's he going to do? Go in there and get them out? From what you tell me, no one can do that."

"Michelet has someone coming to him who might be able to do that," Foreman said. "Also, with the shifting in phase, they might be able to get in and out when the plane is uncovered." If it ever was uncovered now, Foreman thought but didn't add. "First, though, we have to get its exact location."

"Jesus, Foreman, is it that important?"

Foreman bit back the first reply that came to his lips. "Sir, I believe it is of utmost importance."

69

"I don't see it," Bancroft said. "All these years and you've yet to give us anything solid. You know the story of the boy who cried wolf, don't you?"

Foreman stared at the fuzzy, triangular image. "I know the story, sir, and it would do us well to remember that in the end, the boy was right. There were wolves."

"Wolves in Cambodia?" Bancroft said. "Who gives a rat's ass?"

"I think it's much bigger than Cambodia," Foreman kept his voice under tight control.

"You think, you think," Bancroft said. "You sound like those damn UFO people in Area 51 I've got to listen to all the time, worried about little gray men showing up and blowing Earth away. You know how much we spend on those people? And you know how many little gray men they've found? There are real problems that are here and now that I and the President have to worry about."

Foreman remained silent.

"Go ahead, use Bright Eye," Bancroft finally said. "But it's your responsibility."

The satellite phone went dead. It was always his responsibility, Foreman thought as he put the phone back in its holder.

CHAPTER THREE

Ariana Michelet had never been so aware of the simple act of breathing. It was the first thing she felt: air sliding in her throat, expanding her lungs. The texture of the air was strange, almost oily, and thick, although how she could describe air as thick she didn't know but that's what it felt like. She could still taste the acidic trace of vomit in her mouth and along the back of her throat.

With the awareness of breathing, she suddenly remembered. Going down, crashing. She opened her eyes and saw nothing. Complete darkness. Was she blind? Was she dead? That unnerving second question trampled over the first one.

Ariana closed her eyes and brought her breathing under control as she'd been taught by her personal trainer. She felt something diagonally across her chest, holding her. She realized it was the shoulder harness for her seat and that feeling brought immediate comfort as she knew she was still sitting in her seat. She was alive and inside the plane. There was no sound of engines, no throb of power coming up from the seat, so she knew they were down.

She opened her eyes again and this time caught the faintest of glows, from a small battery powered emergency light. She blinked, her eyes slowly adjusting to the dimness.

Ariana reached forward, her hands touching the keyboard. She could work that in the dark but she paused as nothing happened. She remembered ordering Carpenter to shut Argus down. Ariana pressed a button on the side of her console and accessed the back-up emergency computer. She hit one of the keys and was rewarded by the glow of her screen. It worked and that meant there was juice coming from the banks of batteries in the cargo hold.

She quickly accessed the emergency program. The computer worked, slower than Argus would have, but eventually the back-up emergency program was up. She hit the command for the emergency lights and the interior of the plane was bathed in a dull red glow. She checked the time and blinked. According to the back-up computer it was over fifteen hours since they'd gone down.

Fifteen hours! Ariana slowly processed that fact in her head. How could she have been out that long? And why had a rescue party not arrived yet? With fumbling hands she unbuckled her harness. She noted as she stood that the plane was resting slightly canted to the right and forward. If they'd crashed, it had to have been a very controlled crash, since the body of the plane seemed intact.

She staggered through the passageway to the console area. As she entered she could hear ragged breathing to the right. She reached out and felt warm flesh. It was Mark Ingram, still strapped to his seat.

Looking down the length of the plane she could see that the crash had had another effect. Ariana hurried to a body laying up against the bulkheads holding the computers. It was one of the imaging camera operators and he was dead. His seatbelt must not have been fastened and his neck had broken when he hit the wall after his chair had slid down the plane.

Ariana looked at him, remembering what she knew about him. She remembered a company picnic less than two months ago. He had a family. She glanced over at his normal console position. There was a photo of a woman and two children that he kept taped to the edge of his computer station. Ariana took a flight jacket that was lying on the floor and put it over the man's face.

Everyone here was still unconscious, but some were starting to stir. Ariana retraced her steps going back forward, passing through her office to the communications center.

There was someone moaning behind a bank of equipment as Ariana turned the corner past her office. Mitch Hudson, strapped to his seat, was pressed up against the back side of equipment. A large rack holding radios had fallen over and slammed on top of his lower body, pinning him into his chair.

"Mitch, are you all right?" Ariana asked as she leaned over him.

Hudson opened his eyes. "My legs."

Ariana looked down. The sharp edge of a receiver had cut through his flight suit. Blood was oozing from torn flesh. Ariana grabbed the metal and strained but it didn't budge. Then she tried his chair, but the sharp intake of breath as soon as she moved it a fraction of an inch told her that it might be better to leave him motionless for now.

"Let me get some help."

Hudson weakly nodded, closing his eyes.

She went back to the console area. Ariana tried to remember but the last thing her mind played back to her was giving the command for everyone to lock in and prepare for crashing. She grabbed Mark Ingram's shoulder and shook him. Soon he was blinking, looking about.

"What happened?" he asked as he unsnapped his harness and stood up.

"I don't know," Ariana answered. "We're down but we seem to have made it all right."

Ingram unbuckled and stood, looking about. "The pilot's must have managed to make it to a landing strip somewhere." Then he spotted the body under the jacket.

"It's John. He's dead," Ariana said. "Mitch is pinned against a console up front. He's hurt."

Others were standing up now, stretching, trying to get oriented, thankful to be alive. She directed two men to the front to help Hudson.

George Craight, a camera tech moved toward her and Ingram. "Where are we?" he asked.

Ariana had been thinking about Ingram's comment that they'd made it to a landing strip. If that were the case, why weren't rescue personnel cutting their way in? For once she wished they had windows in the bay. Given their location when the trouble had started, she knew there were no landing strips marked on the map within a hundred kilometers. The last thing she remembered was the pilot shouting, but he had made no sense.

Ariana turned toward the front of the plane. "Let's find out."

Ingram and Craight followed her as she passed through her office into the communications area. Hudson's legs had been freed and he was carried to the rear to be bandaged. Ariana grabbed the latch that led from the commo area to the cockpit. It seemed reluctant to give way, then turned with a sudden snap as Craight added his strength to hers. A gust of thick air blew in. Ariana took an involuntary step back as she saw that the top half of the cockpit had been cut out, leaving exposed metal edges and wiring. Beyond, a thick yellow-gray mist was swirling about. She thought she could see what appeared to be the faint outlines of some very tall trees in the fog just in front of the plane, but it was hard to make out. Ariana remembered the scene the forward video camera had showed her just before it went dead--the same fog. Her eyes lowered to the seats.

"Oh God!" Ariana staggered back another step. The pilot's body was still strapped in; what was left of it. The top half was gone, leaving just legs and the beginning of a torso ending in a red, gooey mess where the stomach should have continued. Loops of entrails trailed from the body to the torn out metal and disappeared over the edge. The co-pilot's seat was empty, but the cloth was covered with bright red splashes of blood. The seatbelts ended abruptly.

Craight and Ariana tentatively stepped forward into the cockpit, Ingram edging up behind them. Ingram mutely pointed to the right. The navigator wasn't in his seat. Ariana followed the line of Ingram's finger. The navigator must have tried to get away from whatever had happened to the other two in the cabin. His body was crammed under the console holding the plane's flight radios. One arm was wrapped around a stanchion, the fingers rigid. The other arm and half his chest was gone, cut off smoothly as if by a surgeon's knife. His face was contorted with a look of pure terror.

"What happened to them?" Ariana asked, more to push away the horror than expecting an answer.

"It must have occurred during the crash," Craight offered.

Ariana didn't believe that. The cargo bay was relatively intact. How could the top of the cockpit be ripped out? She looked more closely at the edge of the metal: it was cut smoothly, as if removed by a blowtorch, not torn apart by a crash. It was as if someone had popped the front of the plane off to look inside. What could have cut through metal like that, Ariana wondered? Surely not the force of impact, since it was on top of the plane, but there was no other way she could logically explain it to herself.

She staggered as if she'd been hit in the back of the head and a bolt of pain ripped across her consciousness. For a second she thought she'd been hit in the head, but when she turned there was no one there. She realized that the pain was inside her head.

"Let's get out of here," she said.

Craight was moving forward toward where the front windshield had been, trying to see where they were. Ingram edged back toward her and the door.

"Craight!" Ariana snapped. He half-turned and all that did was allow Ariana to be able to see the expression on his face as a beam of golden light touched him in the back. The light expanded and covered his entire body. Craight's left hand was grasping the edge of the pilot's seat and the light touched the metal, backed up and snapped shut at his wrist, neatly severing his hand.

Craight screamed as blood gushed from the wound but Ariana could see that the blood was kept in by the field around Craight, bizarrely flowing up along his arm as if there were a transparent golden cap on the wound. Ariana focused on Craight's eyes, seeing the pain and shock that they expressed. The light rose up, lifting Craight with it so that he was suspended five feat above the plane's floor. Then he was swiftly withdrawn out of the cockpit into the mist. As he went, Ariana could see that his mouth was open, his throat working as if he were screaming, but there was no sound. Then he was gone. She looked back inside. The hand was still clutching the top of the pilot's chair.

Ingram staggered back toward her. She grabbed him and pulled as another beam of light narrowly missed him. They jumped into the commo area, the wind slamming the door shut behind them, but they didn't pause there, continuing through her office, stumbling into the console area where the others were gathered.

Everyone inside the cargo bay looked up as a loud noise grated through the interior. It sounded as if something impossibly large was sliding across the top of the plane.

"Where the hell are we?" Ingram whispered.

Patricia Conners had a wonderful imagination, her husband had always kidded her about that, but she was also very conscientious. The blurs on the three pictures of Cambodia had been bothering her as she worked on other projects and taskings. Finally, her in-box empty, she decided to check everything one more time. Maybe she had missed something the first time around.

She ran a diagnostic on her own computer and printer. Everything worked fine. She went over the KH-12, both the imaging gear and the satellite's on-board computer. Both checked out.

Conners took a pad of paper and put it on her desk. She drew a circle at the bottom of the page and labeled it Cambodia. Then she put a smaller circle in the middle of the page and labeled it KH-12. She drew a line from the bottom one to the middle one. That was the imagery path. It was processed by the on-board computer which had just checked out. She drew another small circle at the top of the page and labeled it "ME". She drew a line from the middle circle to the top one. But she knew that that line was composed of several elements. She turned to her computer to find out exactly what they were.

"KH-12 bounced to MILSTARS 16," she muttered, tracing the data's path. She checked an index binder. MILSTARS 16 was one of the numerous satellites put in geosynchronous orbit by the military to sustain their secure global communications network. This particular one stayed in place over the South China Sea. It covered all of Southeast Asia and the Philippines.

Conners was very aware of both the capabilities and specifications of MILSTARS satellites and the communications system they supported. They were designed to be extremely secure and interception/jam resistant. They could antenna-hop, frequency-hop and burst-transmit. They were also hardened against nuclear attack and electro-magnetic pulse (EMP).

She knew it was a long shot, but she decided to check MILSTARS 16 to make sure it had not garbled the data from the KH-12. She requested a self-diagnostic from the satellite's computer. Two minutes later, the data was displayed on her screen. She read it through, interpreting the numbers and codes as only one who had spent many years reading the mathematical codes of the machines of space could.

All was correct--Conners paused. She looked through once more. The data from the KH-12 had been relayed without disturbance, but there was something about the MILSTARS diagnostic that bothered her. She tried to find what it was, but it eluded her, just a nagging suspicion that something was wrong somewhere else in the system. After a half-hour trying to figure it out, she had to give up and take two of the Tylenol's she carried in her purse to fight off a splitting headache.

CHAPTER FOUR

Lawrence Freed had so far refused to answer any of Dane's many questions. Dane was particularly interested in how Freed and Michelet Technologies knew about his escape from Cambodia thirty years ago. Freed also disclosed no further information about the plane that had crashed. Other than the lack of answers, Freed was a courteous, if distant, escort. Dane knew Freed had military somewhere in his background. There were too many of the little indicators in his demeanor for it to be otherwise.

On board the private jet, Dane had washed up and even given Chelsea a quick cleaning, her hair fouling up the drain in the small shower on board, but Dane figured whoever could afford such an aircraft could afford to get the shower unplugged. Freed had had fresh clothes ready for him that fit perfectly, a subdued look of khaki pants and black shirt. Already, if nothing else, Dane was impressed with the efficiency and wealth of Michelet Technologies, a company he'd never heard of, not that he kept track of such things.

The only conversation they had on the plane was initiated by Freed.

"I heard you were with Special Forces during Vietnam ," Freed said.

"Yes." Since Freed wasn't exactly a fount of information, Dane felt no pressure to give anything away.

"MACV-SOG?" Freed asked.

"Yes."

"Tough unit."

Dane looked at the small black man. He finally noticed the ring on Freed's hand and the triangular symbol carved into the stone, indicating he had served with the Army's elite Delta Force, a symbol only someone in the know would recognize. "Very."

And that was it. The rest of the ride was spent in silence, although Dane suspected he might have snored a bit as he slept most of the way, Chelsea at his feet, also napping. Dane woke up as the plane touched down at Los Angeles International. There was a limousine waiting for them on the runway.

As they rode through Los Angeles to the north, Dane pondered the unusual situation. He knew it wasn't the money that had brought him to Glendale, California. It was the desire for information. Freed and Paul Michelet knew things about him. Dane wanted to know how much they knew. With the mention of Cambodia, Freed had opened the lid on something that Dane had locked tight for three decades. His exhaustion from the search had kept his emotions from boiling over, but now he felt them all sliding about. He'd tried to forget about what had happened on that last mission over the fence and now it seemed it had remembered him.

The expensive shrink Dane has seen ten years ago had told him that one couldn't let go of the past until one faced it and dealt with it, but Dane had assumed he had been speaking metaphorically. Apparently not, Dane mused as he watched the freeway roll by until they exited in Glendale and pulled up to a large black and chrome building with the word MICHELET prominently displayed in front.

Freed escorted Dane and Chelsea through security checkpoints and into the executive elevator. They bypassed the first twenty floors and stopped at the top. The stainless steel doors silently slid open and they walked into an ante room where three secretaries were manning desks. Freed led Dane past them and into a massive office, dominated by a large desk, one of the secretaries following.

A distinguished looking man turned from looking out over the city and strode forward. He extended a hand. "Mister Dane, I'm Paul Michelet."

Dane took the hand, surprised at the strong grip. Michelet leaned over and patted Chelsea on the head. "And this must Chelsea." He straightened and gestured toward a conference table on the left side of the room. Another man was already over there. "I'd like you to meet Professor Beasley."

Dane shook the professor's hand. He noted that Chelsea didn't seem to be alarmed by anyone present which was a positive sign. He himself felt different waves of emotions coming off each man and it was hard to sort out who was feeling what exactly.

Michelet had moved to the end of the table. "Let's sit down. Can I get you anything? Coffee, soda, a drink?" The secretary hovered, ready to fill the order.

"Coffee," Dane said as he took a seat. He immediately noted the maps taped to the table top with acetate overlays covering them. All that green, the contour lines, the rivers, the language. Cambodia.

"Mister Michelet, I'd like to know what's going on," Dane said. "Your man," he indicated Freed who sat across from him, "hasn't told me much."

"He was authorized to tell you as much as necessary to get you to come here, no more than that," Michelet said. He waved a hand and the secretary left, closing the door firmly behind her.

"Perhaps I should have played harder to get then," Dane said. "Maybe I'd know more."

"Please," Michelet looked tired. There were dark rings under his eyes. "I am sorry about the manner in which we are forced to operate, but there are lives and a great deal of money at stake."

"Which is more important to you?" Dane asked.

"One of those lives is my daughter's," Michelet said.

"You didn't answer my question," Dane said.

A red flush spread over Michelet face.

Freed leaned forward. "A specially modified 707 from our company carrying Mister Michelet's daughter and an imagery survey crew went down over Cambodia yesterday. Our last contact with it as it was going down put its position here," he pulled a piece of acetate up from beside his seat and laid it over the map.

Dane checked the spot. As he had expected, it was in the area of his last mission.

"Do you have a transponder beacon?"

"We have nothing," there was an edge to Michelet's voice. "No beacon, no radio contact, nothing."

"Doesn't the airplane have an automatic transponder?"

"Yes, but we're not picking it up," Michelet said.

Dane wasn't surprised. "How many people were on board?"

"My daughter, three in the flight crew and eight in the scientific crew."

"How do you know they weren't killed in the crash?"

"I don't know that, Mister Dane," Michelet answered. "But while there is any possibility of someone being alive, I will pursue every option I have to rescue them."

"What about the Cambodian government?" Dane asked. "With your money, you ought to be able to get them to launch some sort of rescue operation."

Michelet's snort of derision preceded his reply. "What government?"

Freed was more explicit. "There is a lot of turmoil in the Cambodian government right now. Also, we did approach some of our contacts in the military and they flatly refuse to have anything to do with this particular area of their country."

"I don't blame them." Dane looked across the table at the old man. "You said that I was the last person to come out of there alive. How do you know that?"

Freed fielded that question. "We have it from good sources that you went on a covert mission in that area during the Vietnam War."

Dane put his finger on the map. "*I* don't even know for sure if that's where I was. The CIA ran that mission and I presume they're still in the secret business. How do you know that's where I was?"

"I have extensive contacts throughout the government," Michelet said.

Dane wasn't buying that. "The CIA wouldn't give up that information without a reason."

"I have supplied them with data from my surveys in the past," Michelet said, "so it is not unusual for them to supply me with information in return."

"That was a long time ago," Dane said. "No one's been in there since 1968?"

"There have been reports that some people have gone in there," Beasley spoke up. "There was even a report that a Khmer Rouge battalion fleeing government forces retreated into this area. The battalion disappeared to the last man."

That comment earned Beasley a nasty look from Michelet.

Dane sat back in his seat. "I still don't get it. Why me? You've got so many contacts and so much money, even if the Cambodians won't cooperate, why don't you just charter a plane with a whole bunch of rescue guys and go there yourself?"

"As I told you," Michelet said, "you've been there. I don't believe in going in blind."

"It's jungle," Dane said. "Mountains, rivers. There's plenty of people who've been in that kind of terrain."

"But not that specific area," Michelet repeated.

"No one's been in there in the past thirty years?" Dane asked again, believing it, but not wanting to.

"No one we know of who has come back other than you," Freed said. "We've done an exhaustive inquiry."

"What's so special about that specific area?" Dane asked, thinking of the nightmares that woke him drenched with sweat in the middle of the night.

"We don't know," Michelet acknowledged Beasley. "Mister Beasley is an expert in ancient cultures, with an emphasis on Cambodia, its history, its geography, its people. He says that area might once have been part of an ancient kingdom that had its capital at a place called Angkor Kol Ker, somewhere in those mountains."

"What does that have to do with a plane crashing?" Dane demanded, but the words echoed through his brain. He could see Castle lying on the jungle floor and he remembered the CIA man muttering those words with his dying breath. Dane had done some checking over the years but all he had learned was that Angkor Kol Ker was a legendary city that historians and archeologists gave little credence to.

Beasley ran his fingers through his beard. "This area of Cambodia is very unusual. Air Force aircraft overflying it during the war on missions between Thailand and North Vietnam experienced numerous instrument difficulties. So much so that the Air Force specified routes to the north or south and put the airspace off limits. This was after two B-52s and a SR-71 spy plane disappeared without a trace over the area."

Dane controlled his breathing. Foreman hadn't said anything about B-52s going down. Or the area being off-limits to overflights.

But maybe Angkor Kol Ker was the name the Air Force and the CIA had used for that area, taking it from the legends, and that explained why Castle had whispered it. But Dane remembered the look on the dying man's face and knew there was something much more to all of this. There was also the last thing castle had said: The Angkor Gate.

"I understand your team--RT Kansas--went in there looking for the SR-71 crash site," Freed said.

Dane knew there was no point in playing dumb with these people. "That's what we were told."

"Did you find it?"

"No."

Beasley continued. "Since the end of the war, several other aircraft have been lost over the area. No trace of them has ever been found. A Royal Cambodian helicopter that was searching for a missing commercial plane also simply disappeared. Twice search teams were sent in and never returned. The Cambodian government has had much else to worry about for the past several decades and has adopted an informal but very strict quarantine of the area."

"You can see my reluctance to send men in there without knowing what the exact situation is," Michelet said.

"What makes you think I know what the situation is now?" Dane asked. "It's been thirty years."

"You went in there and you came back out," Freed said. "That makes you an expert."

"Expert?" Dane shook his head.

"You are all we have," Michelet said.

Dane laughed, but there was a nasty edge to it. "Then you're screwed. I can't tell you what's going on in there now, but you want to know what the situation was? It was a whole 'nother world. It's like you aren't even in Cambodia anymore." He met Michelet's eyes and locked into them. "There's monsters there. That's what the situation was and probably still is. Monsters you can't even begin to believe in your worst nightmares. And there's something more than monsters. Something even worse. Something intelligent and powerful. That's what wiped out my team. I don't know what's screwing with the planes, but it's monsters who are on the ground that are killing the search parties." He shoved back his seat. "Can I go now?"

Chelsea was on her feat, whining. The other three men in the room were startled into silence.

Finally, Michelet spoke. "My daughter was on that plane and I need to know whether she's alive or dead."

"Then I'll tell you," Dane said. "She's dead. If she's lucky, she died quickly when the plane crashed."

"You're alive!" Michelet threw back. "You went in there and came out. She can come out!"

Dane shook his head. There was no way he could make these people understand. Chelsea was moving around Dane in a circle, upset, her tail wagging wildly. She gave a low whine.

"Someone's alive there," Freed said. He was looking at Michelet and Dane could read that look clearly: Freed did not want Dane involved and now his talk of monsters strengthened Freed's position.

Dane's head swung to Freed. "How do you know someone's alive? I thought you said you haven't heard from the plane since it disappeared?"

"Just before she went down the *Lady Gayle*, that's the name of the plane, was forwarding everything its numerous data collectors were picking up to our IIC, imaging interpretation center, in the basement of this building." Freed pushed a button on the table top in front of him. "They picked up an FM transmission from the ground just before we lost contact with them."

There was a hiss of radio static, then a badly garbled voice spoke, the transmission very broken. "This . . . . Romeo . . . . Verify . . . Not . . Kansas . . . more . . . . Prairie . . . Repeat . . . Fire."

"I understand the name of your reconnaissance team was Kansas," Freed added unnecessarily.

Dane looked down at his hands. They were shaking. After all these years, it couldn't be. But that voice, it was Flaherty. There was no doubting it. "We're not in Kansas anymore," Dane said quietly.

"Excuse me?" Freed was leaning forward.

"It was our verification to the SFOB, Special Forces Operating Base. To verify that it was indeed us and that we were in E & E mode."

"E and E?" Beasley asked.

"Escape and evasion after a Prairie Fire was called." Dane looked up. "But it can't be. That was thirty years ago."

"The message is less than two days old."

Dane looked at Michelet. He could sense there was much the old man wasn't telling him but he could also sense that this radio transmission was real. He didn't know how that could be, but it was.

Dane stood. "When do we leave?"

Deep in the bowels of the National Security Agency, Patricia Conners reread the incoming sat-mail on her computer. The authorization code was correct, but still it bothered her; both the tasking request and the order to destroy any hard copy and computer back-up of the images she had had the KH-12 do over Cambodia. On top of the strange discoloration on the original Cambodia imagery and the nagging suspicion something was wrong with MILSTARS 16, it was turning into one hell of tour of duty for her.

Conners printed out a copy of the request and walked out of her office down the hallway to her supervisor, the head of remote imaging, George Konrad. The door was open and Conners entered, sliding the paper onto Konrad's desk, while settling down in the chair across from her boss.

Konrad put his reading glasses on and read the tasking, then glanced over the top of the rims at her. "And?"

"Who or what is Foreman?" she asked.

"Why do you want to know?" Konrad asked.

"Because he's ordering me to break standard operating procedure by destroying the computer back-up."

Konrad shrugged. "Do it. This order has the proper authorization to do that. You know it's been done before."

That was not the response she had expected. "What about the tasking?"

"What about it?"

"He's asking us to burn a lot of fuel and energy," Conners replied.

Konrad gave her an indulgent smile. "That's not the real reason the tasking bothers you."

Conners sighed. He always saw through her. "All right. How about I don't like using Bright Eye on an operational tasking? I thought it was just a test-bed? And how the hell does this Foreman guy know about Bright Eye?"

Konrad picked up the fax and looked at it once more. "Well, I suppose he knows about Bright Eye because he has the highest security clearance possible; higher than you or I."

"Clearance isn't the issue," Conners argued. "Need to know is." She pointed at the paper. "Earlier today this guy tasked me for a large-scale view of north-central Cambodia using a KH-12. That was a waste of time and resources and he wants me to get rid of all record of it. Now he wants Bright Eye to look at the same area."

Konrad leaned back in his seat. "'Tasked me'?" he repeated.

Conners flushed. "All right. Tasked *us.*"

"You take everything too personally," Konrad said. "You can't do that working for the government."

"So you keep telling me."

"What was on the KH-12 shots that make him want to use Bright Eye?"

Conners had been expecting that question. She pulled the three images out of a file folded and gave them to her boss.

Konrad looked at them. He slumped back in his chair as he slowly went through the images one by one. Finally he put them down. "You aren't supposed to have these."

"You wouldn't have asked for them if you didn't tacitly accept and know that I download all my imagery," Conners said.

Konrad pointed at the discoloration. "Well?"

"I have no idea what caused that," Conners said. "I've run through diagnostics on the KH-12 and my own system and it all checks out." She didn't add her suspicions about MILSTARS 16. One thing at a time, she thought, and also, that satellite was the Pentagon's worry, not the NSA's.

Konrad shrugged. "Well, looking at these I know why Foreman wants to use Bright Eye. If anything can punch through whatever that is, Bright Eye can."

"Getting back to the problem of using Bright Eye for an operational mission," Conners prodded.

"It's not a problem," Konrad returned. "You don't think we spent eight hundred million dollars just to put a prototype up there, run a few tests and then let it float in space, do you?" He shoved the tasking back toward her. "Get Bright Eye moving."

Conners stood. She took the paper but didn't move. "Do *you* have any idea what caused the interference on those shots?"

A flicker passed across Konrad's face. "I have no idea."

Conners frowned. "Have you ever seen anything like that before?"

Konrad glanced past her at the open door. He looked troubled.

"George?" Conners pressed. "You've seen this interference before, haven't you?"

"Yes," he said in a low voice.

Conners turned and swung shut the door without being asked. She walked over to his desk and leaned forward. "Where?"

Konrad laughed nervously. "You're gonna think I'm nuts."

"Where?"

"Off the East Coast. South of Bermuda, on a line running down to Puerto Rico and across to Key West, then back up to Bermuda."

Conners mentally processed that, then blinked. "The Bermuda Triangle?"

"I told you--" Konrad began but she cut him off.

"I believe you. When did you see this?"

"We pick it up every once in a while when we do a standard weather scan for NAOA. A haze blocking out all imaging covering a triangular shaped area. The size varies from nonexistent to a maximum of the triangle I delineated. We never forward

it." He pointed at the paper in her hands. "By orders of Foreman."

"When?" Conners wanted to know.

Konrad laughed. "Hell, I don't know. Every so often. The interference doesn't last long, maybe a couple of hours every few years. We can always get good shots on either side time-wise so no one's really noticed. Been happening ever since I've been here."

Conners blinked. Konrad had been at NSA imaging for over twenty-five years. "You mean Foreman's order on that has been in effect that entire time?"

"You're getting the picture," Konrad said, "no pun intended."

"But what's causing it?" Conners asked.

"I don't know," Konrad said, "and since Foreman wants to use Bright Eye, I would say he doesn't either yet, but he damn well wants to find out."

"Bright Eye has been up over a year," Conners said. "Why now?"

Konrad merely shrugged. "Your guess is as good as mine."

"Do you have any idea who Foreman is?"

Konrad lifted his hands toward the ceiling in a helpless gesture. "Jesus, Pat. You know how much this government spends every year on classified projects? You know how compartmentalized all those projects are? We get taskings all the time from various code-named organizations without a clue to their purpose. Foreman is just another one. All I know is he's CIA."

"Who just happens to be interested in the Bermuda Triangle," Conners said. "And a similar triangle in Cambodia." She was thinking now. "Any place else?" She waited. "George?"

"He's requested other shots over the years. I've seen something like what you have there on imagery taken off the coast of Japan."

"The coast of Japan?" Conners considered that. "Where else?"

"Other places." Konrad pointed to the door. "I suggest you get moving on that request. I've already said too much."

CHAPTER FIVE

Taking stock of the situation had only served to increase the fear and gloom inside the *Lady Gayle*. Ariana had gathered the six surviving members of the crew around Ingram's console after further securing the door to the cockpit by pushing a table and several spare chairs up against it. There's been no more noise or activity outside the plane as far as they could tell, but being blind to the outside world deepened the anxiety inside.

Ariana had explained, as best she could, what had happened to the crew and Craight. To forestall further inquiry into things she couldn't explain, she'd had everyone do an inventory of the supplies inside the cabin.

There was some food in the galley, enough for perhaps a week if eaten sparingly. Water was more critical. They had enough for about four days if rationed. There were two fire axes. They had three first aid kits, one of which had been opened already to treat Hudson's legs. There were two pistols, Berretta 9mm's. She took one, and gave the other to Mark Ingram.

She knew the most critical factor was the people. Some of them she knew quite well, but several were new. Mark Ingram was at her side and she felt comforted by his solid presence. They'd bandaged Mitch Hudson's legs and he was seated at a console, his face taut with pain despite the pills he'd been given. He was good with radios, one of the best, but outside of that she wasn't sure about his capabilities.

The remaining four survivors were a mixed group: Mike Herrin was the senior geologist. In his mid-fifties he was a long-time Michelet employee but Ariana feared he would be the first to crack. He had been unusually quiet but he was constantly rubbing his hands through his thinning gray hair. He was short and pudgy and in Ariana's opinion he was too soft physically and emotionally to deal with the unexpected.

Daniel Daley was the junior geologist and new to the team. He was young, in his mid-twenties and a hulking presence standing behind the others. He had blond hair and looked fresh from the surf off LA, which indeed he was, having earned his PhD at UCLA. To Ariana, he appeared a little scared, but otherwise solid.

Lisa Carpenter was also new. She was the computer expert and electronic troubleshooter. A black woman in her early thirties, she had a bulky, athletic build, with hair cut tight against her skull. She was seated at her console just below Ariana's position, looking up, her face betraying nothing of what she felt, waiting on her next instructions.

The last member was Peter Mansor, the imaging specialist. He was the one who had bandaged Hudson's legs, using his experience from two tours of duty in the military where he had been a helicopter pilot. Mansor had been on several missions with Ariana and she knew he was steady if somewhat unimaginative.

"All right," she said, feeling the focus of six sets of eyes on her. "What do we have in here other than the food, water and first aid kits?"

"A lot of computers, communications and imaging equipment," Ingram said dryly.

"Which we can run only as long as we have power," Lisa Carpenter added.

"What good does that do us?" Herrin asked irritably. "Computers aren't going to get us out of this."

"Communications might," Hudson said.

"Status of that?" Ariana asked him.

"I've got nothing right now," Hudson said. "I've tried sending but we lost our HF antenna in the crash. It was on the roof of the cockpit. I can't access the SATCOM dish on the rotodome. Diagnostics tells me the cable from my radio to the dish has been cut."

"Cut?" Ariana repeated.

"Probably severed in the crash." Hudson looked up at the roof of the cabin. "Hell, the rotodome with the dish might not even be up there any more."

"What else?" Ariana asked, not wanting to dwell on the external condition of the plane.

Hudson ran a hand over his wounded legs, grimacing. "FM is pretty worthless as it's limited by the horizon. If someone comes close, it might work. Our FM antenna still seems to be attached."

"There are search teams looking for us," Ariana said. "So keep the FM ready and broadcast every once in a while."

Hudson nodded.

"Maybe we should leave here and look for the search parties," Daley suggested.

Ariana looked at Mansor who had been trained for such situations in the military.

The former pilot firmly shook his head. "No. We stay with the plane. That's a basic law of survival training. You always stay with the plane. It's the best way to get found. It's a lot easier to find a downed plane than a small group of people wandering around in the jungle."

Herrin laughed, a manic edge to it. "I'm not going out there." He jerked his head toward the cockpit. "We'll end up like Craight."

"What *exactly* did happen to Craight?" Hudson asked.

Ariana glanced at Ingram but for once he had nothing to offer. "We don't know any more than we told you earlier." Ariana had not wanted the conversation to go in that direction but she knew it wasn't something she could avoid forever. "Right now we worry about what is inside here. We seem to be safe for the moment."

Ariana had no desire to open the door leading to the cockpit again. They had the regular door in the left front and the emergency hatches over both wings and one on the roof, but she didn't want to open any of those until they absolutely had to.

"You don't have a clue do you?" Herrin demanded. "You don't know what's going on, do you?"

"Let's take this one step at a time," Ariana said.

"One step at a time? We've goddamn crashed!" Herrin exclaimed. "Craight is dead, his hand cut off and according to you he was whisked away by some sort of strange beam. John died in the crash, his neck broken. The pilots and navigator are dead. We don't know where we are or how we got here. *Something's* out there! Something that wants us!"

"Shut up, Mike," Peter Mansor said it in a low level, but in a tone that seemed to get through to the other man. "Running around screaming and yelling isn't going to do a thing for us right now."

Herrin moaned and sat down, his head in his hands.

Ariana knew she had to get them on some sort of productive path, if only to take their mind off their predicament. "Anyone have any idea what happened to cause us to crash?" she asked.

"The pilots reported losing power and instruments," Ingram said.

"Why?" Ariana asked.

Ingram shrugged. "Could be an on-board computer failure."

Ariana looked at Carpenter. "Can you run through data on the main computer and check that?"

"The mainframe system went down just before we did," Carpenter said. "I'm going to have to reboot Argus. We can't be sure that its hardware wasn't damaged in the crash and we also can't be sure that Argus will reboot."

"Just try, Lisa," Ariana said

Carpenter turned to her computer and began to work.

"How much power do we have in the plane's batteries?" Ariana asked.

"If we just use computers and lights," Ingram said, "we ought to have about fifteen hours worth. If we turn lighting down to emergency levels, we can up that to

about fifty or sixty hours."

"Let's get lighting down to just the emergency setting," Ariana ordered.

"I'll have to do a systems check to make sure nothing else is drawing power," Ingram said.

"Do it."

Ingram threw a switch on the console he was at and the interior went dark except for several red lamps every ten feet or so. In the dim glow, Ariana looked around. "I want you all to go to your stations. I want to know what caused the crash. And I want to get an idea of what's going on outside of this plane without actually going out there. Clear?"

There were no verbal replies, just everyone heading back to their places, Mansor helping Hudson forward to the commo area. Ariana followed and after Mansor left, she took the other seat and spoke so only he heard her. "If we get a cable run to the satellite dish, can you make contact with the IIC?"

Hudson shrugged. "I don't know. I lost SATCOM before we crashed so even if we get a cable from my radio to the dish, if the dish is still there, it still might not work. And who is going out there," he pointed to the roof of the plane, "to run the cable?"

"We might have to do that," Ariana said, "but not yet. I just want to know what my options are. Keep monitoring FM. There are search parties out there."

"We lost FM too before the crash," Hudson pointed out.

Ariana leaned close. "Just because we lost it then, doesn't mean it's down now, right?"

"Well--" Hudson began, but she cut him off.

"Your job is communications. The only way we're getting out of here is by talking to someone, so I don't want to hear what you can't do, I want to know what you can do. Clear?"

Hudson's jaw quivered and his hands went down to his wounded legs. "Clear," he said through clenched teeth.

"Good." Ariana put a hand on his shoulder. "I know you're hurting, but we need you Mitch. Hang tough."

"Yeah," Hudson turned his back to her.

Ariana left him and went to console area.

"I've got something strange," Carpenter called out as she walked in. Ariana and Mark Ingram hurried over to her position.

"What is it?" Ariana asked.

Carpenter was staring at her screen. "You turned on the emergency program to get the lights on," she said. "That's run off a separate, smaller, back-up computer from the mainframe to keep the two systems from contaminating each other in case one gets a virus or malfunctions."

"I know that," Ariana said.

Carpenter looked at both of them. "I took Argus off-line just before we crashed, but--" she paused.

"But what?"

"But it didn't go off. It's been on this whole time."

Ariana frowned. "So?"

"Well, first, it should be off. I know I hit the shut-down. But that's only the first weird thing." Carpenter pointed a long black finger at the massive racks containing the hardware for Argus. "It's on and I can't access it."

"I don't understand," Ingram said. "What's it doing?"

"I don't know."

"Take a guess," Ariana pressed.

Carpenter frowned. "Well, it's like someone's taken it over. Maybe planted a Trojan Horse program in it that got activated or, I don't know, sending commands into it some other way."

"Goddamn Syn-Tech," Ariana muttered. "Could that have been what caused the crash?"

"I don't know," Carpenter said. "I don't think so, but it's possible."

Ariana pointed at the computer. "Shut it down."

"I told you I can't get access from my console. The only way I can do that now," Carpenter said, "is to cut the power coupling going to Argus's base unit. Pull the plug."

"Do it."

As Carpenter walked over to the racks, Ariana walked Ingram to his position. "What do you have?"

"I'm putting together the data we recorded just before we went down off of tapes," Ingram said. His eyes were on his screen. "As you know we lost SATCOM, GPR, and FM first. I've got our last transmissions and our last GPR position. After--" he paused, squinting at the screen.

"What?" Ariana prompted him.

"There's something funny about the GPR data," Ingram said.

Ariana frowned. The GPR was just a link from the plane to the nearest three global positioning satellites that gave them their location. She waited as Ingram worked his computer.

"Someone piggybacked on the GPR signal in and out," he finally said.

"What does that mean?" Ariana asked.

"It means someone in the crew was sending a secret message out that we weren't supposed to know about," Hudson said. "Someone was sending our data to another location via the GPS satellites just as

93

we were sending it to the IIC." He looked up at her. "We have a spy on board."

"Great," Ariana muttered.

"Oh God!" the yell came from the computer racks.

Ariana raced there, the others following. Lisa Carpenter held a gray panel in her hand, but she was frozen, staring at the bulky metal rectangles that held the core of Argus.

Ariana immediately saw what had caused Carpenter's reaction: a golden beam about eight inches in diameter had punched through the skin of the plane underneath the main computer console. A foot from the computer hardware, the beam split into four smaller lines of two inches diameter, each one going into a different box. The gold lines pulsed and rippled and as they watched a new two inch line split from the main beam and probed its way blindly to the left, finally hitting another piece of Argus. There was a brief hiss, then the line was in. The main gold beam widened by a couple of inches.

"What the hell is that?" Ariana demanded.

"I have no idea," Carpenter said. "But I know why I can't access Argus now. This thing is taking control of it."

"Cut the power!" Ariana ordered.

Carpenter pointed at a black cable lying on the floor. "I already did that.

Whatever that thing is, it's not only controlling the mainframe but it's also powering Argus."

Conners had given the order for the satellite carrying Bright Eye to change orbit over twenty minutes ago. Since it was in a fast polar orbit, execution required a firing of booster rockets to maneuver the angle of flight over the target area. The computer told her that she had a TOT of another twenty-two minutes before Bright Eye made the pass, which gave her time to reflect on the secretive history of the equipment she was about to use.

She knew that Bright Eye had gone into orbit a little over a year ago. Although Star Wars had been officially cut when the Democrats took over the White House as part of the 'peace dividend', Conners knew what had really happened. The Black Budget people had simply kept Star Wars, renaming it the Odysseus Program, and kept eighty percent of the funded programs alive behind a veil of secrecy that had existed in bureaucratic Washington ever since the end of World War II.

Conners knew now that the military-industrial complex Eisenhower had railed against as he left office had been only the tip of the iceberg. Very little of what was really going on was visible to the public eye. Billions and billions were spent every year on classified work.

What Conners also knew, having worked at the National Security Agency and being affiliated with the NRO, National Reconnaissance Office, which oversaw almost two-thirds of Black Budget operations, was that many of these projects were valid national security endeavors and not a waste of money. In fact, many great strides had been made in varied scientific fields through Odysseus Projects, the results slowly filtered out to the rest of the scientific community to not draw suspicion.

Much of the laser work for Bright Eye project had helped other scientists in the medical field. But no one outside of the intelligence community had any idea that something like Bright Eye was beyond the conceptual stage and actually in orbit.

Bright Eye had evolved from a Navy program which in itself had begun with a problem that needed to be solved. With the growing advancement in the threat posed by submarines, particularly missile carrying ones, the Navy had begun to place greater and greater emphasis on being able to track enemy submarines, especially those that carried ballistic missiles.

The first step in that process had started in the fifties and sixties when the Navy had developed a sound surveillance system, codenamed SOSUS, to track submarines. The first SOSUS systems were laid along the Atlantic Coast. Then the Navy put in a SOSUS system codenamed Colossus along the Pacific Coast. Then, with further advances in technology, the Navy moved part of the system toward Russia to catch Soviet subs as they put to sea, putting systems off the two major Russian submarine ports at Polyarnyy and Petropavlovsk.

Over the years the Navy added to the SOSUS system. They put a line of hydrophones off Hawaii in the Pacific. Each of these individual listening devices was as large as an oil storage tank, towed out to the designated point, sunk to the bottom of the ocean and linked by buried cable to the next listening device in line, eventually being brought to shore in Hawaii, an intricate and expensive project.

Then, having achieved the ability to listen to activity in both major oceans, the Navy went a step further, tying the various systems together. Prior to that, SOSUS could only give a rough idea of a sub's location. By linking the various systems, the Navy could now pinpoint the exact location of any sound emitter in the ocean using triangulation from various SOSUS systems. The Navy hooked all the SOSUS systems together using FLTSATCOM--the Fleet Satellite Communication System and downlinked it all to a computer at Fleet Headquarters.

All in all, a most efficient system, Conners knew, except for one major problem the Navy had had from the very beginning: they could tell where submarines were, but the system couldn't tell if the submarine contact was friendly or enemy. When Conners had first heard of that problem she had wondered why it was a problem at all, since she had assumed, as most people did, that the Navy knew where all its submarines were and if it wasn't ours, then it must be their's.

She was surprised to learn that the Navy didn't know the specific locations of its own submarines for a deliberate reason: to insure their security.

The boomers, as the Navy called them, patrolled at the discretion of their own skippers within a large designated area. That way no one could find them. But the Navy realized after hooking the SOSUS system together that they had to be able to tell friendly subs from unfriendly or else they could end up sinking their own submarines in time of war.

The solution to *that* problem became the seed idea for Bright Eye. Some whiz kid at a Navy lab happened on the answer, which at first was greeted with disbelief. Every US and NATO sub was given an ID code which was painted in large letters and numbers with a special laser reflective paint on the upper deck. The Navy could read the codes by pinpointing a sub's location using the SOSUS, then using one of the FLTSATCOM satellites firing a laser downlink. Using a high intensity blue-green light, the laser could penetrate the ocean to submarine depth. The paint reflected the laser beam and the satellite picked up the reflection, forwarding the code to fleet headquarters. No code was a bad guy.

The Odysseus scientists studied the results of this laser program. The key to Star Wars had always been finding and tracking enemy planes and missiles in the first place. You couldn't hit it if you couldn't find it. Surveillance was the critical link and they were looking for the next step beyond the infrared and thermal imaging used aboard the KH-12. Lasers, operating at the speed of light and capable of great power, seemed the next logical progression and thus Bright Eye was born.

Bright Eye consisted of a large circle of laser emitters. By varying the focal length of the emitters, the operators could vary the color of the beam emitted. Using a special computer, the lasers could cycle through a spectrum of colors in rapid succession. Depending on what colors were reflected and how quickly, an accurate view of Bright Eye's focus could be developed. The advantage of the lasers over other emitters was their more powerful beam could cut through severe weather conditions. They were also effective at night. Having a power source in orbit strong enough to fire the lasers from orbit down to Earth was solved by lifting a small nuclear reactor into space, a move made in the utmost secrecy. There was of course the possibility of nuclear disaster if the launch vehicle had exploded going into orbit. Fortunately, no mishaps had occurred.

The second problem was a substantial one. The lasers were so powerful that they would blind any humans in the area who happened to look up into the beams at the moment they came down; therefore Bright Star's use was limited.

And this was why Conners had gone to Konrad. She didn't want to be responsible for hundreds, if not thousands of blinded Cambodians.

The computer beeped, letting Conners know that Bright Eye was rapidly approaching the target area. She ran through the final checks one more time. She sensed Konrad had joined her. He was looking over her shoulder waiting to see what happened.

One hundred and twenty miles up, the dual satellite combination sped through space, north to south over the globe, China passing beneath rapidly. The reactor was working perfectly, a large cylinder, lacking the shielding of its cousins on the planet's surface below. Next to it, the circular satellite containing Bright Eye was also functioning properly. The twenty foot round door that covered the laser array smoothly slid open, revealing the tips of the emitters. A large flat panel, the laser receiver, was extended on a mechanical arm to the right of the array, unfolding until it was over a hundred yards long by fifty wide, its cells ready to receive the bounceback.

Power flowed from the reactor to the lasers, accumulating in capacitors as the countdown dropped below twenty seconds. As Bright Eye passed over north-central Cambodia, the on-board computer went into hyper-drive. Bolts of laser light flashed out, each individual laser immediately firing again and again as the computer rotated both the frequency of the laser itself and the direction the tip was pointed in, making minute adjustments at the base of each. Those tiny adjustments, when multiplied over the one hundred and twenty-five mile down trip each laser beam traveled, allowed Bright Eye to take an accurate picture of a large area.

Traveling at the speed of light, the first beams reached down and hit the target area.

"We're getting something," Conners announced as she read the data on her computer screen, a real-time downlink from Bright Eye, showing what the receiving panel was getting. "I think we've got a--"

She paused as a large glow showed in the middle of the screen. "What the heck?"

A bolt of energy, in the shape of large glowing golden ball, over fifty meters in diameter, punched out of the mist covering the triangle and raced up through the down-firing lasers, scattering them in all directions.

As it gained altitude, the ball's diameter slowly grew smaller, but it was covering the distance between it and Bright Eye at a rapid pace.

"Shut it down!" Konrad yelled.

They could both see the large golden ball on the sighting scope downlink that was part of Bright Eye. The laser image had gone completely haywire.

Conners fingers flew over the keyboard, turning off the lasers, but the ball continued to gain altitude toward Bright Eye, until it filled the entire screen. Then suddenly there was a gold flash of light and nothing. The data that had been on the computer screen suddenly went dead.

"Do you have contact?" Konrad demanded.

Conners felt the bottom of her stomach fall out as she realized what she had seen. "Nothing. I've got nothing. Bright Eye is gone!"

"Oh, man! I've got to call the Director," Konrad was running from her office.

"Dear Lord," Conners whispered.

CHAPTER SIX

"Monsters? What exactly did you mean by that?"

Dane had been waiting for that question and as he'd expected, Freed was the one to pose it. There'd been no time for it to be asked earlier. Since Dane had accepted the mission they had been busy, getting ready to depart and heading to the airfield.

They were in Michelet's private jet, the same converted 707 that had flown Dane and Chelsea from the disaster site to LA. Now they were over the eastern Pacific, heading west at maximum speed. Paul Michelet and Roland Beasley were seated in deep leather chairs on the other side of a small table. Freed was next to the window on Dane's right and Chelsea lay in the aisle at Dane's other side, sleeping.

"If the CIA told you about me," Dane said, "then you probably saw the after-action report for that mission. I told them the truth."

Michelet shook his head. "We never saw a copy of the after-action report. But if you told the CIA that monsters were responsible for the mission's failure, that would explain a lot."

"Like my getting chaptered out of the army on a psych eval?" Dane asked.

"Yes," Freed said, meeting Dane's gaze. "We knew about your discharge, but all we could find out was that it was listed as combat stress."

Dane's laugh had a bitter edge to it. "I was on my second tour and I'd been running cross-border recon missions for six months. I'd had more than my share of combat stress, but when I got debriefed in Laos by the CIA field rep, he didn't back up a word I said, just passed me to their army liaison who thought I was bonkers."

Dane hadn't been worried about keeping his army career. Not after what he had seen. Surprisingly, Foreman had listened to him carefully, asking many questions, expressing no opinion one way or the other. But the army had definitely had a negative reaction and with no back-up from Foreman, they had quickly dumped him.

"What kind of monsters?" Freed asked, ever the professional, trying to size up the opposition no matter how strange.

Dane wondered why they believed him. Of course, he reminded himself, maybe they didn't and were just humoring him.

"If we're going in there," Dane said, pointing at the ever-present map on the table in front of him, "then you need to hear what happened on that mission."

He told the story, from leaving the CCN camp in Vietnam, through the CIA base in Laos, the flight in, the landing zone, the movement and the crossing of the river. He wasn't interrupted once, not even when he tried as best he could to describe the encounter on the other side of the river. When he finished describing Flaherty being dragged away into the fog by a blue beam of light, he had to stop for a moment. He had never told another person the complete story after being debriefed by Foreman thirty years ago.

There were many times he had wondered if it all hadn't been a nightmare, but always the reality of his memory came was reflected by the scar on his forearm.

"How did you get away?" Freed asked.

"I ran," Dane said.

They waited for an elaboration, but Dane added none.

"How did you get out of immediate area and escape the monst-- whatever it was that did that to your team?"

It was hard for Dane to know what Freed believed by the tone of his voice. "I was lucky." The voice in his head, Dane decided was something he best keep to himself. Over the years working with Chelsea, he had learned to keep silent about the voices and the things his mind saw and heard that others didn't. He'd known since he was very small that he was different. He'd learned early on that people feared and distrusted different.

"Lucky?" Michelet repeated.

Dane shrugged. "I was chased to the river. Once I got on the other side, out of the mist, there was no problem."

"No monsters?" Freed said, his voice flat.

"No monsters."

"No beams of light?"

"No."

"How did you get out of Cambodia?" Freed pressed. "You said you didn't know where the CIA pick-up zone was."

"I used the river as my left guide. I knew it would flow east, eventually emptying into the Mekong. Then I followed the Mekong to South Vietnam. I was picked up by friendly forces there and immediately flown back to Laos for debrief."

"You make it sound simple," Freed said. He tapped the map. "It's over five hundred kilometers from where you were to South Vietnam. Through territory thoroughly infiltrated by the Viet Cong and the NVA."

Dane shrugged, but didn't elaborate. He felt no need to share that hellish trip with these men, safely seated in the comfort of the Michelet corporate jet. The nights spent pushing through the jungle. The days hidden, covered by leaves, insects crawling over his body. The grubs he'd eaten for nourishment. The feeling of sitting totally alone, sensing there wasn't anyone within miles, listening to the sounds of the jungle, falling into fitful sleep, nightmares jolting him awake, hearing the cries of his teammates.

"What do you think it was that burned you and Flaherty?" Freed asked, bringing the conversation back to possible threats. "The beam of light?"

Dane thought it interesting that of everything he described that was the threat Freed focused on. He could feel the scar tissue on his forearm. "I have no idea. I just saw the beam of light."

"A laser?" Michelet asked.

"I don't know."

"You say there were two colors of light. One gold, one blue?" Michelet asked.

"Yes."

"Perhaps the other things--the monsters--you saw were holograms," Michelet suggested. "One of my divisions has been doing some work on those for the movie industry. Very realistic. In fact," he added, "this strange fog you're talking about, it would help with the projection process considerably."

Dane wasn't surprised at that response. "It wasn't a hologram that killed my team. The thing Flaherty shot died. I don't think you can do that with holograms. The bullets would have went right through it. And it was almost thirty years ago. I don't believe anyone had

102

technology that could have produced those things back then or even now."

"Did it ever occur to you that you might have imagined the whole episode?" Freed quietly asked.

Dane stared at the black man. "Yes. It occurred to me."

"The CIA has done quite a bit of work on hallucinogens," Freed said. "Perhaps you were part of an experiment. I know that some of those cross-border teams used chemical warfare agents, some of it pretty cutting edge stuff."

Dane shrugged. "If you think I hallucinated the whole thing then you made a big mistake bringing me here. Unless of course you've hallucinated your plane going down."

"I'm not doubting you," Freed said. "I'm just doing my job."

"I know that," Dane said, "but remember you came to me."

"I've heard that MACV-SOG used to issue drugs to its people," Freed persisted, ignoring him.

Dane nodded. "We used amphetamines sometimes on missions, after we'd been in for a few days, but I hadn't taken anything on that mission. We weren't in long enough."

"Did you carry any chemical agents to use on enemy personnel?" Freed asked.

"No."

"But--" Freed began, when Dane interrupted him.

"Listen," he said, pointing at the tape recorder on the table. *"You're* the one who told me that message from my old team was real and only two days old. And that it came from here," Dane's fist thumped down onto the map. "So unless *you're* lying, then you have to believe I'm telling the truth."

"Uhh--" Beasley caught everyone's attention. "Could you describe the thing that your team leader shot a little more clearly?"

Dane ignored Freed's look of irritation and gave as much detail as he could.

Beasley pulled a folder out of his briefcase when Dane was done. The professor thumbed through then stopped on a certain page. "Did it look like this?"

Dane looked at the picture of carved stone, then up at the professor. "That's it exactly."

"Hmm," was Beasley's only comment.

"Where was that picture taken?" Freed demanded.

"Angkor Wat," Beasley replied. "Off a temple wall."

"What is it?" Freed asked, taking the book and looking at it more closely.

"A creature of Cambodian myth," Beasley said. "It seems the legends are coming alive."

Dane flipped pages, looking at other carvings. There were no representations of the cylindrical objects that had gotten Castle. He paused at one page. "What's this?"

Beasley looked down. "That's a *Naga*."

"There was a sculpture of that on each corner of the watchtower we found," Dane said.

Beasley nodded. "That's not uncommon. *Naga* is Sanskrit for snake. The *Naga* in this part of the world is a sacred snake. It plays an important part in the mythology of Southeast Asia and in Hinduism. In fact, it is probably the most important symbol in that part of the world. In Hindu mythology, the *Naga* is coiled beneath and supporting Vishnu on the cosmic plane. The snake also swallows the waters of life, these being set free when Indra hits the snake with a bolt of lightning, rupturing the snake's skin.

"What's interesting," Beasley continued, "is that the word has meaning far beyond the borders where the Sanskrit language is used. In Egypt and even Central and South America, the word *Naga* is used, but in those places it means one who is wise. In China the word *Naga* is representative of the dragon and is associated with the Emperor or the 'son of heaven.'"

Beasley continued. "There are some fringe groups that believe the word *Naga* is one of the few words from an earlier, universal language, that has survived into 'modern' language. The language of Atlantis." Beasley ignored the looks that statement brought him. "Of course, the serpent myth is larger than simply the Sanskrit word *Naga*. Even Christianity's oldest myth features a serpent."

"You say this thing was what you shot?" Freed was staring at the first picture.

"Yes," Dane answered.

"I want a full brief-up on Angkor Wat before we land," Michelet said. "I want to know everything there is to know about it."

Beasley shrugged. "I can do that in ten minutes because we don't know much about it at all."

"Just get it ready," Freed said in clipped voice, before turning back to Dane.

They questioned him in more detail but despite the nightmares that he'd had over the years, he wasn't able to elaborate much. He sensed that Freed knew he was holding something back, but Dane told them as much as they needed to know. What was his own, Dane felt he could keep to himself.

"I've got a question," Dane said during one of the brief pauses between questions directed his way. "How do you propose to get us into the area?"

Freed pulled a piece of acetate from under the map and laid it on top. "This is an outline of the no-fly area that the Air Force imposed during the Vietnam War."

It showed an inverted, triangular shape covering several hundred square kilometers of north-central Cambodia. Dane examined it. The eastern angle of the triangle ran along the river that he had crossed so many years ago.

"Where exactly did your plane go down?" Dane asked.

Freed used an alcohol pen to mark a spot on the overlay. It was about five kilometers inside the eastern edge of the triangle. "Right about there," Freed said.

"When did the plane start experiencing trouble?" Dane asked.

Freed marked another spot, this one about ten kilometers further east from the last dot, just outside the triangle.

"It's bigger," Dane said.

"What's bigger?" Michelet asked.

Dane pointed. "The triangle. It's crossed the river, if it affected your plane that early."

The other three stared at the map.

"This ancient guard house you saw," Beasley prompted.

"Yes?" Dane said.

"Where was it?"

Dane looked at the map. "If this is where you say I was, then it was on the high ground, here to the east of this river." Dane allowed his mind to project the contour lines of the map into a three dimensional mental image. "It was right here."

Freed noted the position. "It might be a good place to start."

"That's your job, Mister Freed," Michelet said. He turned to Beasley. "Now it's time for you to earn your money. Tell me about Angkor Wat and this carving of the creature that Dane says his team leader shot."

Beasley nodded. "If you want to know about Angkor Wat, I have to give you an overview of Cambodia's history first, because Angkor Wat comes later." Beasley waved a fat hand over the map. "Around 800 AD this entire area was under the control of the Khmer Empire. Most people have heard of Angkor Wat, which is the massive temple complex built in the ancient city of Angkor Thom right here, but the first capitol of the Khmer was at Angkor Kol Ker."

"I thought you said that was a legend?" Michelet interrupted.

"Sometimes all we have to work with are legends," Beasley said. "And often there is quite a bit of truth in legend. After all, they just don't spring up from nothing. There is always a seed of something real at the core of every legend."

"Where did the Khmers come from?" Dane asked.

Beasley shrugged. "If I could answer that, I'd have solved one of the greatest debates about that part of the world. No one really knows. Historically, the Khmer seem to have appeared out of nowhere and then a millennium later the kingdom disappeared and the city was deserted. From the Fifth to the Fifteenth centuries the Khmer empire was the greatest in Southeast Asia and the city of Angkor Thom, which contains the temple of Angkor Wat, was one of the greatest cities of the world."

Beasley continued. "But at the very beginning of the empire, before Angkor Thom was founded, the Khmer capitol was reportedly at Angkor Kol Ker. The city was abandoned and the king moved south in 800 AD to found Angkor Thom. It has always been a subject of debate among Cambodian scholars as to the reason for that move and the location of Kol Ker."

"When was Angkor Kol Ker founded?" Dane asked.

"The Khmer Empire was first mentioned in Chinese histories in the 5th Century which is why I said earlier that the Empire lasted a thousand years. But even those histories say the Khmer Empire existed long before then. Some suggest for several thousand years before that, which is quite remarkable if you think about it. In fact," Beasley seemed to be relishing his role as resident expert, "in an ancient Chinese text about the Xia State, usually considered the first Chinese unified state in the third millennium BC, there is an obscure reference about an Empire far to the south whose people came from over the large sea."

Dane frowned. "What large sea?"

"I would assume the Pacific," Beasley said, "given the geography of that part of the world, although for the ancient people of that time, even the Sea of China would have been considered a very large body of water."

"If it was the Pacific," Dane said, "then that's saying the Khmer came from the Americas three thousand years before Christ was born?"

"Possibly much earlier than that," Beasley said.

"But--" Dane shook his head. "But I thought the Pacific wasn't crossable given the state of navigation and ships of that time."

Beasley shrugged. "It isn't just ships. *Civilization* itself didn't supposedly start anywhere on the planet until about 3,000 BC, in China and Mesopotamia. So how did this people obviously coming *from* a highly civilized place, cross the Pacific and settle in Cambodia at a time when historians tell us civilization didn't even exist? Quite a puzzle, eh?

"All of you gave me a strange look when I mentioned Atlantis, but there may be more to the legend if you start connecting the dots world-wide. I wouldn't be the farm on it with what I know right now, but I wouldn't rule out the possibility of such a place really existing and the founders of Angkor Kol Ker being refugees from it."

"Where was Angkor Kol Ker supposed to have been?" Dane asked, remembering the dying words of the CIA man and wanting to stay focused on the immediate problem.

Beasley's hand made a wide swath over the map. "No one knows exactly. Best guess is to the north and east of Angkor Thom and the later palaces built in that region. Most likely in the area where we are going, the remote Banteay Meanchey Region. The jungle can completely cover a place in a few years and there certainly has never been much detailed mapping of the area done."

"Why was Angkor Kol Ker abandoned?" Dane asked.

Beasley leaned forward in his seat. "Whatever's going on there now would certainly have been a reason enough to leave then, wouldn't it? The blockhouse you describe sounds like it was set up to oversee this triangle."

"How long was Angkor Kol Ker the capitol of the Khmer empire?" Michelet asked.

"I don't know," Beasley said. "No one does. The only official and agreed upon history we have of the Khmer's starts with the establishment in 802 AD of Angkor Thom. As I've said, they could have been in Angkor Kol Ker for hundreds, if not thousands of years prior to that. And God knows where they were before that."

Michelet stood up and began pacing. "This is all nonsense. You're talking about events over a thousand years ago," Michelet said. "What could be in there for a thousand years?"

Beasley smiled, his fat lips revealing crooked teeth. "Have you ever seen old maps? Maps made when men still had to venture out into the unknown, where as far as they knew, no man had been before them?"

Beasley didn't wait for an answer. "There used to be large white spaces on those maps, areas no one knew anything about, or where those who had gone exploring never returned. For lack of anything else to put in those blank spaces, the cartographers would write: 'Here there be monsters.'"

Beasley tapped the map. "Well, I think here there be . . ." he looked at Dane, ". . . monsters. If there's any place on the face of the planet where monsters could still be hiding, it would be here, in the middle of the Cambodian jungle, a place that is practically inaccessible."

"But you don't think there are monsters, do you?" Dane asked.

"I think things can be explained scientifically," Beasley said. "For years people thought there was a monster in Loch Ness. They even had a photo, or so the supporters of that theory said, but it turns out the photo was a fake. There was no monster."

"People and planes didn't disappear into Loch Ness," Freed observed.

"Yes, that is a troubling aspect," Michelet said.

"I think it might be worthwhile to take the analogy I made a little bit further," Beasley said. "In ancient days they marked the blank spots on their maps as being filled with monsters and demons. As these areas were explored, what was really there was filled in." He tapped the map. "Perhaps, all we have here is a natural phenomenon in this area that we do not yet understand."

"You have to be able to get there to examine it," Dane said. "So far that plan hasn't worked well for anyone."

"But just think," Beasley said. "If we could find Angkor Kol Ker, we might be able to prove the existence of a civilization that predates the commonly accepted start-point for civilization! And, if the Chinese legend is true, that civilization might have even crossed the Pacific and come from somewhere in the Americas or even beyond! That would throw our accepted course of the history of civilization completely in disarray. It opens up all sorts of exciting possibilities."

Freed leaned forward, ignoring the academic's enthusiasm, and focusing on Dane. "The things you describe, how could they affect an aircraft? Interfere with navigational devices and radio?"

"I don't know," Dane said. "That beam of light that lifted Flaherty up. That certainly had some power to it. The thing he shot was a monster or some sort of creature, maybe even," he said glancing at Beasley, "some animal that's remained hidden deep in the jungle all these years, but the other stuff;" Dane paused. "Well, the sphere that got Castle, that was something else. I don't think that was natural but it wasn't a machine either."

"I just want to get my daughter our of there," Michelet said. "All this speculation does us no good."

"It gives us an idea of what we're up against in an unprecedented situation," Freed said.

"But there is perhaps a precedent," Beasley said. "There is another place on the planet where people and planes and ships disappear and monsters have been reported. I'm sure you've all heard of the Bermuda Triangle."

"Oh, Christ," Freed muttered, finally letting his feelings show and dropping his professional shield.

"Think about it!" Beasley said excitedly. "The Bermuda triangle encompasses water. What if there were something like it on land?"

"What exactly is the Bermuda Triangle?" Dane asked, interested in this new theory. He had never made this connection.

Beasley shrugged. "No one really knows. But a lot of weird happenings have been documented in the area. The few times in recent memory that people have tried to penetrate this area in Cambodia, weird things have also happened. Plus," he added, "they're both shaped like triangles."

"Gentlemen," Paul Michelet cut in. "Let's stick to what we do know and not go off on tangents." He looked at the clock on the wall of the cabin. "We will be in Thailand in six hours."

"You still haven't told us about Angkor Wat," Dane prompted Beasley, intrigued that there was a relief of one of the things that attacked his team on a temple wall there. It was the first solid proof besides the scar he had that his memory wasn't a combat induced nightmare. It was also a link to sanity in another way: perhaps these creatures of legend had once been real and some of them had survived over the course of the centuries, hidden deep in this forbidden land they were heading towards.

"Angkor Wat is the central temple in the city of Angkor Thom," Beasley said. "Angkor Thom was the capitol of the known Khmer Empire starting in 802 AD. At that time the Khmer Empire stretched from the Dangrek Mountains in the west to the Cardomon Mountains in the east and south to coast.

"Cambodian legend has it that at one time the entire area was part of the Gulf of Siam, but that a prince fell in love with the daughter of a seven-headed serpent, the *Naga* King, as I've already mentioned. The snake drank all the water to make a place for his daughter to live and thus Cambodia came into being."

Beasley paused, sensing the disinterest on the part of both Michelet and Freed. "Gentlemen, it is good to remember that much truth is hidden in legend."

"A seven-headed snake?" Michelet growled. "My only concern is getting my daughter."

"Go on," Dane urged.

"All right," Beasley said. "Just the facts. Besides the mountains surrounding it, the two major geological features of Cambodia are Tonle Sap Lake and the Mekong River. Tonle Sap is the largest freshwater lake in Southeast Asia. It is connected to the Mekong via the Tonle Sap River. During the rainy season, when the Mekong floods, the river reverses course and flows back into the lake, doubling its size. This phenomenon is most interesting and has lead to a massive amount of land, some of which is inside your triangle," Beasley added, pointedly looking at Michelet, "being flooded for half the year. Tonle Sap, when it floods, comes within a few miles of Angkor Wat. I don't think the positioning of the temple or the city was coincidence."

Beasley leaned forward. "Water is the key. Not just Tonle Sap and the Mekong, but in the way the Khmer built their cities and temples." He reached into his leather briefcase and pulled out some imagery. "These are the pictures taken by the space shuttle in 1994 of Angkor Thom and Angkor Wat. Notice the moats. Nowhere else on earth has man put such effort in building such massive structures with water barriers as an integral part.

"The moats separate the sacred world from the outer world in Khmer mythology. Look how the temple of Angkor Wat is completely surrounded."

Dane saw what Beasley meant. A very wide dark band surrounded the temple

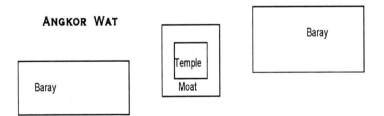

Beasley nodded. "More water. Those are Barays or reservoirs, which is rather interesting considering there is no need for reservoirs

for agriculture in that area, given that there is normally sufficient water already present. Those Barays, each over 16 square kilometers in size, can feed into the moats surrounding both Angkor Thom and Angkor Wat. Keeping those moats filled must have been of tremendous importance to the Khmer."

Beasley's thick finger centered on the square representing Angkor Wat. "The temple is considered one of the world's foremost architectural wonders. If it were any place other than in the jungles of Cambodia, it would be as well known as the Great Pyramids of Egypt.

"In fact, the amount of stone used in building Angkor Wat is estimated to be equal to that used in the Great Pyramid at Giza. The temple covers a square kilometer and the central spire or Prang as it is called, rises over 213 feet above the moats. It is the largest temple of any kind in the world, easily dwarfing the great cathedrals of Europe.

"Unlike the pyramids, though, the surfaces of the temple are not smooth stone. The Khmer covered every available surface with finely carved bas-relief and figure sculpture."

Dane noted that even Michelet and Freed had been drawn in by Beasley's voice and were now listening carefully.

"Angkor Wat was supposedly built with a very specific idea in mind: to be a schematic interpretation of the Hindu Universe. The Prang in the center represents mythic Mount Meru, while the surrounding moats supposedly represent the ocean."

"Why do you say supposedly?" Dane asked.

"You have to remember that Hinduism and Buddhism came to Cambodia *after* these temples were built so those explanations of the architecture and layout that are commonly accepted could not have been the motivating factor in the design or building, but rather added on after the fact, something many of my colleagues fail to acknowledge. What they view as the result of a myth, may in fact have given rise to the myth.

"It is that motivation, gentlemen," Beasley said, "that I believe to be critical to solving whatever this mystery is."

"We don't have to solve a mystery," Michelet said. "We just have to get my daughter and the others out."

Beasley shook his head. "I think you are mistaken, Mister Michelet. I think this mystery has ensnared your daughter, and the members of your team," he added, nodding toward Dane. "And we won't be able to accomplish your goals unless we have a much better understanding of what we are up against."

Bangkok was known in the Orient as Sin City. From its early days catering to divisions of American soldiers on furlough from Vietnam, to the present-day battalions of Japanese businessmen who took sex junkets from their island kingdom, Bangkok had slid into a cesspool of crime, prostitution and corruption that, truth be known, the men in power in Thailand were quite glad to have. Vice brought in hard currency and since it wasn't likely that Disney was going to open a theme park on the muddy banks of the Cho Prang River that ran through the city, the sex industry would have to suffice. Human bodies were not worth much in Thailand and despite having perhaps the highest rate of HIV per capita in the world, the government was not overly concerned with stopping the trade in flesh despite occasional press releases to the contrary.

Nestled among the darkest depths of the red light district off of Patpong Road, the "street of a thousand pleasures," among the bars, whorehouses and massage parlors, a renovated two story hotel squatted, its recent coat of white paint already dank and dirty. Men slid in and out of the ground floor side entrance, greeted by young girls and boys who would take them along dark corridors to fulfill their desires.

Upstairs was different. There was only one way to the second floor, a single staircase in the back of the building. In the shadows around the stairs several men dressed in black waited, automatic weapons slung over their shoulders. They made sure that only those who were invited went up the stairs and turned away the occasional drunken staggerer.

The staircase opened onto an anteroom with steel walls and a large vault door at the end. Going through the heavy reinforced door, a visitor would come upon a scene that could quite as easily have been drawn up underneath the Pentagon on the other side of the world.

State of the art satellite radiotelephones lined one wall, their dishes hidden among the pigeon coops and plywood shanties on the roof. An electronic map of Southeast Asia eight feet wide by six high rested on another wall. Three rows of computers manned by earnest young men and women faced the map. At the back of the room, furthest from the door, was a raised dais, surrounded by bullet and soundproof, darkly tinted, glass. There was one chair inside, facing a computer console.

The chair was currently occupied by an old man who slowly cracked the shell of a peanut between wrinkled fingers, letting the shell fall to the floor. Taped to the glass were the three sets of imagery he'd had faxed in during his flight to Thailand.

He turned as a red light beeped on the handle of one of the phones in his booth. He picked it up.

"Foreman."

The voice on the other end was harsh with barely restrained anger. "Foreman, this is Bancroft. I just wanted to let you know we lost Bright Eye."

A white eyebrow arched on Foreman's face. "Lost it?"

Bancroft's voice was clipped, the tone curt. "It's gone, Foreman. Destroyed. It was imaging down, trying to do what you wanted, and something came back up and destroyed it. Some sort of energy weapon. What the fuck is going on over there?" Bancroft's voice went up several notches at the last sentence.

"I don't know," Foreman said. "That is why I wanted Bright Eye to give me a picture. Did it get any data?"

"I don't have all the information yet," Bancroft said. "I'll have NSA forward whatever they've picked up. But the big issue right now is that I've got some very powerful people on my back because we just had a rather large nuclear reactor explode in a hundred and twenty-five mile orbit. Do you know what that means? Do you have any idea what that means?"

"It means there's something in Angkor Gate that hates pictures," Foreman replied. "It also means for the first time something has come *out* of one of the Gates. That we know of," Foreman added.

"Fuck your Gates!" Bancroft yelled. "We weren't supposed to have this reactor in orbit. We weren't supposed to have *any* nuclear reactor in orbit. It violates every treaty this country has ever signed regarding the exploitation of space. Never mind the fact that the reactor was tied to a down-firing laser. That little fact violates every space armament agreement we ever signed also."

"I didn't blow up your satellite," Foreman said in a level tone. "But I'm going to find out who did."

"Damn right, you'd better."

Foreman leaned back in his chair and fought for control. "Mister Bancroft, I suggest you forget about what the press is going to say if it should discover this and consider the fact that *we* don't have a weapon capable of firing one hundred and twenty-five miles into orbit and destroying a satellite but someone, or something, inside Angkor Gate does. I think that is the more pressing concern at the moment."

There was a moment of silence on the other end. "All right, Foreman. I'll get back to you. I've got to go brief the Old Man and he's not going to be pleased."

The phone went dead. Foreman would have smiled but for the current state of affairs; he'd tried to get to the President for the last twenty-five years but had been blocked at each turn by Bancroft and other muddle-headed bureaucrats like him, none of whom had believed the threat. Well, now it was here.

Foreman looked to the figure which had silently appeared to his right. His voice was barely above a whisper as he spoke to the woman who moved to stand in front of him. "Sin Fen," Foreman greeted her.

The woman was striking, both for her height and beauty. She was six feet tall with oriental features. Jet black hair framed high cheekbones above which almond shaped dark eyes were focused on the man in the chair. "Michelet will be landing at the airport in two hours," she said.

"Dane?" the man asked.

"He boarded the plane in America. It would be logical to assume he is still on board."

"Can you sense him yet?" Foreman asked

"He is coming," Sin Fen said. "I feel him getting stronger."

"And the others?"

"The others here or the others that went there?" the woman asked cryptically but Foreman understood.

"Here."

"I have eyes watching them. I believe they will act to stop Michelet before he even gets started."

"And those who went into Cambodia?"

"As you predicted. Which is why the elder Michelet has brought Dane here."

"Do you have any data on their disappearance?" he asked.

"A rescue team coordinated by a man named Lucian who represents the Michelet interests in this city crossed the Thai-Cambodia border within three hours of the *Lady Gayle* going down," Sin Fen said. "The team was on board a CH-53 helicopter." Her eyes looked past Foreman at the papers taped to the glass. "Once the helicopter crossed the Gate boundary all contact with it ceased. There have been no reports since."

Foreman quickly updated Sin Fen on what had happened to Bright Eye. Her face betrayed no emotion as to how she felt about the news. As he finished, the fax machine next to him spewed out several pieces of paper.

Foreman picked up the top sheet and looked at it. It appeared that Bright Eye had worked, if only for a short period. He squinted at the paper, making sense of what it showed, then he held it out to Sin Fen. "At least we have a location for the *Lady Gayle*."

Sin Fen looked at the paper, then up at Foreman. "Most strange, the plane."

"An understatement," Foreman said.

"There must a specific reason why this was done to the aircraft," she held up the imagery.

"That's exactly what I'm afraid of," Foreman said.

"Should I give it to Michelet?"

"At the appropriate time," Foreman said.

He picked up the other paper. He closed his eyes briefly, then handed it across to her.

"Where is this?" Sin Fen asked.

"Bermuda Triangle Gate," Foreman said. "The Bermuda Triangle."

"It is activating once more," she said, a statement, not a question.

Foreman nodded. More paper was coming out of the machine. Foreman looked at each piece, then at her. "We've got disturbances at eight of the Gates. Not an open Gate yet at any of them, but give it more time at the rate it's going and they are going to open. Two near the States. Some near populated areas."

"How can that be happening?" she asked.

"I don't know, but we have to find out."

"You might wish to inform your Mister Bancroft," Sin Fen said.

"I will. I think we have his attention now. Or rather I should say that Angkor Gate has his attention now."

"What will you do about those other places?" she asked.

"My primary concern is Bermuda Triangle Gate near Miami. I will move some forces near the area to be ready, but since we really don't know what we are facing, it's difficult to know exactly what our response should be. I am hoping we can get some of those answers out of Angkor Gate."

"What about the Devil's Sea Gate?" Sin Fen asked. "How are the Japanese reacting?"

"Intelligence reports indicate the Japanese are dispatching several submarines and ships to the area to stand by. I've been in contact with Professor Nagoya and we are

prepared to exchange any information we acquire."

"The Russians?"

"They are monitoring their two known Gates. At Chernobyl, naturally, they can only work remotely. And at Lake Biakal they are deploying their on-site survey team. I am in contact with them also but I think they will be less forthcoming than Nagoya if they discover anything." Foreman grimaced. "The old ways die hard. There are too many suspicions and by the time we work together, it might be too late." The woman turned to go, but he spoke again. "Sin Fen."

She paused, her body still, only her head turning so that she could see him out of the corner of her eye. "Yes, Mister Foreman?"

"Stay close to them."

"Yes, Mister Foreman."

He held up the papers. "There is not much time."

"No, Mister Foreman, there is not."

"Sin Fen," he said once more halting her. "I think this is the beginning of mankind's worst nightmares and we are the only ones who know it."

Sin Fen nodded. "But remember, too, how little we know."

"That is what really frightens me," Foreman acknowledged.

117

ATLANTIS

CHAPTER SEVEN

"Any idea who the spy is?" Ariana asked in a low voice. Ingram had been deciphering data for over an hour.

"No," he said. "Once it hits the GPS satellite, the signal goes everywhere. Anyone with a GPR anywhere on the planet can receive it."

"What about the message? Wouldn't that make our data accessible to everyone?"

"Like I said, someone's got to look for the piggyback. And then the data's encoded. It would be gibberish to anyone else who doesn't know the code or the original data to match against the code. That's the only way I was able to figure it out. It's a really smart method."

"Any ideas?"

"Most likely Syn-Tech," Ingram said. "They've got the technology and they've got the money to get access to the GPS transmitter."

"Great," Ariana muttered. "Just what we need. Could Syn-Tech have sabotaged the flight?"

Ingram shook his head. "That wouldn't be too smart if they had a spy on board. I'd assume they'd want their spy back. Plus they have nothing to gain by sabotaging us this way. They would want the data as much as we did. Remember, we went down before we were directly over the target area." He held up a disk. "We got maybe twenty-five percent of what we wanted."

Ariana took the disk and slipped it into the vest pocket of her shirt. "Maybe the spy screwed up. Syn-Tech wanted the data but they wouldn't want us to get the data. Maybe the spy cut it too close."

They both looked down the body of the plane at the other members at their stations, illuminated by the dim red glow of the emergency lights, the glare of their computer screens and the golden glow emanating from the vicinity of Argus's mainframe.

"The spy could be dead," Ingram noted.

"Could be, but we don't know," Ariana replied. "Any idea who'd have the expertise to do this type of messaging and encoding on our end?"

"Anyone with the proper training," Ingram said. "And anyone who has access to the main computer could have put the message in."

"Damn," Ariana muttered. "That's everyone."

"They must have paid someone off at the NSA to get their messages piggybacked on the GPS signal," Ingram noted.

"They could afford it," Ariana said. "We paid forty million for this gear and several million in bribes to get it here. They could afford to spend quite a bit to steal our data after we do all the work."

"Don't you think we have bigger problems right now," Ingram gently suggested, looking back where Carpenter was watching the golden beam infiltrate more of Argus's hardware, "than figuring out who the spy is?"

Ariana didn't say anything in reply, which was her only acknowledgment that he was right. She would deal with the spy issue once they were out of here.

"Do you have any clue what that could be?" she asked Ingram, pointing back at Argus.

He sighed. "Based on what I can see it seems to be pure energy in the form of an atomic laser."

"Atomic laser?" Ariana asked.

"An optical laser operates by emitting photons, which have no mass and move at the speed of light," Ingram explained. "An atomic lasers emits atoms, which not only have mass, but also have a wavelike nature. I know that there are some people who have been experimenting with such things as part of a super-computing system, but nothing I've heard of is beyond the theory stage."

"That's no theory back there," Ariana said.

Ingram rubbed his forehead. "The problem with developing an atomic laser has always been that you have to super-cool the atoms so they will act in a coherent manner by entering a collective quantum state."

"How can someone here in the middle of Cambodia be able to super-cool atoms?" Ariana asked.

"I don't know," Ingram said. "There's only two labs in the States that have the equipment to do it. And it's not exactly transportable."

"What advantage does the atomic laser have over an optical one?" Ariana asked.

Ingram shrugged. "I don't know exactly. The possibilities are limitless; from super-computing like I said, to who knows what."

"You think it's hooked in to Argus for a purpose?"

"I'm sure it is," Ingram said. "The way that beam is spreading through the computer's hardware is not random."

"Why?"

"That's the key question along with who," Ingram agreed.

"Why would someone who had an atomic laser be wasting their time with Argus?" Ariana asked out loud. "For our data? But as you said we didn't even have a chance to gather much before we went down."

"Same problem our spy has," Ingram noted. He ran a hand through his thinning hair. "I'm not too sure that this is about our survey. I think it's something else entirely."

"Like what?"

"I--"

"Don't know," Ariana finished for him. "Go through what we do have and try to get me some ideas," Ariana said.

"All right."

Ariana went forward to Hudson's commo area. "Anything?"

Hudson looked tired. Between the stress and his injuries, he was wearing down. "Remember we picked up a transmission just before we crashed?"

Ariana nodded.

Hudson flipped a switch. "Here it is:"

There was loud hiss of static, a voice coming in brokenly. "This . . . . Romeo . . . . Verify . . . Not. . Kansas . . . more. . . . Prairie. .. Repeat . . . Fire."

"It was low on the FM band," Hudson said. "That part of the spectrum is usually reserved for the military."

"Any idea what it means?"

"None. It's too broken to make much sense of."

"Anything else?" Ariana asked.

"I've got my computer scanning the FM waveband. I think the radio is working, but we're not picking up anything. You'd think if there were search teams in the air they'd have zeroed in on our last reported location and they'd be broadcasting. We've been down over twenty hours now."

Hudson had raised a point that was weighing heavily on her mind. A chopper out of Phnom Penh could have reached their position in a couple of hours. She was sure her father knew the plane was down. The lack of any indication of a search party could mean any of several things, none of which were good.

"All right. Keep monitoring," Ariana said, then went back to the others in the main console area.

"Any indication what caused us to crash?" she asked Ingram upon reentering the console area.

He had some papers in his hand. "As far as I can tell from the data, we experienced a cascade of systems failures just before we went down. I can give you the exact order that things failed, but basically all equipment that operated in the electromagnetic spectrum failed in rapid succession. Why, I have no clue, except that there must have been some sort of massive interference." He walked over to a table holding a chart. "I do have our last plotted position before the GPR went down."

Ariana walked over, along with the others, and stared at the map sheet pinned to the table. Ingram placed his finger on the map. "This is the last plot point. The main computer went off-line five seconds after that plot. I estimate, as best as I can from memory, that we crashed less than thirty second after that. The back-up computer also gave me our last heading." He picked up a pencil and drew a short line. "I think this is where we are. Somewhere in here."

"Jesus," Mansor exclaimed. "Look at that terrain! There's no way the plane could have come down intact in those hills and jungle."

"Maybe the pilots found a landing strip?" Daley suggested.

"Where?" Mansor asked. He ran his hand across the chart. "There isn't even a town within a hundred kilometers of this location, never mind a landing strip. We should be scattered across the countryside in tiny little pieces."

"But we *did* get down relatively intact," Ariana noted. "How?"

"I'd have to go outside and take a look," Mansor said.

"No way!" Herrin exclaimed. "There's something out there." The old man looked around at the other with wild eyes. "Can't you feel it? Something is out there waiting for us. Something that's into Argus now. It's finding out information about us. If you go out there it will get you like it got Craight!"

"We're blind in here," Mansor argued. "I want to know what the hell is going on outside."

"I think the time has come to at least--" Ariana began, but Hudson's voice suddenly came over the intercom.

"We're getting something on FM!"

The other six on board all rushed forward toward Hudson's position. The commo man had pulled on a set of headphones as he worked the controls on one of his radio sets. "It's Morse," he said in a hushed tone as he strained to listen, his right hand writing out dashes and dots with a pencil, as the others crowded into the small area.

His left hand was fumbling through a cabinet drawer underneath his console. He pulled out a strange device, which he snapped down high on his thigh, above his wound. His rested his left hand on top and began tapping out a reply.

They waited for almost a minute before Hudson took off the headphones and the knee key. "It's gone now."

"What did they say?" Ariana asked. "Who was it?"

"I don't know yet," Hudson said. "I've got to decipher the Morse. I haven't done that in a long time."

"What did you send in return then if you didn't what the message was or who was sending it?" Ariana asked.

"I sent an international SOS. But I don't think it was acknowledged. The message I was picking up just kept recycling then cut out."

"Shit," Ariana exclaimed. She pointed at the pad. "What does it say?"

Hudson had been printing in large block letters. He checked the message once, then held up the pad of paper:

L-E-A-V-E-O-R-D-I-ET-W-E-L-V-E-H-O-U-R-SL-E-A-V-E-
O-R-D-I-ET-W-E-L-V-E-H-O-U-R-S

"That's the entire message. It kept repeating those letters," Hudson said.

"Leave or die, twelve hours," Ariana read, unconsciously checking her watch which wasn't working.

"Doesn't sound very friendly," Ingram offered.

"Who sent this?" Ariana asked.

"Your guess is as good as mine," Hudson said.

"Could it have been the same guy who made that radio transmission we picked up before we crashed?" Ariana asked.

"Maybe," Hudson said. "He might be sending in Morse now because it has greater range than voice and uses less power."

Ariana read it once more. "The important question is: Was that message directed at us?"

"I'd say so," Hudson said. "There's no one else on the radio in this area."

Ariana looked at the skin of the aircraft. "We're going to have to find out what's going on and make our own help. It's been too long since we crashed. We can't just stay in here and hope someone stumbles across us."

She didn't add her fear that whoever had sent the message knew something they didn't and that the aircraft gave them a false sense of security. Whatever had ripped open the cockpit could rip through the side of the plane just as easily. And then there was the golden beam feeding into Argus. She had no idea what it was or why it was doing what it was doing, but she had a very strong feeling that it wasn't a good thing. Ariana's analytical mind had too much data that she didn't understand and she was willing to go with her gut instincts.

"All right," Ariana said. She looked at each person, catching their eye for a few seconds, then moving to the next one. "What we're going to--"

Suddenly there was a hissing noise on the left side of the plane. Everyone spun and looked. A small hole, about two inches in diameter suddenly appeared at about knee level and a beam of bright gold light crossed the console area, touched the edge of a computer desk, slicing right through it, then hit the far side of the plane, hissed for a second, then was through. The beam remained in the air, like a bar, crossing the compartment.

"Jesus!" Herrin scurried behind a console, putting it between him and the light. "They're coming in for us!"

"Calm down!" Ariana yelled. After a few moments to see if anything else would happen, she walked up to the beam. She'd seen top of the line lasers but, like the other golden beam, this was something different. Every few seconds she thought she could detect a change to the flow in the beam, but it was hard to be sure.

"Another atomic laser?" Ariana asked as Ingram came up next to her.

"Probably, but I couldn't tell you what the other one is so I don't know for sure," Ingram said. "Anyone have any idea what this is?"

Carpenter took a piece of paper and slid it down into the beam. The paper was neatly cut where the beam touched, the material simply disappearing. "I don't know, but whatever it is, I wouldn't want to step into it."

"Maybe it's a rescue team, trying to get in?" Daley offered.

Mansor snorted. "It would be a lot easier for them to just open the hatch," he said, pointing to the emergency door above the wing. "Or knock on the door."

"I think--" Ariana began when the slithering noise they'd heard earlier when Craight had been taken suddenly filled the cabin, as if something incredibly large was sliding across the top of the plane.

As Ariana watched, the gold light faded somewhat for a couple of seconds, then suddenly there was a noise that tore through her skull. It was a high pitched squeal but of tremendous volume as if the very air were being ripped at several different frequencies.

The noise was gone after three seconds to be followed by another hissing noise. "Watch out!" Ariana yelled, but it was too late.

A gold beam punched through the top left corner of the console area and caught Daley in the upper left chest. Flesh slowed it down not the slightest as the beam came out his lower right back and pierced through the skin of the aircraft on the forward right side of the console area.

125

Daley's eyes were wide with shock, then he screamed as he toppled over, the beam slicing flesh as easily as the paper had been cut. He was dead and the scream silenced before he hit the floor in two pieces.

"Everyone freeze!" Ariana ordered.

The interior of the plane was silent. Eyes turned toward the left side of the plane, waiting for another hole to be punched. After a minute, Ariana slowly walked over to Daley's body. She draped a cloth over it, avoiding the gold beam.

There was a long period of silence as everyone watched Daly's blood soak through the cloth.

Ariana fixed Hudson with her gaze across the light. "Will the SATCOM radio work if we reconnect the cable to the dish?"

"It should," Hudson said.

"I'll do it," Peter Mansor said.

"You're crazy!" Herrin yelled. "Did you hear that thing that went across us? Don't you think they can get you with the light beam if you go outside?"

Mansor ignored him. "Where does the cable run?"

"Come to my area and I'll show you," Hudson said.

By moving to the left side of the plane and ducking, they were able to get under the beam and go forward.

Hudson reached into a drawer and pulled out a binder. "It's not as bad as you think," he said. "There's a chance the cable's failed before it goes up to the rotodome. That means it's cut along the access corridor in the inside top of the plane. You might not have to go outside at all."

"Luck doesn't seem to be coming in bunches here," Mansor noted.

"Hey, we're alive," Ariana countered, aware that the others were listening. "We should have died in the crash, but for some reason we didn't. So let's keep a positive attitude. We get the SATCOM working, we can get a hold of my father and he'll get us out of here, no matter what it takes."

Herrin gave a sharp laugh at that, but he didn't say anything as the glares of the others kept the words from coming forth.

Hudson pointed at a small panel above his work station. "That's how you get into the access crawlspace."

Mansor stood on the front of the desk and pushed the panel out of the way. He stuck his head into the darkness and then turned a flashlight on and looked about.

"Do you see a group of wires to your right?" Hudson asked.

"Yes."

"That's the commo leads to the rotodome. The HF goes forward, so all you have there are the SATCOM and FM. The FM goes down to the FM antenna in the belly. The ones that go to the rear; those are the SATCOM cables. Just follow them."

Mansor looked down. "Mighty tight up here."

"You can make it," Hudson assured him. "When the cables disappear up, you'll be right below the rotodome. Let's hope the break is before then."

"Yeah, right," Mansor said. He grabbed the edge of the small opening and pulled himself up.

The last glimpse Ariana and the others had of him were his boots disappearing heading toward the rear of the plane. They could hear him slowly moving above their heads and as he began making his way to the rear, they followed inside the plane, just below him, everyone tensed, waiting for a hissing noise.

The door to his glass cubicle was shut, isolating Foreman from the others in his operations center. He flipped a lever putting the satellite call he had just received on the speakerphone.

The voice that echoed off the glass walls was incredulous at what Foreman had just told him. "You've been doing this since 1946 and you don't have any idea what you're dealing with?"

"Mister President, I have some idea of what we're dealing with," Foreman's voice was level. He had long anticipated this moment and he had known it would not go pleasantly, but that was not a concern of his.

There was the sound of paper rustling on the other end. "I'm looking at a report here from 1968. It tells me we lost a nuclear submarine checking out, what do you call it, this Bermuda Triangle Gate?"

"That's correct, sir. The USS Scorpion. "

"This Bermuda Triangle Gate is the Bermuda Triangle, isn't it?" The President didn't pause for an answer. "A myth for Christ's sake."

"No, sir, it's not. The crew of the *Scorpion* was not killed by a myth."

"What were they killed by?"

"I don't know, sir."

The explosion from the other end caused even Foreman to stiffen in his hard backed seat. "Jesus Christ, man! Fifty years and you don't know? An entire submarine lost with its crew and you don't know? And what else? I see here a spy plane working for you was also lost. And a special forces team that you sent in to recover the spy plane's black box never made it back out."

Foreman leaned forward. "Someone came out from that special forces team, sir."

"One man? So?"

"It looks like he's going back in, sir."

"And?" The President's voice was sharp. "We just lost a satellite and a nuclear reactor. God help us if any of that radioactive material comes down over a populated area."

Foreman glanced at the papers taped to the glass wall. "Sir, we've got a bigger problem than that."

There was a long pause, then the President's voice came back, under tight control. "And that is?"

"Our spy satellites are picking up electromagnetic and radioactive disturbances at various places around the globe." Foreman paused, but no one interrupted him so he continued. "The signature of these disturbances is the same that always presages activation of the Angkor, Devil's Sea or Bermuda Triangle Gates but this is occurring in greater quantity than we've ever seen and at some locations where we suspected there might be Gates but weren't certain."

"How many signatures?" the President asked.

"Sixteen, sir."

"Where?"

"All over the globe."

"Where in United States?" the President clarified.

"The readings aren't exact, sir, but Bermuda Triangle Gate appears ready to open again. If it expands twenty percent from the largest perimeter we've recorded, it will touch Miami. But we've also got two new sites, one on the Baja Peninsula south of San Diego and one just off the shore of Alaska, near Valdez, the southern terminal of the Alaskan Pipeline. There's also one in Canada, north of Calgary. From what I'm reading, the Gates that could open at each of these sites would be roughly triangular and almost two hundred miles along each side."

Silence reigned for a few moments, then the President spoke again. "Going back to the start of this conversation, Mister Foreman, can you give me any idea what these Gates are, other than whoever and whatever goes into them never comes out? A Gate indicated to me that you think these things lead somewhere. Where?"

"Sir, I've had the best minds study the available data, unfortunately we don't have much information given the facts you just stated. As far as we can determine, we believe Devil's Sea, Bermuda Triangle and Angkor Gates to be any of several things:

"One possibility is that they could be a door to another dimension that we don't recognize yet with our current level of physics. Another is a gateway to an alternate universe coexisting with ours. Another could be an attempt by an alien culture to open an interstellar gateway from their location to Earth. Another could simply be a physical anomaly of our planet itself which we have not yet figured out. Or it could be something totally beyond our capability to understand."

"That's not helping much," the President said.

"Sir, I haven't been the only one interested in this phenomenon. The Russians and Japanese have also studied them. In fact, over the years, the Russians have been much more interested in this than we had been. They do have two Gates inside their borders."

"And what have *they* discovered?"

"Not much more than we have, sir. Besides investigating their two Events, I know they've managed to lose two submarines investigating Bermuda Triangle Gate and several planes over Angkor Gate. I also believe they've sent two ground elements into the Angkor Gate in Cambodia. One in 1956 and one in 1978. Both disappeared without a trace."

"What about their Gates?" the President asked.

"Naturally, I don't have much information on that. One is in Lake Biakal. The other--" Foreman paused, then plunged in. "The other is located right around Chernobyl. The Russians believe that the disaster at that plant was somehow connected to this."

"Yeah, they'd like to believe anything," the President snarled, "but the fact that they couldn't build a decent nuclear power plant."

"I can't really comment on that," Foreman said. "But I also know that the Japanese have lost some ships and submarines in what I call Devil's Sea Gate and they call the Devil's Sea. The latest intelligence report indicates that they have an active cell inside their government that is keeping tabs on the Devil's Sea Gate, much like what I am doing."

Foreman could sense the growing frustration on the other side of the world. He continued on. "But the Russians do have a theory, sir, and some of this new data our satellites are collecting, these new locations, tends to support that theory somewhat in some of its aspects."

"What do they think it is?" the President asked.

"In the 60's, three Russian scientists published an article in *Khimiyai Zhizn*, the journal of the old Soviet Academy of Sciences. The title was: Is The Earth A Large Crystal?"

There was no comment about that. Foreman knew that the seriousness of what was going on was finally sinking in to warrant the silence after such a statement.

"The three Russian scientists had backgrounds in history, electronics and engineering, a rather eclectic group. They started with a theory that a matrix of cosmic energy was built into our planet at the time of its formation and that we can still see the

effects of this matrix today in such places as Angkor Gate or Bermuda Triangle."

"Jesus Christ," a new voice exclaimed, "I've never heard such poppycock."

"That's Professor Simmons, my science adviser," the President informed Foreman. "He just got here a few minutes ago and I wanted him to listen in on this."

"Should I continue?" Foreman asked, "or perhaps Professor Simmons has a better theory."

"I'll discuss what he has to think when I'm done with you," the President said shortly. "Continue."

"The Russian theory divides the world into twelve pentagonal slabs. On top of those slabs are twenty equilateral triangles. Using this overlay, they point out that these triangles have had a great influence on the world in many ways: fault lines for earthquakes lie along them; magnetic anomalies exist; ancient civilizations tended to be clustered along some of them.

"What's most interesting to our current situation is that there are places called Vile Vortices at the juncture of some of these large triangles. One such place is Bermuda Triangle Gate also known as the Bermuda Triangle. Another is Angkor Gate in Cambodia which we believes centers around an ancient city called Angkor Kol Ker. Devil's Sea Gate, called the Devil's Sea off the east coast of Japan is another. Chernobyl was built adjacent to one of these sites. The Lake Baikal site is also at one of these junctures. These new Gates that are now showing magnetic anomalies are also at Vile Vortices."

"Why are these places acting up now?" the President asked.

"I don't know, sir. Over the years I've seen quite an ebb and flow to Devil's Sea, Bermuda Triangle and Angkor to the point where there is no trace of them at all at certain times. The Russians feel that there is an internal mathematical harmony to this entire crystalline structure and that explains the rhythmic nature of the disturbances."

"Do *you* believe this Russian theory?"

"I don't disbelieve it, sir, until I know exactly what is causing it."

"Ahh--" Simmons' voice sounded in the background.

"Go ahead, Professor," the President said.

"The Earth as a big crystal theory is a bunch of poppycock," Simmons said. "The lithosphere, the outer surface of the planet, which is where these Events are located, has been moving for millions of years. Thus any crystal formation would be so disfigured by continental drift as to make such patterns unrecognizable. Also, there is no evidence in the first place of the planet having any sort of massive crystalline structure."

"Anything to say to that, Foreman?" the President asked.

Foreman could picture the President sitting in his office with his advisers; a man who had not even been born when Foreman was flying combat missions in World War II; sitting among other men who had not known the strife of world-wide conflict. "No one has conclusively proven the continental drift theory or--"

"What is your degree in?" Professor Simmons demanded.

"I don't have a degree," Foreman said. "I was discussing a theory and all I want the President to know is that you were discussing a theory also. I think we take too much for granted as fact that, although most evidence points that way, might not indeed be fact. I've been studying these Gates for over fifty years. I would say I know more about them than you do, Professor Simmons, but at least I can admit what I do know isn't much."

"So obviously you knew something was strange about this area in Cambodia before Michelet Industries sent its plane over the Angkor Gate?" the President asked.

"Yes, sir, I did."

"You didn't think it proper to warn Mister Michelet?"

"Sir, how could I warn them? You've seen the data on Bright Eye getting destroyed and still you doubt what I am telling you about these places. We gave Michelet the data on the Angkor Gate area. The planes lost. The special forces mission lost. We *did* warn him as best we could. He still went ahead."

"What happened to his plane?"

"It's down, sir, inside the borders of the Angkor Gate. Bright Eye did manage to get a picture of it and pinpoint the location. I am having that picture forwarded to Mister Michelet to aid him in trying to recover the plane and his daughter."

There was a short silence, then National Security Adviser Bancroft spoke. "You wouldn't just have happened to have set all this up, would you have Foreman?"

"Set what up?" Foreman asked.

"Michelet sending his survey plane over Angkor Gate?"

"Sir, Michelet Technologies has been interested in that area for many years. It was inevitable that they would eventually send some sort of reconnaissance. As I said earlier, there was no way I could directly warn Michelet against doing that. I did send him enough information so that he had an awareness of the danger."

"A very carefully worded reply," the President noted. "What if these Gates appear elsewhere? What happens?"

"I can only make an educated guess at that, sir, based on Devil's Sea, Bermuda Triangle and Angkor. There is a legend of an ancient capitol city of the Khmer Empire,

a city called Angkor Kol Ker. Apparently Angkor Gate overran it in 800 AD."

"And?" the President impatiently demanded.

"And the city was devastated. An empire that was perhaps the strongest on Earth at its time disappeared and its capitol is now only known as a legend.

"And that was only one Gate, not sixteen, like we're seeing now. I also have a suspicion what is happening now predates even that long ago event. I've talked with Professor Takato Nagoya, who runs the Japanese team that is investigating the Devil's Sea Gate. Based on various data, he thinks that what is happening now happened once before in Earth's history."

"When was that?"

"Ten thousand years ago. Nagoya believes that the legend of Atlantis, as related by Plato in the Timaeus and Critias, two of his dialogues, tells a true story of what happened when all these Vile Vortices grew into Gates and tried to connect. He believes that a highly advanced human civilization was destroyed to the point where it is only a legend. That one of the Vile Vortices, now known as Bermuda Triangle Gate or the Bermuda Triangle, opened on top of Atlantis and destroyed it."

"Hogwash!" Simmons exploded.

"Doctor Nagoya does has several doctorate degrees, Professor Simmons; in fact he is one of Japan's foremost scientists. Mister President, I believe we are facing a dire threat not only to these specific areas but to mankind as a whole. It wasn't hogwash or poppycock that destroyed Bright Eye; or made the Scorpion disappear so many years ago; or that knocked Michelet's plane out of the sky.

I believe we are being invaded through these Gates, sir, and we cannot sit on our current level of scientific knowledge insisting that it can't be so, when in fact, it is already happening. We can not intellectually appease this threat. Something's happening, sir, and I don't believe we have the time or the latitude to stick our heads up our asses and ignore what is going on." Foreman noted that several people in the control room were looking at him and he realized that he had shouted the last sentence.

"Sir, there is a long history of men in power, men who have the responsibility given to them, of not waking up to threats before it is too late. Remember Chamberlain in 1939 with Hitler. They had facts then, which they chose to ignore or squeeze into their own fanciful imaginings."

"You're walking a very dangerous line there," the President's voice was ice cold.

"Sir, if you think I am worried about my career or my pension or my position or anything else other than this threat, you are wrong. This invasion is real and this time there won't be anywhere for people to run to and our country won't be left alone."

There was a long silence.

"And now?" the President finally asked. "What do we do now?"

"Sir, I'm hoping to find out what is on the other side in the Angkor Gate and then to formulate a plan of action."

"How the hell are you going to do that? Nothing has come back from there."

"As I told you earlier, sir, one man did. He is currently with Mister Michelet. When he went in, he was contacted in some manner by something or someone inside that area. There was also a radio transmission to him just before Michelet's plane went down from what appears to be one of his old teammates inside the Angkor Gate. I don't know how that could be, but it's the best lead we have. The man went in once and came out. I'm hoping he can do it again, this time with more information. In the meanwhile, I do have a list of actions that will put us in position to respond in a variety of ways once

we find out what is really going on." "And if we don't find out what is really going on?" the President asked. "God help us then, Mister President," Foreman said.

CHAPTER EIGHT

Even though it was three in the morning, a blast of heat hit Dane as he stepped onto the short staircase pressed up against the plane's door. But more than the heat, the smell brought back a cacophony of memories. An odor of exotic food, human sweat, and the faint tinge of disease and dirt made him feel for a moment that he was back in Saigon thirty years ago.

Dane looked at the lights reflecting off the runway: Don Muang Airport was not that much different than it had been three decades ago when he'd come here on R & R. Dane felt the same rush of bad feelings come over him that he had then. This was a sick place. Dane had only spent a day in Bangkok, holed up in a motel room before catching the first flight back to Vietnam and, for him, the peace and security of MACV-SOG's base camp. There was too much human misery in Bangkok, too much hopelessness and he couldn't block it out.

"There's our man," Freed said, nudging him and bringing him back to his present circumstance.

Dane saw the black limousine that waited for them. Chelsea at his side, he followed Michelet, Freed and Beasley to the car. Chelsea leaped in and curled up in the spacious center between two wide leather seats that faced each other.

An old man was waiting for them inside. Michelet sat next to him, shaking his hand. "Lucian, it is good to see you."

Dane estimated that Lucian was at least 70, if not older. Dane's guess was the he was one of the original French ex-patriots, booted from Vietnam when the communists took over and shifting his business two countries west.

"You've met Mister Freed," Michelet made the introductions. "This is Mister Beasley and Mister Dane."

Lucian turned clear blue eyes on each man and nodded his liver spotted bald head, before returning his gaze to Michelet. "I reported to

Mister Freed about what--" he paused as Michelet raised a finger ever so slightly.

"Is the equipment we requested ready?" Michelet asked.

Lucian inclined his head. "The plane and helicopter are here at the airfield, fueled and ready. The crews are on standby. The men are with the plane. They are the best I could get under short notice so they may not be as good as you would like." Lucian seemed ready to say something more about that, then changed his mind. "I had the bomb you requested already put on board the plane. As far as the specialized equipment you asked for, I have arranged a meeting with a man who can supply you with what you require."

Michelet's face darkened in the dim glow inside the compartment. "I don't have time to barter. I told you to take care of that for me. The gear should be here!"

Lucian met his gaze. "I never deal directly in weapons or drugs. That is how I have survived in this part of the world all these years. I might not have much life left in me, but I wish to have it end by natural means. You will not be overly delayed. This man is most efficient. We must make a short sidetrip to pick up the equipment."

Lucian rapped a walking stick on the thick glass separating their compartment from the driver and the limousine began moving.

Dane reached down and curled his fingers in the hair on Chelsea's rump, slowly massaging the thick muscle underneath. She turned her head toward him and gave a low whine.

The old Frenchman was hiding something, Dane was sure of it. Whatever it was that he had been about to say when they first got in the car was important, but something that Michelet didn't want Dane to know about. Dane glanced out the back window and noted a pick-up truck following them, three men in the bed, a heavy caliber machine-gun mounted on the roof of the cab. Lucian had a strong desire to remain healthy.

They wound their way through palm-lined street which were crowded even at this early hour. There were more cars on the street and no American GIs, but it reminded Dane very much of Saigon. Southeast Asia was a place where the hands of time moved very slowly. They passed farmers pulling carts loaded with produce for the markets that would open soon.

The limousine turned a corner and went down a narrow alley. Dane tensed, a feeling he had not experienced in a long time stabbing through him.

"It's an ambush," he said quietly to Freed.

The security man looked at Dane, then out the tinted windows at the buildings looming close overhead on either side. His hand slid inside his jacket but other than that, he did nothing. Dane thought briefly of the reaction such a statement on his part would have brought from the members of RT Kansas, then he forced himself to relax. If they were attacked he was going to have to trust Lucian's men to protect them, unless of course, it was Lucian who was setting the trap. Dane doubted that with the man in the car with them.

A set of warehouse doors swung open at the end of the alley and they were inside. Dane tensed, ready to roll out the door, but surprisingly, the feeling abated slightly as the doors closed behind them. Lucian stepped out, followed by Michelet.

"What was that about?" Freed hissed at Dane, before exiting.

Dane just shook his head and pushed his way past the other man. "Stay," he ordered Chelsea who looked none too thrilled with the order, but complied, burying her nose between her front paws in the heavy carpeting inside the car and furrowing her eyebrows at Dane.

The pick up truck with the heavy machine gun had followed them in, but it immediately turned around in the confined space behind the limo, ready to lead the way out. The interior of the warehouse was lit by naked lightbulbs, spaced twenty feet apart and hanging down from the ceiling. The far wall was about forty meters away and the interior was full of crates.

Five Cambodian men stood waiting behind a long table on which were laid two large footlockers. Lucian walked up to the table and waved his cane over the lockers. "Your equipment," he said simply.

"Check it, Freed," Michelet said.

The Cambodian in the center raised his hand. "The money first."

"Freed, check the gear," Michelet repeated as he slid the metal briefcase onto the table.

The Cambodian grabbed the case and his fingers worked at the latches as Freed swung open the first locker. Dane walked up next to Freed. Inside were six M-16A2s, still in their original wrappings. Thirty round magazines were stacked in the corners along with several cans of 5.56 ammunition. There were also a dozen green canvas bags which Dane immediately recognized as Claymore mines.

"The key!" the Cambodian hissed angrily, holding up the briefcase.

Michelet reached into his pocket and held up a small metal key. "You have the money in hand. You get the key when we finish checking the equipment we have purchased from you. If you try to open that case without the key, a special charge inside will incinerate the money."

Lucian looked from the men on one side of the table to the other. "The money is in the case, Sihouk."

Sihouk hissed something in Cambodian and the other four men spread out, their hands hovering near the waistbands where the handles of large caliber handguns were prominently displayed.

"The money is in the case and you will get the key," Lucian said again. "Let them make sure they have what they need."

Sihouk said something else and his men halted, ready.

Freed threw open the second locker. Several bulky packs were inside along with some plastic cases. Dane reached in the first locker and pulled one of the M-16s out. He grabbed a 30 round magazine, made sure it was loaded, then slid it into the well of the weapon, seating it home with an audible click that edged the tension in the warehouse up a few more degrees.

"What the hell are you doing?" Michelet demanded.

"Playing the game with you," Dane said. He wasn't overly worried about Sihouk and his men. They had their money and Dane knew Michelet would give them the key. He was concerned with the feeling he'd had coming into the warehouse. "I'm not going to stand here with empty hands while you guys play who's more manly."

Dane held the M-16 casually at his side, the muzzle pointing toward the ground. He smiled at Sihouk. The Cambodian met his gaze, and then slowly the other man smiled also, revealing two gold teeth. Dane could read the betrayal behind that smile, but he knew no one else could.

"All here," Freed announced.

Michelet tossed the key. Sihouk caught it. As Freed and Dane carried the gear to the trunk of the limo, Sihouk opened up the briefcase. He smiled once more, hissed a command and then the five Cambodians were gone, disappearing into the darkness.

"Let's get out of here," Lucian said. "I do not like even transporting this sort of equipment."

Dane had pulled out a second M-16 when putting the weapons in the trunk along with several magazines. He tossed the weapon to Freed as they got back in the limo. "Don't say I never gave you anything," Dane said as he followed the weapon with four magazines. "I think getting out of here is going to be more difficult than getting in was."

Freed loaded his rifle as the limo turned around. The doors opened and the pickup truck drove out into the alley, the limo following closely behind.

Dane felt the sense of dread even more sharply than before. "Stop!" he yelled as the front edge of the limo passed between the doors. The driver reacted automatically, slamming on the brakes.

The pick-up truck exploded in flames as a rocket propelled grenade slammed into it. Several lines of tracers roared down from the surrounding rooftops peppering the street and truck. A second grenade slammed into the street just in front of the limo. Dane kicked open his door, weapon at the ready as Michelet, Beasley and Lucian hunkered down inside, protected from the bullets by the car's armor plating and bullet proof glass while Freed went out the other side.

Dane used the side of the car for cover, firing an entire magazine in quick three rounds bursts at the sources of the tracers. Freed was on the other side of the car, shooting across his field of fire, covering him.

Dane recognized the chatter of AK-47s, a sound he'd heard many times before. He slid a new magazine home. A man with a rocket launcher on his shoulder stood up, aiming down. Dane fired a quick burst, slamming the man back out of sight.

Dane paused as he recognized a slightly different sound of automatic fire coming from the rooftops. Someone up there had a

139

weapon other than an AK. Dane raised the M-16 to his shoulder when suddenly a body tumbled over the edge of the roof and fell to the street between the front of the limo and the burning pick-up truck. Another quick burst from the same new gun followed. Then two more.

Suddenly, all was silent. Dane glanced over the hood of the trunk at Freed, who raised his eyebrows in question. "Let's get out of here," was all Dane said.

As Freed slid in the door on his side, Dane ran forward and grabbed the body that had fallen. He tossed the slender Cambodian over his shoulder and carried him with him, tossing the body into the back to the consternation of Michelet and Lucian and Chelsea who whined and cowered as far away from the corpse as possible.

"Go!" Dane ordered.

The driver needed little prompting. He pushed the wreckage of the truck out of the way with his front bumper, then accelerated.

"Easy girl," Dane whispered to Chelsea as he knelt next to the body.

"What is the purpose of this?" Michelet demanded.

"It's always good to know who's shooting at you," Dane said as he quickly searched the man's pockets. All he found was a thick roll of local currency. He didn't know what the going rate for murder was in Bangkok but even with high inflation it looked like the roll would meet the going rate anywhere in the world. Other than that, there was nothing.

"Know your enemies," Dane said as he ripped the man's shirt off, "and know who the enemies of your enemies are. Because they might be your friend but then again they might not. They might be even worse enemies."

"What the hell are you talking about?" Michelet demanded.

"You tell him," Dane told Freed.

"Someone busted the ambush for us from behind," Freed said.

"How do you know that?" Michelet asked.

"We heard a different weapon from what the ambushers had being fired on the rooftops and there's no way we killed them all from our position," the security man explained.

Dane pulled a Leatherman out of the leather case on his belt. He extended the large knife blade and dug into the mangled flesh around one of the bullet wounds. He pushed in, then with his free hand,

140

pressed two fingers into the hole. He felt the hard knob of a bullet between the two fingers and with great difficulty pulled it out.

He put his bloody hand under one of the small lights. "9 millimeter. The Cambod's were firing AKs; 7.62 mm. Someone hit them from behind with a submachinegun."

"Who?" Lucian asked, his face still pale from the bloody incident.

"Someone who knew we were going to the warehouse. Someone who knew we were going to get ambushed. Someone who must have been following us from the airport," Dane said. He was tired. The bad feeling was gone and now he was drained. He sat back in the deep upholstery and closed his eyes.

"We were followed?" Michelet asked. He turned to Lucian. "What do you know of this?"

Lucian sputtered out a protest, but Dane's weary voice cut in. "Sihouk sold us out to someone. He got your money, and then he got money from someone else to give us up. It was just a good day's work or him, nothing personal. You got any enemies?"

"Syn-Tech," Freed said.

"What's that?" Dane asked.

"A rival company."

Dane opened his eyes. "They'd try to kill you?"

Michelet gave a harsh laugh. "We're talking hundreds of millions, if not billions of dollars involved here. Yes, they'd kill for that. Wouldn't you?"

"No," Dane said, which prompted another laugh from Michelet. "Actually, I think you were paid considerably less when you were in the army."

Dane stared over Chelsea at the old man. Their eyes locked, then Dane leaned back and nodded. "You're right. I was paid considerably less then." He turned his body away from the others, placed his hand on Chelsea's neck and closed his eyes to rest.

They made it back to the airport without further incident, but instead of pulling up to Michelet's plane, then went around the main runway to an old hanger. Dane opened his eyes once more as they pulled inside. A battered two engine C-123 transport plane and an aging Huey helicopter rested inside.

The limousine came to a halt. Lucian did not get out with them. He looked at Michelet. "Our business is concluded. Contrary to your feelings, I believe there is much that money cannot replace or buy. Please do not ever call me again."

Freed and Dane barely had time to get the lockers out of the trunk before the limousine raced away. A figure detached itself from the shadow of the C-123 and ambled over.

"Good day," the man said in a deep Australian accent. "Or good morning, I should say as the day is not yet upon us. I'm Porter, your pilot."

"Is the plane ready?" Michelet demanded.

Dane noted that Michelet had recovered well from the events of the past couple of hours. Dane imagined a person did not get to be in the position the old man was in without having hard nerves.

"Aye, it's ready." Porter glanced over his shoulder. "But these fellows your friend in the limo lined up. Not too sure about them, if'n I was you."

"You aren't me," Michelet brusquely said. More men were coming out of the shadows. There were four of them, dressed in plain green jungle fatigues that had seen better days and were stripped of all insignia. Their boots were encrusted with mud and they had large knives prominently strapped to their belts. Rambo knives, Dane noted. Such weapons looked very impressive but were impractical for either slitting a man's throat which took a small commando stiletto, or cutting through the jungle, where a machete worked best. Each man had several days worth of beard on their face and their eyes were red. Dane picked up the odor of alcohol.

"I'm McKenzie," the largest of the four introduced himself. "Major McKenzie."

Dane watched as Freed stepped forward. "I know who you are, McKenzie. You're not a major any longer."

"These are my men," McKenzie said, looking over the small black man in front of him, trying to size up the situation.

Dane walked over and stood off of Freed's left shoulder. Two of the men wore faded red berets with an insignia pinned over the left eye:

a set of jump wings surmounted with a maple leaf. From that Dane knew these men were formerly with the Canadian Parachute Regiment. He also knew from reading the newspaper that the Canadian Parachute Regiment had been disbanded amidst allegations of various atrocities during peace-keeping missions in Somalia and Bosnia.

"Break a pile of shit apart and you never know where the flotsam will surface," Freed said, which confirmed to Dane where the mercenaries had come from and their circumstances.

McKenzie popped a lightning quick jab with his right hand, but Freed was already moving, sliding under the punch and delivering four quick blows to McKenzie's ample gut. The larger man doubled over gasping for breath.

"Easy," Dane said, holding the M-16 generally pointed in the direction of the other paratroopers. "I think the fight is one-sided enough as is."

As McKenzie straightened, wheezing for breath, Freed hit him again, a stinging blow to his nose, bringing forth blood. Freed nimbly moved behind McKenzie and a hand snaked around his neck, the hold tightening, causing the Canadian to labor for breath.

"You're not a major anymore," Freed hissed in his ear. "Clear?"

"Fuck you, nigger."

"Mistake," Freed said. He dug the knuckle of his free hand into McKenzie's temple, bringing a yelp of pain as he hit the nerve. Freed pressed down harder, bringing tears of agony from the Canadian's eyes.

Dane saw McKenzie's left hand grasp the handle of his large knife. As McKenzie whipped the knife out, Freed let go of him and stepped back out of reach. McKenzie swung wildly twice, before settling down into a fighter's crouch, eyeing his opponent with much more wariness.

"Now listen here!" Michelet started forward, but Dane swung his arm out, hitting the old man in his chest and holding him in place.

"Wait," Dane said.

McKenzie slowly straightened out of his crouch. The point of the knife wavered, then went down. "Hey, I just didn't like you coming in here trying to piss on me and my men."

"You've already pissed on yourself," Freed said.

McKenzie's face got even redder, something Dane thought wasn't possible.

"You're hired help," Freed said. "Clear?"

McKenzie smiled, a twitch of his lips that no one in the hanger bought. "Sure. Just a misunderstanding."

"My name is Freed. Mister Freed to you. That clear?"

"Clear." McKenzie slid the knife back home in its sheath.

"Clear, what?"

McKenzie again twitched a grin. "Clear, Mister Freed." McKenzie stared at the smaller man, the hand going up to his head and tenderly touching the spot where Freed had elicited such agony.

"You've been well paid up front," Freed said. "You get the same when we return. You do exactly what I say when I say. Clear?"

All four men sullenly nodded.

"Any booze in your gear, you dump it now or I dump you out of the plane without a chute. Got it?" Freed stepped closer. "I can't hear heads shake. Got it?"

"Yes, sir!"

"Get the gear on board," Freed ordered.

As the Canadians carried the footlockers to the C-123, Freed turned to Dane. "Thanks for the help at the warehouse."

"Next time I tell you there is an ambush," Dane said, "I suggest you listen." He gestured at the Canadians. "I'm not being paid to back you up."

As Freed turned away, Dane froze both him and Michelet with his next words. "I want to know what happened to your first rescue team and I want to know what our plan is to get to the plane. I want to know who your enemy is that attacked us and I want to know who attacked them. Otherwise, I am not going anywhere."

One entire wall in Patricia Conners office was covered with a mosaic of satellite imagery. She'd gone to the NSA Imaging Communications Center and pulled up all requests for imagery from Foreman for the past twenty-four hours. She wasn't surprised to discover that there had been other requests besides the two she had handled. What did surprise her was the nature of the requests: they were directed to a comrade of Conners, the ELINT or electronic intelligence specialist just down the hall from her. ELINT also included magnetic and radioactive data, so it covered a lot of ground.

144

She'd printed out the results gathered by the string of ELINT satellites the US had circling the globe and now she had a mosaic that encompassed the entire planet. She had no clue, of course, what the various colors and lines overlaid on top of the basic geo-data meant. She knew it represented various spectrums in the electromagnetic realm, but that was the extent of her knowledge in that area.

Conners walked down the hallway and stuck her head in a doorway. "Jimmy, dear," she smiled.

A young man with long hair pulled back in a pony-tail looked up from his computer screen with a slightly unfocused stare. "Yes?"

"Jimmy, I need your help interpreting something."

Jimmy blinked. He wore a loose-fitting t-shirt and a pair of jeans that had seen better days. His eyeglasses were thick, the metal frames holding the lens almost sagging

under the weight.

"Interpreting? Interpreting what?"

"Come to my office, Jimmy. I'll fix you a cup of that special tea that you like."

Conners led the way. Jimmy walked in the door to her office then paused. He whistled seeing the mosaic. "Whoa, Pat, when did you do that?"

"Just now."

Jimmy walked over and started tracing lines with his fingertips, peering intently. "This data is new. I got the request this morning. Forwarded it all. You're not supposed to have this."

"You didn't look at it?" Conners plugged in her small hot water heater.

Jimmy turned away from the wall in surprise. "We're not supposed to look at it unless directed to do so. We're supposed to forward and file." He paused in thought. "Do *you* look at everything you're requested?"

"Of course, dear."

Jimmy's bottom lip curled in as he chewed on it. He reached over and swung Conners' door shut. "Actually I look at everything too. I mean what's the point in doing this if you don't. Hell, *I'm* supposed to be the expert. It's not that--"

"Jim," Conners gently interrupted, "you don't have to explain it to me. Remember--I do the same thing. The point is, that means you've looked at this data, right?"

Jimmy turned back to the wall. "Yeah. Foreman. I don't know who the hell that guy is, but he's into some weird shit--Uh, sorry, stuff."

"What kind of weird shit?"

Jimmy's hand were back on the mosaic, tracing various colored lines as if his fingertips could feel what they represented. "These blue ones are electromagnetic flux lines. The reds ones are geomagnetic. The green ones show radioactivity."

"And?" Conners prompted when Jimmy fell silent.

"Well," Jimmy tapped the mosaic, "this isn't right."

"What do you mean it isn't right?"

"It's not the normal patterns for any of those images. Something's happening. On a global scale."

"What kind of something?" Conners asked with forced patience.

Jimmy shrugged. "Something is upsetting the natural flow of the earth's geo-and electro-magnetic fields. That something also carries a trace of radioactivity with it, although how that could be I have no idea."

"Radioactivity?" Conners repeated.

"Yeah, but I've never seen anything like this. Really weird. Bizarre. In fact, downright impossible."

Conners was startled by this information. "Have you told anyone about this?"

At that Jimmy in turn looked surprised. "Why?"

"Because according to what you just said, something abnormal is going on," Conners said in exasperation.

"But if I told someone, they'd know I was looking at data I wasn't supposed to be looking at," Jimmy said simply.

"Good God," Conners shook her head. "We have met the enemy and they is us."

"What?" Jimmy frowned.

"Forget it." Conners focused her mind. "All right. What do you think is causing this?"

"I don't have a clue," Jimmy said. "The patterns are very regular though and the lines intersect and seem to focus on several spots on the planet's surface. So its not random."

146

"Not random," Conners muttered. "So something's causing this?"

"Of course something's causing this," Jimmy said.

"No," Conners shook her head in exasperation. "What I mean is *someone* is causing this?"

Jimmy squinched his face. "Well, actually no. Nobody could do this. I mean, the pattern is not random, so that would suggest that there is a guiding cause, but nobody could propagate something like this so--" his words tumbled on top of themselves to an awkward halt.

Conners walked over and looked at the lines. "What effect is this going to have?"

"At the current levels," Jimmy said, "not much at all. But it seems to be growing in power."

"And if it keeps growing?" Conners pressed.

"Gee, I don't know, Pat." Jimmy rubbed his chin where a few hairs struggled to hint at a beard. "But it would be bad if it went, say four powers higher. The electromagnetic stuff could knock out power grids, cause certain types of electronic devices to malfunction. You know how they ask people to turn off their laptops and Walkmans when a plane takes off? Well, those things aren't really a problem but the airline doesn't want to take a chance with anything interfering with the plane's systems. Right now, at the center of each of these points, the interference is about four times more powerful than that sort of equipment.

"The radioactive stuff, now that's a whole 'nother ballgame. I don't see how this upswing could be happening, but if it keeps up for a few more days at this rate, we're going to have some very sick and some very dead people at the intersections of some of the flux lines." Jimmy brightened. "But it can't keep growing."

"Why not?"

"Well, cause--" Jimmy paused. "Cause, I mean it just happened and . . . " his voice trailed off.

But Conners had suddenly noticed something about the map. She reached for a three ring binder on her desk and flipped through it. "Oh, God," she muttered.

"What is it?" Jimmy was alarmed at the ashen look on her face.

Conners jabbed her finger into the book. "I think I know how this is spreading. And I think I know where it's coming from." She ripped out a page and carried it over to the mosaic. With a red marker she begin making small X's on the paper.

"It's not all of them, but some of them fit."

"Not all of what?" Jimmy asked.

"MILSTARS satellites. See how these are along the lines of propagation? You have a MILSTARS satellite in geosynchronous orbit at each of these points. Whoever or whatever is doing this is using satellites as a medium." She remembered the strange data on the MILSTARS-16 satellite and now knew what it meant.

"But how can that be? You can't do that," Jimmy said. "It's not technically possible."

"I don't care if it's technically possible," Conners said, "but someone is doing it. This all fits too well."

"But why?" Jimmy asked.

"I don't know why because I don't know who is doing it," Conners said. "But I can tell you exactly where all this power is originating from." She touched a point on the mosaic. "Right here in north-central Cambodia where good old Mister Foreman wanted me to take a look with Bright Eye. And that someone didn't appreciate us taking a look because they blasted Bright Eye right out of space."

Jimmy's eyes opened wide at that. "Bright Eye blew up?"

"Damn right."

Jimmy shook his head. "These lines aren't originating from just the one point. Not anymore. They were, I mean, from what was requested before, but not now."

"What do you mean?" she asked.

"The colors," Jimmy said. "The shades. They tell--" Jimmy paused, as if trying to figure out how to explain to her. "All right, just trust me on this. I can read these colors and patterns, OK?"

Conners nodded.

Jimmy went on. "OK. I went back when I saw all this, trying to get a read on how quickly the power was growing." He gave a slight smile. "And not only was I able to get an estimate on the growth rate, but also the path the propagation is taking. It did indeed start in Cambodia, but it seems to be picking up power from a couple of other places now."

"Where?" Conners asked.

Jimmy's long finger tapped the spots as he called them out. "Here, off of Bermuda. Here, in western Russia, right about Lake Baikal, and here in the western Pacific off the coast of Japan. It started in Cambodia and that is where the most powerful force is generating, but these others are growing in strength and propagation ability, feeding off of whatever is in Cambodia."

"But--" Conners paused. She had been about to ask why, but she knew it was a pointless question. "Maybe Foreman knows what all this is. I sure hope he does."

The USS *Wyoming* was part of the Second Fleet, headquartered at the naval base at Norfolk, Virginia. It was not due to put out to sea for another three weeks as part of its normal rotation of duty. But one phone call from the Chief of Naval Operations to Captain Rogers, the submarine's commander, changed all that.

For the last two hours phones had been ringing all over Norfolk and the naval base, alerting members of the crew and ordering them to report to duty.

Standing high on submarine's sail, Rogers watched his crew arrive in spurts, grumbling about the strange alert. He wasn't concerned about morale--submariners were the elite of the Navy and he knew he could count on his men. He was, however, concerned about the strange nature of the tasking the CNO had given.

First was the fact that it had bypassed every link, and there were many, in the chain of command between Rogers and the CNO. Second, the CNO had simply ordered Rogers to put to sea as quickly as possible, and go at flank speed to a set of coordinates in the ocean and await further instructions. Rogers had had the distinct and troubling feeling that the CNO himself wasn't quite sure why he was giving these orders and was acting on orders himself. And to Rogers that meant the orders could only come from one of two places: the Secretary of Defense or the President. Either way, it meant whatever was going on was dead serious.

But Rogers had plotted out the coordinates in the chart room and they puzzled him. They were for a point about 600 miles from Norfolk, to the southwest of Bermuda.

Rogers rubbed a hand over his freshly shaved face as another bus pulled up to the gangplank, disgorging a pile of sailors. Now why, he wondered to himself, would someone need a ballistic missile submarine at those coordinates. Rogers could feel the thrum of the engines through the steel plate under his feet, as the reactor got up to power. He looked to his rear, along the massive desk of the *Wyoming* at the 24 sealed hatches that walked to the rear fin in pairs. Inside those silos he had enough nuclear power on board to destroy the world, or at least a very good chunk of it.

"Eight hours to be on station at the designated coordinates," his executive officer, Commander Sills, reported to him, coming up the hatch out of the conning tower.

"Crew status?" Rogers inquired.

"Sixty-seven percent accounted for."

"Let's get under way," Rogers ordered.

Sills' face showed his surprise. "But what about the rest of the crew, sir?"

Rogers put a foot through the hatch and felt the rung. "The CNO said ASAP and sixty-seven percent makes us mission capable. Radio the harbormaster and tell him we get under way in five minutes."

CHAPTER NINE

"You can go one of two ways," Hudson said.

Ariana looked from the communications man to Mansor who had just climbed down from the small opening, his mission to find a break in the cable unsuccessful. The three of them were gathered around a small table on which were spread the blueprints for the plane.

Other than Mansor's mission, the last hour had been uneventful, for which Ariana was grateful. No more beams of light had gone through the plane. Nor had there been any noises outside of the plane but none of that helped the atmosphere inside much. The bodies of Daley and the engineer killed in the crash were in the rear of the plane, covered in blankets, reminders of their perilous situation, as if they needed any.

Ariana looked across the table. Mansor was layered with dirt, grime and grease and looking none-too-happy. It had taken over an hour for him to traverse the crawl space to the base of the two stanchions that held up the rotodome. The SATCOM cables had been intact the entire way and disappeared up into the right stanchion, out of sight. Ariana was running out of options; that left going outside to check the rotodome. For all she knew, the entire system might have been sheered off in the crash and the satellite dish lost.

"You've got the emergency overwing escape door or the emergency overhead hatch," Hudson pointed out the two doors on the chart, one opening onto the right wing, the other onto the roof of the aircraft just behind the pilot's cabin.

"Do you think the overhead one might have been damaged with the cockpit?" Mansor asked.

Ariana remembered the way the metal had been cut. "I don't think so. The opening ended before the back of the cockpit."

"What about the beams?" Ingram asked. "What if they're being aimed by someone outside and once they spot you--" he stopped, the others knowing the end to the sentence.

"I don't think we're in a stable situation here," Ariana said. "I think we have to act and act quickly. My father would have sent a rescue party as soon as he lost contact with us. It is long past the time for such a party to have reached us, so we have to assume we are going to get no outside help. I don't know why, but that's the situation. And the message we received told us we had only twelve hours. We've already wasted some of that.

"The first step is to try to get satellite communications and see if we can contact someone. If that doesn't work, then I've made the decision we're going to have to leave the plane. I say we try the radio first."

Given those choices, the others nodded their heads. Mansor stood, shaking some of the dust off his clothes.

"I'll go with you," Ariana said, grabbing a mini-mag light and sticking it into her pocket.

"There's no--" Mansor began, but he was silenced by the flash in her eyes.

"Let's do it. We'll go out the top hatch," Ariana decided. "That way we won't have to climb up from the wing."

Mansor held up a reel of co-axial cable. "I'm ready."

Ariana turned and walked toward the front of the plane. The emergency overhead access door was in the ceiling of her office. They unhooked her heavy metal desk and pushed it underneath. Mansor climbed up, after tying off one end of the coaxial cable to a leg of the desk. He grabbed the emergency latch and twisted it. With a loud popping noise, it opened inward, swinging down, revealing a pitch black rectangle. There were no stars visible, nothing but utter blackness. He glanced down. "Ready?"

"Ready," Ariana said, climbing on top of the desk and crouching next to him.

Mansor pulled himself into the darkness. He disappeared for a second, then his arm reappeared. Ariana grabbed his hand and he pulled her up and out of the plane.

"We had a rescue team on standby," Freed said. "Lucian coordinated it."

"And?" Dane asked. Chelsea was rubbing against his leg. The four Canadian mercenaries were waiting by the plane, as was the pilot, out of earshot.

Freed laid the facts out. "As per our emergency plan, Lucian ordered the team in once he got word the plane went down. It went toward the last plotted position we had for the *Lady Gayle*."

"And you never heard from it again," Dane summarized.

"Contact was lost and has not been reestablished," Freed said.

"Who were the lucky sons-a-bitches?" Dane asked.

"Cambodian Special Forces," Freed said. "A twelve man A-team, plus two men in the helicopter crew."

"That explains why the Cambodian government is so eager to support you now," Dane said.

"Screw the Cambodian government," Michelet said. "I want my daughter out of there."

"Those Cambodian soldiers had lives too," Dane said. "Families."

"Their families have been well compensated," Michelet said. "It was the nature of their job."

"Running missions for rich Americans?" Dane asked.

"They took the money quite eagerly," Michelet said.

Dane ignored the old man and stared at Freed. "Why didn't you tell me?"

"We don't know what happened to the team, so there wasn't much we could tell you," Freed said. Seeing Dane's stare, he sighed. "All right. We didn't think you'd come if we told you the team had disappeared."

Dane was thinking of something else. "The tape. Was it real?"

"Yes," Freed assured him. "The *Lady Gayle* picked up and forwarded that message before it went down."

"Maybe someone taped us back in '68 and . . ." Dane's voice trailed off.

"And saved it thirty years to use?" Freed asked.

"Who ambushed us at the warehouse?" Dane asked. He knew Freed and Michelet weren't lying about the tape. He'd known it from the moment he heard it. But he'd known the two men were withholding other information.

"It must have been people hired by Syn-Tech," Freed said.

"Maybe they were Cambodians pissed about the Special Forces guys," Dane suggested.

Freed shook his head. "No. There wasn't enough time. It had to be Syn-Tech. And we did pay a considerable amount of money to the Cambodians and their families."

"What else don't I know?" Dane asked.

"You know everything now," Freed assured him.

Dane grimaced. "That's assuming *you* know everything, which I don't think is the case."

To that, Freed made no comment.

"What's the plan now?" Dane asked.

Freed jerked a thumb over his shoulder at the Canadians. "We jump with them-"

"Who's we?" Turcotte asked.

"You, me, and Professor Beasley."

"Jump?" Beasley asked, a worried frown appearing on his forehead.

"You signed on for the whole deal," Freed said. "All you have to do is fall off the ramp. The parachute will do all the rest."

"Fall off the ramp?" Beasley repeated.

Turcotte turned to Michelet. "And you?"

Freed answered for his boss. "Mister Michelet will go on the flight with us, make sure we're down OK, clear a landing zone, then return here and bring the chopper back to the landing zone and wait for us to contact him for exfiltration or arrive at his landing zone."

"Where the LZ?" Turcotte asked.

Freed pulled out his map. "This hilltop five kilometers from the watchtower where we're jumping."

Dane stiffened. He looked down at Chelsea who had turned her head and was looking to the side of the hanger. "Someone's coming," Dane announced.

The barrel on Freed's M-16 rose.

"No," Dane shook his head. "No danger." He cocked his head. He'd sensed many peoples' auras over the years, but whoever was approaching now was different, very different. Dane felt a strange thrill race down his spine. Chelsea picked up something also, because her tail was up and wagging rapidly, whacking against Dane's leg.

"Easy, girl," Dane whispered, but he knew the dog wasn't indicating danger.

A woman came around the corner of the hanger. She was tall with oriental features, her face strikingly beautiful. Dane was unable to figure out exactly what part of the Orient she came from; he sensed she had the blood of several races in her, perhaps some European ancestors also. She wore black pants, a gray turtleneck and a thin black, tailored jacket. She carried a nylon bag over her shoulder. She walked right up to Dane and stopped a few feet away, staring at him.

"Who are you?" Freed asked.

"Her name is Sin Fen," Dane said, his eyes still locked on to hers. He smiled very slightly. "Am I right?"

The woman inclined her head to the left, indicating he indeed was.

"You know her?" Freed was confused.

"Just met," Dane said. "But she know things we need to know, don't you?"

Again the slight incline and the hint of a smile on her lips now. Her right hand extended forward, long fingers with nails tapered to a point and painted bright red, reaching out.

Chelsea stepped forward and dipped her head. The woman bent at the waist, like a tall tree in a stiff wind and her fingers slid through Chelsea's mane. "A good dog," she spoke for the first time. Her accent was hard for Dane to fix, but he could tell she had been educated in Europe at some point in her life.

"Yes, a very good dog" Dane said. He glanced at Freed and Michelet. Behind them Beasley was watching. Dane listened inside his head, marveling at what was happening, then spoke aloud. "It was Syn-Tech who hired the men to attack us at the warehouse. And they are organizing a team to try to beat us to the *Lady Gayle*."

"How do you know that?" Michelet asked.

Dane raised his hand toward Sin Fen. "She told me."

"But she didn't say anything," Freed argued.

Sin Fen turned toward the others. "The Syn-Tech team is already at a staging camp in Cambodia, just north of Angkor Wat. They have a helicopter and will be heading north at first light."

"They won't be able to--" Michelet began, but Sin Fen held up her free hand.

"They may know exactly where the *Lady Gayle* is. There is a spy among the crew."

"A spy!" Michelet exploded.

Sin Fen turned back to Dane. "There is not much time." She reached inside her black jacket with her left hand, still stroking Chelsea's neck with the other, and pulled out a glossy piece of paper. "Imagery from a satellite. Your plane."

Michelet grabbed the paper, Freed at his side, Beasley looking over their shoulders. "Jesus!" Michelet exclaimed. He looked up at Sin Fen. "What happened to it?"

"I don't know," Sin Fen said.

"But--" Michelet was shaking his head. "This can't be right. The fuselage would be broken apart if--" he stopped in confusion. "It could never have landed like this."

"But it is right," Sin Fen said. "And the coordinates are listed on the bottom. Not far from where I believe you plan on jumping."

"How do you know where we're jumping?" Freed asked.

"She knows many things," Dane said.

"How did you get this?" Freed demanded, holding the imagery.

"A mutual friend," Sin Fen said.

"You were on the roof at the warehouse," Dane made it a statement.

"She busted the ambush?" Freed's tone indicated his disbelief.

Michelet wasn't even listening, his entire being focused on checking the coordinates on his map. "It's near where we thought it went down. Let's load!" Michelet yelled, handing the imagery to Freed and turning toward the plane.

Dane didn't move. He took the imagery from Freed. The other man followed his boss, but still Dane waited. He stared at Sin Fen and her fingers running through Chelsea's hair. Sin Fen straightened. Chelsea seemed startled, then bounded back to Dane and rubbed her side against his leg.

"Who are you?" Dane asked quietly.

"I am Sin Fen."

"I know that. Where are you from?"

"From near where we are going," she said. "No," she held up her hand. "Not inside. But near. I have felt it also, what you have felt. And I have heard the voices, not as well as you, I believe, but enough to know they are real."

The engines of the C-123 coughed as they started. The others were all up the ramp, waiting.

"The plane," Dane said. He held up the imagery. "How did this happen? It's not physically possible."

Sin Fen shrugged. "There is much that is not possible that happens in the Angkor Gate."

"Angkor Gate?"

"It is what we call this place in Cambodia," she answered.

"Who is we?"

"We'll get to that," Sin Fen said.

"I need more information," Dane said out loud. Then he focused his thoughts:

I need to know how we can talk without speaking.

A hint of a smile played around Sin Fen's blood red lips.

Theories, nothing proven.

The words came in a strange mixture of images, but Dane could make sense of what she was trying to impart to him. It reminded Dane of when he would be driving in his car and a melody would come into his mind and then he would turn on the radio and that song would be playing. Sin Fen's word were like the first part of that, a melody of words that came unbidden but that if he concentrated he could make sense of.

"I'll take theories," Dane spoke aloud.

"I think we should go," Sin Fen said. "I will tell you what I know on the way."

Foreman looked down at the small LED screen. He didn't recognize the name but he did recognize the call sign: National Security Agency, Satellite Imaging. He pressed a button, activating the speaker phone inside his bullet and sound proof cubicle.

"Foreman here."

A woman's voice filled the room. "This is Patricia Conners. I'm with--"

"I know who you're with," Foreman said. "I am very busy, Ms. Conners. What do you want?"

"A little courtesy would be appropriate," Conners said.

Foreman sighed and waited.

"I've reviewed the data you've been getting from us," Conners said.

"You're not supposed to be doing that," Foreman warned.

"Do you want to play games or do you want to figure out what is going on?"

"Why don't you tell me what's going on?" Foreman asked.

"You have the world-wide electromagnetic imagery?" Conners didn't wait for an answer. "You also have the radioactive pattern that is overlaid on top of that. You also know that it is coming out of the area in Cambodia you requested Bright Eye to take a look at earlier."

"Please," Foreman's hand reached down for the cut off switch, "don't tell me I know what I know."

"Do you know how the electromagnetic waves and radioactivity are being propagated?"

Foreman's hand paused. "Why don't you tell me?"

"Some sort of strange power signal is being uplinked to a MILSTARS satellite, then being broadcast through the MILSTAR network," Conners said, "using those satellites that fall along lines between what appear to be critical points."

Foreman pulled his hand back. "Go on."

"I've checked with a friend of mine over at the Pentagon. They've lost all communications on the MILSTARS network. They don't know why, but we do, don't we Mister Foreman?"

"Are you sure the power is being sent through MILSTARS?" Foreman asked. "How do you know MILSTARS isn't just picking it up from ground readings?"

"I've checked the propagation," Conners said. "It follows the MILSTAR satellites from Cambodia out. It started there but there now also seems to be weaker uplinks near Bermuda, in the western Pacific, and at several other locations."

Foreman leaned back in his chair and tapped a pen against his lower lip. "But how can that be done?"

"I don't know that yet, but I've got a friend working on it." There was a short pause, then Conners continued. "If you gave us what you know, it might help."

"There's not much information," Foreman said.

"Do you know what destroyed Bright Eye?" Conners asked.

"No."

"Do you know what is in Cambodia that causes distortion on our imaging?"

"No."

"Well, this seems to be very much a one-sided conversation," Conners said. "Let me continue my end then. My friend has done some number crunching using the data that was forwarded to you. He predicts that if the electromagnetic and radioactive disturbances at these sixteen locations continue to grow and increase in intensity at the rate they are doing so now, that the first deaths will occur in less than twenty-four hours at the critical nodes where the power is most focused.

"It's a geometric progression so the power increases by a factor," Conners continued. "He predicts that these sixteen sites are situated so that they will eventually link up with each other and blanket the world."

"When does he predict that will occur?" Foreman asked.

"Total coverage in two days."

Foreman thought about that. Two days to the end of the world.

"Does your friend have any ideas how we can stop this propagation?" Foreman asked.

"We haven't gotten that far yet," Conners answered.

"I am trying to get to the source of the power," Foreman said, "but if I fail, it would be most helpful if you could come up with some way to stop it from spreading."

"If you can't stop the source," Conners said, "then you have to stop the conduit of propagation."

"You're sure the MILSTARS satellites are being used?"

Conners voice was steady. "Yes."

Foreman almost smiled. It was nice that someone was certain of something. "What can we do about that?"

"Shut the affected satellites down."

"And if that doesn't work?"

"Destroy them."

"How?"

"Using an HMV fired from Thunder Dart."

Foreman was impressed. This woman knew what she was talking about.

"The Pentagon will not be too thrilled to destroy their own satellites."

"According to the taskings you send me," Conners said, "you have sufficient clearance to get the SR-75 and Thunder Dart airborne."

"I was under the impression that control of the HMV came from the ground, though. Which still means I'd have to go through the Pentagon."

"I can control the HMV," Conners said. "We worked with the Pentagon on the deployment of the system and I've done the simulation many times."

Foreman was impressed for the second time. "I'll take the option under advisement. I appreciate the information and the offer of help," Foreman said. "Can you keep the area in Cambodia under surveillance?"

"We can't see in," Conners said.

"I know that, but just in case. Plus, even knowing how much we *can't* see is helpful."

"With your authorization I can put a KH-12 right over the spot and keep it there."

"Do it. I will be in touch."

Foreman cut the connection, then sat back and stared at the imagery he had taped to the glass. He was beginning to see some of what was going on and although he didn't understand most of it, an unsteady feeling in the pit of his stomach warned him that he might already be much too late to stop it, whatever it was, from occurring. He knew it would take others a long time to wake up to the reality and by then it would be too late, but there was no doubting what the information was pointing to: The Gates were expanding and getting ready to link up. Earth was being invaded.

He looked at the display board in the front of the operations center. It showed the C-123's current location, nearing the border with Cambodia. He flipped another switch.

"Anything from Sin Fen?"

"No, sir."

"Keep the line open."

Then he proceeded to check on the military forces he's had Bancroft ordered in motion. Submarines, ships and planes were all converging on the Gates. What they could do once they got there, Foreman had no idea, but he felt it was better to be prepared.

He looked at the world map. If whatever was in the Gates was using MILSTARS then there was only one card he could play now to slow things; the card Patricia Conners at the NSA had thrown on the table; a card he knew that would cause blood vessels to burst in the Pentagon but time was getting short.

Ariana swore she could feel the texture of the air outside the plane on her skin and even sliding down her throat into her lungs. It reminded her of the strange mixtures she had used in tanks on deep sea dives, but this feeling was a slightly nauseating one.

She stared into inky blackness. All she could see were the two lines of gold that sliced into the left side of the plane and came out the right along with a third golden beam that came from a different left angle, lower and further to the rear. The first two beams began in a haze about forty feet away and ended the same distance on the other side as if the plane was surrounded by a fog.

She started as she looked about. Near the rear of the plane, a thick golden beam blazed straight up into the sky, about twenty feet above their current elevation. Other than that, there was nothing. Ariana could hear Mansor's breathing and the beat of her own heart sounded loud inside her head. With the glow from the four beams and her eyes beginning to adjust, she noticed there was a very faint visibility, but nowhere near enough to really see anything further than a few feet away.

She reached into the pocket of her jumpsuit and pulled out the flashlight. A firm grip came down on her wrist. She could just make out Mansor's silhouette next to her.

"I wouldn't," Mansor said. "I don't think we want to attract any attention."

"All right," Ariana agreed, peeling his hand off her wrist. "Let's go."

They moved down the top of the plane by feel, staying on top of the center of the curvature, Mansor reeling out cable as he went, Ariana keeping one hand on the cable, letting it drop behind her. Ariana concentrated but she could hear nothing. The total lack of sound was unnerving, as much as the lack of light. She wondered when dawn came whether the sun would be able to penetrate the strange mist that enveloped the plane.

They made their way about twenty feet along the top of the fuselage. Ariana could faintly see the top of the plane beneath her feet and about twenty feet ahead as her eyes adjusted to the dark.

Suddenly Ariana sensed something behind them. She turned. A circle of gold light twice as large in diameter as the fuselage appeared at the nose of the plane, lighting up the skin of the aircraft inside of it's circumference. Ariana could see the gaping hole in the top of the cockpit as the circle slid down the plane, covering a few feet every second. The circle was only about ten feet deep, behind it was the same darkness, as if the plane were being run through the beam of a massive searchlight.

"Freeze," Ariana hissed, knowing they couldn't out run it. Mansor needed no further prompting, seeing what was coming.

The two of them stood perfectly still on the top of the plane as the light circle slid down the plane. It reached them and Ariana felt the hairs on her skin energize. Her brain felt as if it were encompassed in a compressing tight band. The pain in her head became unbearable and she bit back a scream, then the circle was past and they were back in darkness, the pain gone as quickly as it had come.

The gold circle was still going down the plane and she followed its progress.

"Oh, man," Mansor whispered as the circle passed the mid point and they could see that part of the plane. Ariana stared in disbelief. The wings were gone, smoothly cut off less than two feet from the body of the plane. The plane appeared to be resting on a tangle of broken foliage, but Ariana knew that the wings had not been torn off in the crash. There was no sign of them and she knew they were gone long before they came down. She began to understand some of the last words she'd heard from the cockpit.

Ariana watched the circle hit the rotodome and she could see the source of the golden beam that was going up. It came straight out of the top of the rotodome.

"Shit," Mansor muttered. "Now we know why--"

He paused as they both heard the sound of something massive moving to their left. Ariana squinted but the only image that came to her was of a darker shadow against the black if such a thing were possible. Its indeterminate form towered over them about fifty meters away. She could tell it was coming closer, the trees splintering underneath its weight sounding like shots. Overriding that sound was the same slithering noise they'd heard inside the plane, with a backdrop of hissing, like steam issuing from massive boilers.

Ariana's heart froze as she began to make out the dark form as it got closer: the forward part of a thick serpent's body, ten meters wide, was raised up off the ground. Thirty meters up the body, it split into seven snakes' heads, well above their level, hissing issuing forth from each open, jawed mouth as they twisted and turned. Each head was over two meters wide and tall, the dark eyes glinting over a foot in diameter each on the side of the mouths. Behind, the rest of the length of the body stretched into darkness.

While Ariana remained frozen, Mansor turned and ran back toward the hatch they'd come out of. One of the snake's heads darted down toward him, foot long fangs bared.

A blue beam flashed out of the dark from the other side of the plane and struck the head a glancing blow. With an angry hiss, the head jerked back, barely five feet from closing on Mansor. The fangs snapped shut in frustration.

With a startling display of accurate fire, the blue beam flashed seven short bursts in less than two seconds, each one catching a different head. While the blue beam fired its last burst at the snake, a golden beam struck Mansor dead on, freezing him in its grip like a deer in bright headlights.

"Ariana!" his voice mouthed.

She broke out of her amazement and moved for him, but the golden beam picked him up into the air, ten feet above the fuselage.

Ariana looked over her shoulder as she heard the creature moving, but it was heading away, disappearing into the darkness. She turned back to Mansor. The golden beam was starting to draw him in the opposite direction, toward its source. She came to a halt directly below Mansor, helpless. She grabbed hold of the cable that he still had in his hands and that was tied to inside of the plane. She twisted a wrap around her left wrist and braced herself, trying to hold against the force, feeling her own feet begin to leave the top of the plane.

The blue beam came out of the darkness again and struck Mansor. Gold and blue flashed around his body in a panoply of color. Ariana noted that he was no longer being pulled toward the gold, but rather seemed caught in a bizarre tug of war, while she dangled below from her left wrist, her toes scraping the top of the plane.

She looked up and caught Mansor's eyes as he desperately twisted his head, gazing down at her, his mouth still open in a silent scream.

Ariana's scream was heard though, as Mansor's body burst apart in an explosion of blood and viscera that rained down upon her.

Both beams disappeared. Ariana collapsed to top of the fuselage. She was vaguely aware that she was being pulled forward via the satellite co-ax cable, but all she could truly register was the wet feeling on her face of Mansor's blood.

CHAPTER TEN

Dane sat in the red web seat and checked out the plane. The Canadians were seated halfway up the cargo bay, near Michelet and Freed. The forward third of the bay was filled with a large green metal canister, something Dane had seen before: a five thousand pound bomb designed to be dropped off the back ramp. When it went off, it would clear an area large enough for a helicopter landing zone. He'd seen them dropped and he'd even been on the ground nearby when one of the "daisy-cutters" as they were called, went off. The shock wave had lifted him three feet off the ground and slammed him back down.

Dane focused his mind and stared across the cargo bay at Sin Fen

How we can do this?

Her dark eyes locked onto his and he knew she'd 'heard' him. She got up and sat down next to him.

"It will be easier if we spoke," she said. "The capability is a genetic throwback."

"Go on," Dane prompted.

"What do you know of the bicameral mind?" His negative answer was instantly in her head and she continued. "All right, let me start with the basics so you can understand.

"First, you're left handed, aren't you?"

"Yes."

"So am I. The majority of the population, of course, is right-handed. Which means that the left side of their brain is the dominant hemisphere, due to the crossover of our central nervous system at the base of the skull. So already you are part of only three percent of the population, in that the right side of your brain is dominant. But I believe you are even more rare, because I think both sides are, in a way, dominant, in that they work together much more efficiently that a normal person's."

She must have sensed his confusion.

165

"Let me back up a little. The issue is at what point in our evolution did humans become different from the other animals? What makes us different from, say a monkey? An ignorant person would say thinking, but that's not true. All the manifest examples of thinking are present in various degrees in the animal world: learning, the ability to conceptualize. True, they may be very basic, but they are there so any line drawn would have to be arbitrary."

Dane found himself listening, mesmerized at the two levels to their conversation-the verbal and the other, deeper, level inside their heads where he knew she was picking up more from him than he was from her.

"There are those who think language is the great divider but several species have a rudimentary language. It is widely accepted that dolphins communicate on some level. Some monkeys have approximately eighty signals or commands that they use-- communication, in effect.

"There is a theory that we only truly broke away from the animal world when we were able to communicate extensively with a verbal language and act as an individual rather than as part of a group. But what you have to understand is that we humans did not start out with a verbal language or even with verbal communication being our primary mode.

"Wait!" Sin Fen cut off Dane's interjecting thought. "Listen to me and you will know all I do.

"There is a physiological theory that prior to having an extensive verbal language, early Homo Sapiens communicated on a telepathic level, which in a way-although it made for an effective group defense in a harsh environment--also retarded progress because it required the group to stay close together and also think somewhat alike. Once we developed verbal language, we were able to explore and have more initiative as individuals. This is the point at which man separated himself from the animal world.

"The interesting thing is that the development of language wasn't dictated so much by external factors but more by the physical evolution of the human brain itself."

Dane felt Chelsea pressing against his leg and he could hear the steady drumming of the plane's engines. He was even aware that Freed was moving about the cargo bay, pulling the parachutes out of their wrapping and preparing them, but his primary focus was on Sin Fen.

"That's where the bicameral mind comes in," Sin Fen continued. "The human brain consists of two halves that are almost identical, but have very little actual physical connection to each other. Scientists believe the two sides developed that way to give us redundancy in critical brain processes.

"The speech centers in the brain are present to almost the same extent in both hemispheres yet in ninety-seven percent of people they are functional only in the left hemisphere. What happened to the speech centers in the right? They are still there, three distinct areas that work together to produce speech: the supplementary motor area, the least important; Broca's Area, in the back of the frontal lobe; and Wernicke's area in the posterior part of the temporal lobe, the removal of which produces a permanent loss of meaningful speech.

"These areas function together to produce speech from the left hemisphere for most people, but they are also present on the opposite side, but apparently non-functioning. Some feel that these opposite side speech centers working together is where the telepathic ability resided. Initially, man's brain was more connected between the two sides and the speech centers worked in harmony so that all humans could 'talk' to each other the way we have."

Sin Fen smiled, revealing even, very white teeth. "You've always been able to sense things, even hear 'voices' sometimes that others can't hear, haven't you?"

Dane nodded.

"Of course, since the verbal language wasn't yet developed, the only messages that could be sent were very basic and really just a surge of raw emotion. Warnings of danger by a burst of fear, for example. In a way, it required the development of a verbal vocabulary for man to add the depth and subtlety to language that allowed us to move forward as a species, yet in losing our telepathic capability we regressed in a certain way also.

"But think if some humans have come full circle! What if some of us have the verbal language in our heads, but also retain the telepathic capability? This is what we are!

167

"Our speech centers are developed equally in both sides of the brain. The two hemispheres of our brains are also more connected than a normal human's. I have seen MRIs of my own brain and know this to be a fact. This is how we can communicate telepathically and how you have your

'sixth' sense that has served you so well. It is simply your brain functioning on a higher level, analyzing more sensory input in a more efficient manner than the normal person."

Dane stared at Sin Fen. He'd always known he was different, but because he hadn't known what normal was, he hadn't known how different he truly was.

Sin Fen continued. "Physiological psychologists at the very least agree that Wernicke's area in the non-speech side of the brain does exist. It can be removed in most people without causing any apparent problems. But there are those who hypothesize that this apparently non-functioning area is the center for our imagination, the place where we hear the voices of the Gods."

Dane started in surprise. He'd heard voices in his head all his life and he knew from the way Sin Fen's voice resonated in his brain that she wasn't referring to 'Gods' in the traditional sense, but more a higher order of awareness.

"Not only does this area give you the ability to 'speak' to me," Sin Fen said, "but it gives you many more capabilities, some of which you are not even aware of yet. You have some of the power that the ancients ascribed to the Gods."

Dane could see Freed running his hand along the steel static line cable that stretched the interior length of the cargo bay from front to rear, checking it.

"What does that have to do with where we are going?" Dane asked, trying to bring this back to a level he could cope with.

"We don't know," Sin Fen said.

"Who is we? Who do you work for?"

Dane started forward as he saw the image that flittered across Sin Fen's consciousness, before a mental curtain came down over it. "Foreman!"

"What?" Freed yelled, barely audible above the plane noises. "What did you say?"

Dane broke contact with Sin Fen, earning an approving bark from Chelsea. "What?"

"You said something," Freed yelled.

"Nothing," Dane said.

"Time to rig for the jump."

Dane looked over at Beasley who appeared to be less than enthusiastic at the moment. As he stood, he projected his thoughts toward Sin Fen:

I want to know the entire truth. Sin Fen's dark eyes met his. *I will you tell you all we know, but it is not much.*

"Where's Mansor?" Ingram was holding Ariana's arm, his fingers squeezing into her bicep. She knew he was afraid she was in shock, but she wasn't ready yet to come back to reality. She *wanted* to be in shock, to forget what she had just witnessed.

They'd hauled her back using the co-ax cable, pulling her into the hatch. Ariana looked up. The hatch was still open above their heads. That brought her back like a slap in the face. "Shut it! Shut it!" she screamed at the others.

Lisa Carpenter jumped up on the desk top and pushed the hatch closed. She spun shut the locking latch.

"What happened to Mansor?" Ingram asked once more as she peeled his fingers out of her arm. "Is he out there? Should we get him?"

Ariana stared at him, choking back the insane laughter she felt welling up in her chest. She spread her hands indicating the blood she was covered in. "This is what happened to Mansor. This *is* Mansor."

"Sweet Jesus," Ingram muttered, sitting down in shock.

"What about the SATCOM?" Carpenter asked.

Ariana held up the cable, where it had gone to Mansor. The end was cleanly cut. She pulled the loose end through and undid the knot she had around her wrist. She could feel pain in skin where the cable had tightened down on her, but it was distant, not sharp. She threw the cable down and collapsed in a swivel chair.

She took stock of the situation, getting herself under control. There were only five of them left. Hudson was in a chair, his wounded legs propped in front of him. Herrin was huddled in the corner, his glazed eyes telling Ariana he was long gone and could not be counted on. Ingram seemed all right, but age was against him. Carpenter seemed ready, muscular black arms folded over her chest. But ready for what? Ariana wondered as she absently ran a hand across her face. It came away sticky and crusted with blood.

"Here," Carpenter said, holding out a towel.

Ariana took it and wiped herself clean as best she could.

"What happened out there?" Ingram asked.

So Ariana told them. When she was done, silence reigned, until Carpenter spoke. "What do we do now?"

"Nothing," Ariana said. "We do nothing. We wait and we pray but I don't even know if that will do any good, because as far as I know, we may already be in hell."

Much as Foreman hated bureaucracy, there were times when he also appreciated it and the blind allegiance paid by those who filled the various nooks and crannies of the government.

Right now he had a live satellite feed to the National Reconnaissance Office representative at the Groom Lake Test Facility, more commonly known as Area 51 in the media and among UFO fanatics. He'd given the order twenty minutes ago and the NRO had reacted with its usual efficient speed.

"The SR-75 is ready to go," the NRO rep informed Foreman.

"Go," Foreman ordered.

Groom Lake had the distinction of being home to the longest runway in the world, built onto the dry lake bed. Over seven miles long, it had been the field from which such exotic planes as the Stealth Fighter and the B-2 bomber had first been tested.

But today, the plane that had just been rolled out of a massive hanger at Foreman's order, made those earlier planes look like toys. Over a 250 feet long, almost the length of a football field, and a hundred feet wide at the tip of its v-wing shape, the SR-75 Penetrator was the most advanced airframe ever built by man. The plane was shaped like an elongated B-2 bomber. The crew of three consisted of a pilot, co-pilot and reconnaissance surveillance officer (RSO). Those three sat in a special compartment in the upper nose. A fourth man sat in the belly of the plane, waiting.

With Foreman's final order, the pilot of the SR-75 rolled up throttle on the plane's conventional turbo-jet engine and the large plane began accelerating down the runway. It took the plane over two and a half miles to gain sufficient speed so that the delta wings produced enough lift for the wheels to separate from the ground.

With the turbojet engine at max thrust, the pilot continued to gain altitude and speed.

"I need you to stay on top of this and tell me immediately if there is any change." Patricia Conners rubbed a weary hand across her wrinkled forehead. "We'll stay on top of it." She glanced across her desk at Jimmy who nodded in agreement. There was a pause, then Foreman's voice echoed through the office. "I appreciate this."

"You're welcome," Conners said. "I'm just glad someone's taking action."

"Are you linked to the HMV?"

"I'm linked through the NRO," Conners said. "I'll take over control once the HMV is launched."

"You only have one shot," Foreman said.

"I know," Conners replied.

CHAPTER ELEVEN

"Hook up!" Freed yelled, curling his forefingers and gesturing up and down.

Dane slipped his static line hook over the cable, snapped it in place, then ran the thin safety wire through the small hole, locking the hook in place. It had been thirty years since Dane had had a parachute on his back, but the routine and feelings that he had first experienced at Fort Benning during his basic airborne training came rushing back. He was getting ready to jump out of a perfectly good airplane. Unlike that first training jump, Dane felt no apprehension about the jump itself. This time he feared the ground.

He was wearing protective gear, designed for rough terrain jumping: braces on his arms and legs, a helmet with a protective grill over his face, a thick, padded vest covering his torso. A 200 foot length of rope was tied off on the outside of his rucksack, to be used to lower himself to the ground if he got stuck in a tree. The M-16, mines, ammunition and other gear, were broken down inside the ruck.

In front of him, Beasley was fumbling with his snap hook. Dane took it out of his hands and hooked it up. Beasley didn't thank him.

"Don't sweat it," Dane said.

Beasley just moaned.

Dane twisted his head. Chelsea was with Sin Fen, looking none too happy. He sent an image of Chelsea to the woman, curled up on her pillow at home

I'll take care of her. Sin Fin's mental projection echoed in his brain.

Dane leaned over and yelled so that she could hear him above the noise inside the plane. "Foreman sent you to be the link, didn't he?" Dane asked. "He thinks you and I can communicate once I go into this place."

"Yes."

"How far away can you communicate with me?"

"I don't know."

"Great."

"Foreman also thinks you are capable of much more than just communicating with me," Sin Fen added.

"A clue about that would be helpful."

"It is for you to discover because it is beyond what we know.

"Great," Dane repeated. "Any idea what this place is?"

"You know more than we do, since you've been in there. But we must know if the MILSTARS satellite system is being used by the force inside the Angkor Gate."

"Used for what?" Dane asked. He started as an image of the entire planet came into his mind, overlaid with various colored lines. There were several glowing spots along those lines. He could also see a spy satellite directly over where they were going and Dane knew, without knowing how, that the satellite was blind, that nothing could see into the Gate.

"That is the power being propagated by a source inside the Angkor Gate. The dots are MILSTARS satellites. The building force will rise to dangerous, lethal, levels in less than day. We have to stop it."

"What does Foreman want me to do?"

"Find out what is causing this to happen. And stop it."

"Sure. I'll be back in time for lunch."

"This is very dangerous, more dangerous than you know. These areas are expanding and they could destroy the world."

"Thanks for letting me know that now."

Dane tried penetrating her mind, to see if there was anything else she was hiding from him, but his psychic probe came up against a black wall that allowed him to go no further. He cursed inside his head and her voice echoed on top of the curse.

It takes practice. I have trained very hard to discipline my mind.

"Then maybe you should be wearing this parachute," Dane said out loud.

No. You are the one.

"One minute!" Freed yelled.

Dane thought about the place in Cambodia expanding. He reached down and made sure the straps to his rucksack were secure, then tightened his leg straps a cinch.

The back ramp began opening, the top half disappearing up into the tail well, the bottom half leveling out. Freed moved toward the platform.

Dane blinked as wind whipped his face. It was still dark, but he knew dawn was near. Freed was kneeling, holding onto the hydraulic arm that moved the platform. The four Canadians and Beasley outfitted in bulk gear were between Dane and Freed, waiting.

Freed stood. "Stand by!" He scooted to the edge, giving a thumbs up to Paul Michelet.

"Go!" Freed stepped out into the darkness, the Canadians hustling behind him. Dane could see their chutes billow out behind the plane, the deployment bags still attached to the steel cable, twisting in the wind. Beasley paused at the edge, but Dane simply shoved him off.

Dane followed, shuffling his feet along the metal until there was no more floor. He felt the familiar sensation of freefalling as his static line paid out behind him, then the abrupt tug of his chute opening.

Dane looked up, checked to make sure he had a good canopy and grabbed his toggles, then he switched his gaze downward. He could barely make out the rapidly nearing dark green carpet of vegetation below. As he got closer, he could see that he was coming down on the side of a ridge, covered in triple canopy jungle. He could also see the other chutes, a couple of which were already in the trees.

Dane wheeled his elbows across his face and tensed his body as he approached the top of the jungle. He hit leaves, then he was in, bouncing off a branch, breaking

another, then suddenly he was still, hanging from his harness. Before Dane did anything else, he closed his eyes.

Sin Fen.

The voice in his head came back immediately.

I hear you.

The SR-75 passed through Mach 2.5 over the eastern edge of the Pacific Ocean at an altitude of 60,000 feet. At this altitude, the radical nature of the aircraft's design came into play as the conventional turbojet engines were now strained to the maximum, gulping for air at the extreme speed and altitude of their design specifications.

In the cockpit, the co-pilot lifted the cover on a series of four red switches. "Ready for PDWE ignition," he informed the pilot.

"Ignite."

The co-pilot flicked the switches from left to right. In the rear of the plane, nestled below the turbojet engine, the pulsed-detonation-wave-engine came to life. The PDWE was a rather simple device, consisting of a group of small chambers in which mini-explosions occurred in rhythm. These explosions caused supersonic shock waves to form and rush out into a larger combustion chamber. The shock waves compressed the fuel-air mixture and thus produced another larger shock wave that was channeled to the rear of the plane, providing propulsion at ranges never before produced by man.

Leaving behind a series of white puffs in the high atmosphere, the SR-75 pulsed its way even higher, as its speed raced through Mach-5 on the way to its maximum speed of Mach 7, or 5,000 miles an hour.

The C-123 was banking across the sky, ten kilometers from the drop zone. The ramp was still down. One of the crewmen was slowly unreeling a set of nylon straps that held the pallet the daisy-cutter bomb was attached to. The pallet was on rollers and the crewman let out slack in the nylon until the pallet was perched the very edge of the ramp. He pulled a large hook off the top of the parachute on top of the bomb and hooked it into the static line cable.

He was listening to the pilot via a headset and when he got the word, and the green light went on, he cut the nylon with a razor sharp knife, allowing the pallet to fall off the ramp.

The bomb and pallet fell, then a large cargo parachute billowed open. The C-123 circled above as the bomb drifted down. It hit the jungle and crashed through the top layers. Just before touching the ground, it exploded in a flash of five thousand pounds of high explosive.

In the C-123 overhead, Paul Michelet saw the instant landing zone they had created. He pressed his intercom. "All right, let's get back to Thailand."

Michelet turned to Sin Fen, who had sat quietly with the dog throughout. "I want to know who you are and who you work for," Michelet demanded, sitting down next to her.

Sin Fen's eyes were unfocused and slowly she seemed to gain awareness of her immediate surroundings. She shifted slightly so she could look at the old man. "What you want is no longer important."

She reached into her bag and pulled out a small SATCOM radio. She began to punch into the handset when Michelet reached out and grabbed her wrist.

"Listen here," Michelet hissed. "This is my plane, this is my--"

He gasped in pain as Sin Fen placed her free hand on his upper arm and applied pressure.

"Do not ever touch me again," she said. "Do not ever get in my way again."

She released her grip and finished dialing.

"They've jumped," she reported as soon as she got a reply. She listened for a few seconds then turned off the phone.

"A helicopter has taken off from Angkor Wat," she told Michelet who was glaring at her, massaging his arm.

"What?"

"Syn-Tech," Sin Fen simply said.

"Goddamn!" Michelet exploded. "Those sons-a-"

"Enough," Sin Fen said. "Syn-Tech is not something that you need worry about."

"My recommendation is that we take out MILSTARS," Foreman said. His eyes

were focused on the computer screen that showed him the display from the SR-75. It was flying at 125,000 feet over the western Pacific now, traveling at Mach-7.

"Jesus Christ man!" Bancroft sputtered. "Do you know how many billions of dollars we have invested in that system?"

Foreman ignored the National Security Adviser. "Mister President, somehow our satellites are being used by this force. We are going to have fatalities in less than twelve hours near some of the Gates. We need to stop this before it's too late."

"Can you prove this?" Bancroft demanded. "We've got nothing here proving that these waves are being propagated through MILSTARS."

"I have proof from the NSA," Foreman said.

"No, you have a theory from the NSA," Bancroft said. "I've seen what they are saying and the only thing they've got is coincidence. Hell, some of the MILSTARS satellites don't seem to be affected at all. That's not conclusive proof."

"By the time we get conclusive proof, it will be too late," Foreman said. "Remember what happened to Bright Eye."

The President finally spoke. "My advisers do not agree with you, Mister Foreman. They neither believe the threat is as great as you claim or that MILSTARS is could be used in this manner. They say it is impossible."

"Nonetheless, Mister President, it is being done," Foreman forced himself to keep his voice level. "Do your advisers have an explanation for what is happening?"

"Not yet."

"Then, sir, we have--" Foreman was cut off by the President.

"You're asking me to destroy billions of dollars worth of equipment," the President said.

"The equipment can be replaced," Foreman said. "People can't."

"We don't even have a way of taking out MILSTARS," the President said.

Foreman looked once more at the computer display. "Actually, sir, we do."

"And that is?"

"Thunder Dart," Foreman said.

"What the hell is that?" the President said.

"Jesus Christ," Bancroft exploded before Foreman could even answer. "You already cost us Bright Eye. Now you propose putting Thunder Dart in harm's way?"

Foreman leaned back in his chair. This was the part of the bureaucracy that he despised. "It's launch platform is already in the air and Thunder Dart is two minutes from deployment."

"Foreman!" Bancroft yelled.

Foreman leaned forward and spoke earnestly as the speaker. "Mister President, let Thunder Dart take out one of the affected

177

MILSTARS, the one closest to the Angkor Gate. The first one affected. Let's see what happens. If it affects the propagation, we know for certain that the MILSTARS satellites are being used. If it doesn't then all we've lost is a non-functional satellite."

There was a long silence. Foreman glanced at the display. Thunder Dart was a minute from launch.

"All right," the President finally said. "Take it out."

A door in the belly of the SR-75 slid forward and upward at the same time, specially constructed adapters bearing the intense stress of the thin air buffeting by at over Mach-7. The opened bay was also aerodynamically designed, so the speed of the plane slowed a mere 500 miles an hour.

Inside, securely locked by two hydraulic arms, rested Thunder Dart, the progeny of the SR-71 and the other half of the Penetrator. With a 75 degree swept wing delta configuration, it too had a PDWE propulsion unit built into it's body, although on a much smaller scale. The Thunder Dart was less than forty feet long from nose to tail, and thirty feet wide at the full extension of the wings.

Nestled inside the specially constructed cocoon cockpit sat Major Frank Mitchell, patiently waiting for his moment. His gloved hand tightly gripped his throttle, thumb poised over a red button.

"Are you green?" the co-pilot of the SR-75 mothercraft asked him.

Mitchell had had his eyes on nothing else for the past ten minutes, but he swept them over the gauges one last time. "All green."

"Free in five," the co-pilot informed him. "Four. Three. Two. One."

Mitchell felt the weightlessness as the hydraulic arms let the Thunder Dart go and he lost the G-force of the SR-75's constant acceleration. The sky below was light, but he was so high he could easily see the curvature of the Earth ahead. This was his third time piloting the Thunder Dart, although he had over 3,000 missions in the simulator. But no simulator could make up for the feel of free-falling at 125,000 feet with an initial forward velocity of almost 5,000 miles an hour. Above, the SR-75 slightly turned and disappeared from sight.

Mitchell's thumb closed on the red button. He was slammed back in his seat as the pulse engine kicked in. Pulling back ever so slightly, he angled the nose of the Thunder Dart up five degrees.

Mitchell looked out the cockpit. He could see that the edges of his craft were already glowing red from heat, but that was normal. Even at this altitude there was enough oxygen molecules to cause friction. The specially designed titanium alloy hull could handle the heat as long as he maintained positive control of his craft.

He looked up higher and saw the blackness of space. He glanced down at the flight path outlined in red on his computer screen. The triangle symbolizing his craft was slightly to the right of center of the path marked in green. Mitchell edged the stick to the left just a tad and centered out.

"I'm on-line with all my systems," Jimmy said. "Anything changes, we'll know."

Jimmy was seated across from her, his laptop open, the line in the back jacked into the central network to allow him to directly access those satellites that channeled the radioactivity and electromagnetic data.

She was seated behind her own desk. A small joystick was next to the keyboard, waiting for her. She picked up the baseball cap with the astronaut wings and placed it on top of her gray hair, rim back.

Jimmy looked at her and smiled. "Ready for warp speed, helmsman?"

Conners grinned. "Ready."

"All systems go," Major Mitchell said into his oxygen mask. The small triangle in his screen was dead center. The altimeter read 155,000 feet, over 27 miles high. Mitchell knew the air was so thin outside that even the pulse engine was having problems now.

He looked down once more. There was the faintest trace of a flashing red circle at the very center of the display.

"Acquisition initiated," Mitchell reported. His free hand went palm down on top of a flat display. The face was specially designed for the pressure glove, each button an exact match.

"Arming MHV." Mitchell had the process memorized and his fingers worked the code perfectly. He felt the slightest of stutters in the pattern of pulses from the PDWE.

"Insure you get both beacon and trajectory lock," a voice ordered in his ear.

"Roger that," Mitchell said. His fingers pressed down. A series of numbers came up on the right top side of the display. "I'm turning on the MILSTARS beacon. Beacon on. MHV is locked on MILSTAR beacon. Locked as primary." He watched as the red circle stopped flashing and became steady. His thumb pressed down on another panel. "Ground, do you have control?"

A woman's voice came back. "This is Ground. I have control."

"Ready to fire," Mitchell said.

"Fire."

"Firing." Mitchell's thumb pressed down on the button on top of his control stick.

Underneath the belly of the Thunder Dart explosive bolts fired, separating the MHV from the body of the aircraft. Less than eight feet long and only eight inches in diameter the MHV was the result of eight generations of anti-satellite (ASAT) development. It's own very sophisticated and miniaturized pulse engine kicked in once it was clear of the Thunder Dart and it angled up toward space.

Major Mitchell had the MHV on his screen as he banked his own craft ever so slightly and began a carefully calculated descent back toward earth. "MHV running smooth and clean," he reported.

Patricia Conners knew the MHV stood for miniature homing vehicle. And she could see the same image from the rocket as the nosecone fell away, allowing the built-in infrared imaging scope to go active. It filled the entire screen of her computer.

"There!" Jimmy said, pointing at a very small dot in the center of the screen. "That's MILSTARS 16. The MHV is homing in on the satellite's secure beacon so there should be no problem of a hit."

Conners hand hovered over the joystick, just in case.

In the nose of the HMV rocket, the guidance computer had the exact location of MILSTARS 16 beacon; the same beacon that the space shuttle used to find and dock with the satellite to refuel it every two years. The beacon was normally silent, except when activated with a special access code, much like the landing lights at a remote airfield were activated by an incoming airplane signaling on a certain FM frequency.

The nose also held an infrared camera. The camera was sending to Conners a picture of MILSTARS and the golden glow growing around it.

"What the hell is that?" Jimmy asked.

"I don't know," Conners said. Her hand was now resting around the manual control. "But it looks a lot like what took out Bright Star."

"Oh, man!" Jimmy exclaimed as the glow expanded. "How the hell does it know the HMV is inbound?"

"The radio," Conners' free hand was typing into her keyboard even as she said it. "I'm going to shut down the radio link from the HMV to Thunder Dart." She hit the enter key as her other hand tightened around the joystick. "I have control of HMV," she announced into the headset.

Jimmy quietly stepped back. He knew that Conners was now controlling an eight inch diameter missile traveling at 4,000 miles an hour toward a target less than twenty feet wide. There were forty, tiny, solid fuel booster rockets lined around the circumference of the rocket that she could fire to alter the course but this was like threading a needle stuck in a mailbox by leaning out a car at 60 miles an hour.

"Thirty seconds out," Conners announced.

The golden glow was growing. "Oh, shit!" Conners muttered, trying to think with one part of her brain, even as she kept the small dot indicating the MILSTARS satellite centered.

"Oh God!" She exclaimed. "Jimmy, tell Thunder to--" she paused as a golden fireball separated from the main aura and raced to the right.

"Stick with the MHV!" Jimmy yelled.

Major Mitchell saw what Conners saw. He immediately slammed down on his throttle, feeling the PDWE engine pick up the pace.

He had no idea how quickly the fireball was coming. He could still see the curvature of the earth ahead and his altimeter read 112,000 feet.

"Get out of there!" he heard the woman screaming in his headset.

"Damn right," Mitchell muttered to himself, then he pushed right on the stick. The Thunder Dart began turning, but Mitchell had no idea whether he was avoiding the danger or not.

A second later he knew it was not. He felt his skin begin to crackle and a golden light suffused the cockpit. Mitchell slammed his fist down on a red lever. The entire cockpit shell of the Thunder Dart separated from the main body of the plane, slamming Mitchell against his shoulder harness with such force that he blacked out.

"Come on, come on," Conners whispered as the MILSTARS satellite rapidly grew on the screen in front of her. The numbers in the upper right hand corner raced down as the rocket ate up the distance. As the time hit three seconds out, she pulled back on the trigger.

The explosive charge in the MHV ignited. The core of the rocket exploded into thousands of one inch diameter steel ball bearings. They spread out evenly, still moving in the vacuum of space with the original velocity of the rocket, now covering an area over two hundred meters wide.

Over two hundred of the bearings ripped into the MILSTARS satellite, shredding it like a shotgun blast to a tin can.

Conners slumped back in her chair. She looked across her desk at Jimmy who was peering intently at his laptop screen. "Well?"

"I'm downloading."

Conners hit the switch on her satellite phone. "Foreman, what about the pilot?"

"He ejected his pod. We're tracking it. I'll get a rescue moving, but we have no commo."

"Damn."

"No one's ever ejected, even inside a pod, at 3,500 miles an hour," Foreman noted. "What about the pattern?"

Conners looked over at Jimmy. She knew from the look that came across his face what the answer was, but she waited.

"Negative," Jimmy said. "The lines cross where the MILSTARS was without interruption. We were too late. There's too many cross connections. Whatever this thing is, it's rerouted and it can probably do that faster than we can take out satellites."

Conners relayed the information. There was a long silence, then Foreman's voice. "Well, then I guess it's down to stopping it at the source."

CHAPTER TWELVE

The sleep of the dead, Ariana thought, listening to the uneasy slumber of her fellow prisoners. Having been awake for over twenty-four straight hours and with no course of action available, they had decided to try to get some rest. She'd also ordered Ingram to turn off even the emergency power lights, trying to conserve their batteries as much as possible, leaving the inside of the plane in darkness, other than the two gold beams crossing the main console area and the golden glow coming from Argus's hardware consoles.

She knew she needed to clear her head and try to come up with a course of action, but her brain was so tired she could barely think. Still, though, sleep eluded her, as images of Mansor dying crowded to the forefront while large snakes slithered about in her subconscious, jaws snapping shut and tongues hissing.

The golden beam in Argus had stopped expanding. Apparently it had accessed everything it needed. They had pulled more access panels off and discovered that a golden beam came out of the back side of Argus's mainframe and disappeared into the ceiling. Ariana had no doubt that the golden beam she had seen coming out of the rotodome was the same one.

No new gold beams had come into the plane, nor had there been a repeat of the sliding noise. Ariana had described the massive seven-headed snake to the others, but she had seen the uncomprehending looks in their eyes. She knew if it had not been for them hearing the noise earlier they would not believe her at all. As it was, she knew they were giving her the benefit of the doubt in an insane situation, something she wasn't too happy about.

Ariana turned on her side, trying to get comfortable in her desk chair when she heard a low noise. Someone, or something, was moving through the passageway. Ariana reached down and pulled out the Berretta. As quietly as she could, she checked the chamber, making sure a round was loaded. Then she pulled back the hammer, locking it to the rear. She picked up a mini-mag light from her desktop. Gripping the light and gun tightly, she got out of her chair.

The noise had gone forward, past her compartment to the radio area. She followed, moving stealthily. There was the muffled metal on metal noise of a cabinet being opened.

Ariana held the butt of the gun in her right hand, finger on the trigger and with her left, the mini-mag alongside the barrel. She pressed the on switch for the flashlight as she turned the corner for the communications area.

She caught movement and her finger tightened on the trigger, stopping a hair short of firing as she recognized Hudson crouched over something on the floor.

"Don't move!" Ariana ordered.

"Jesus!" Hudson exclaimed, blinking in the flashlight's glow. "You scared the piss out of me." He started to stand.

"I said don't move," Ariana repeated. She stepped forward, the muzzle centered on him.

Hudson froze. "What's wrong?"

"What are you doing?"

"Just checking on some things," Hudson said.

"In the dark?" Ariana slid left, keeping the radio man locked in the beam, gun still pointing at him. She wanted to see what he had been working on.

"I didn't want to wake anyone up," Hudson said. He reached down for what was lying on the floor. "I just--"

Ariana rapped the muzzle of the gun on the back of his hand, bringing a yelp of pain from Hudson. "I said leave it." She stuck the gun in his chest. "Back up."

Hudson put his hands up and pressed back against his main console. Ariana briefly shined the beam down at the floor. A small satellite dish was folded open, sitting on a tiny tripod. She shined the light back in Hudson's face.

The emergency lights flickered, then came on. Ingram and Carpenter appeared in the corridor, peering into the room. "What's going on?" Ingram asked, the other gun held uncertainly in his hand.

"I found our spy," Ariana said.

"Listen--" Hudson began, but the next words didn't come out as Ariana stepped close, pressing the muzzle of the gun against his forehead, right between his eyes.

"Did you sabotage the plane?" she hissed.

"No!"

She put pressure on the gun, digging into his skin. "Tell me the truth!"

"I didn't do anything!"

She nodded toward the satellite dish. "Who were you trying to call?"

"Wait a second," Ingram said, stepping next to Ariana. "How do you know he's the spy?"

"It will take just the slightest pressure for me to pull this trigger," Ariana said, keeping her focus on Hudson. "And I really feel like doing just that. If you lie to me now, and I let you live, and I find out you lied, I will make your death very painful. Is that clear?"

Hudson's eyes locked onto hers. He started to nod, but the gun wouldn't allow that. "Yes."

"Are you a spy?" Ariana asked.

"Yes."

"Who are you working for?"

"Syn-Tech."

"You were trying to call them with that?" she again nodded toward the dish.

"It's just a beacon," Hudson said.

Ariana stepped back from Hudson. He slumped down in his chair, sweat rolling down his flabby cheeks. "I swear, Ariana, I didn't do anything." He rubbed his bandaged legs.

"No," she said, "you just allowed Mansor and I to go out there," she swung the muzzle of the gun toward the ceiling, "to run cable to the rotodome satellite dish while you had that in here all the time."

"I couldn't bring it out before," Hudson said. "You would have known then." "So you let Mansor die," Ariana brought the gun to bear on him once more. "I didn't know! How could I have known?" Hudson pleaded. "I'm sorry!" "Hold on!" Ingram said, stepping between the two. "Get out of the way, Mark," Ariana ordered. "Listen to me,"

Ingram said. "He says it's a beacon. Let him turn it on!" Carpenter spoke for the first time. "Who's listening for the beacon, Hudson?" "Syn-Tech has a team near Angkor Wat," Hudson spoke rapidly.

"They'll home in on the beacon and rescue us." Ariana lowered the gun and laughed, but there was a harsh edge to the sound. "Fine. Turn it on. Let them come."

"You didn't have to shove me," Beasley whined, tenderly touching a long scratch on the side of his face. "I was going to jump."

"Shut up," Dane said. His eyes were scanning the surrounding terrain, the M-16 ready in his hands.

The sky above the triple canopy was growing light, but on the jungle floor it was dark, with barely enough visibility to see twenty feet. Dane had gathered in Beasley, helping him climb down. He had heard the blast from the daisy cutter somewhere to the east, then the sound of the jungle had returned.

They were moving along the track of the aircraft, Dane working from his internal sense of direction. He'd already checked and his compass and watch didn't work. He knew the Canadians and Freed were along this way. He could even hear someone climbing down not too far ahead.

He felt all the old skills coming back, becoming part of the jungle, one with the flora and fauna. Other than the irritating presence of Beasley and the others, he felt a peacefulness in the immediate area.

And he also felt the shadow to the east, just as he had felt it thirty years ago.

Foreman watched the master board which showed a downlink from a KH-12 satellite that was tracking the Syn-Tech helicopter. The KH-12 had picked it up as soon as it took off from the company's base camp outside of Angkor Wat. It was flying a route along the limits of the Angkor Gate. Foreman gave whoever was in charge of the operation some credit; the chopper would get as close as possible to the downed plane before darting in.

Still, the helicopter didn't really interest Foreman. What he found intriguing was the beacon signal that was drawing the chopper into the Angkor Gate. That the signal was being allowed to escape the electromagnetic anomaly of the Gate was a fact that Foreman found quite chilling. Someone, or something, wanted that helicopter to come.

"Which way?" Freed asked.

"The watchtower is up there," Dane said, pointing with the muzzle of his M-16. All they could see was dense jungle in any direction but Dane had no doubt about which way to go. "The stream is on the other side. According to the imagery, the plane is another five klicks past the stream."

Freed took point, scrambling up the steep slope, Dane following right behind. The Canadians and Beasley struggled to keep up, all in much poorer shape than the two men setting the pace.

Dane didn't even bother to look over his shoulder. He paused for a second and closed his eyes. He pictured Sin Fen in his mind.

Still there?

He opened his eyes and kept moving.

An image came to him. The airfield they had taken off from. Chelsea and Sin Fen getting off the plane and moving over to a helicopter. In his vision, Sin Fen paused. The image shifted. He saw the satellite overhead. It exploded. Overlaid on the image was the unmistakable message from Sin Fen that the attempt to stop whatever was coming out of the Gate by destroying the satellite had failed.

Dane checked to make sure that he was still right behind Freed, then returned to what he was seeing internally. The scene shifted. He saw a helicopter taking off and he knew from the subtext that Sin Fen was projecting, that the helicopter was heading his way and that it was from Syn-Tech.

The helicopter was riding a line. Dane frowned trying to make sense of the image, then he realized the line was a transmission, a radio beacon coming out of the Gate.

He paused, realizing the implications of that. He looked over his shoulder, at Beasley's sweating face, then turned back to the front.

Dane leaned into the climb, feeling sweat pour down his back, soaking between his shirt and backpack. Then suddenly he broke into the clear, a fresh breeze brushing against his face, drying the sweat. He looked up. The watchtower.

He quickly climbed the remaining distance and joined Freed at the base of the wall. Dane reached out and touched a massive stone block. The stone felt smooth under his fingers, comforting.

"You can't see a damn thing," Freed said.

Dane's momentary good feeling left as he looked in the same direction. The sun was behind them, casting long shadows down into the river valley, but beyond was the same thick fog that Dane had seen so long ago. It was even thicker and more impenetrable than he remembered. It stretched south and north as far as he could see on the far side of the river valley.

"Let's get up top," Freed startled Dane out of his contemplation.

The Canadians and Beasley broke into the open on the ridge back, all breathing heavily.

"Beasley," Freed called out. "Come with us. McKenzie, I want a perimeter around the base of this building."

Dane could see Beasley's fatigue fade as the scientist took in the watchtower and the ancient stonework.

"This is unbelievable," Beasley said as he came to the stones.

Freed led the way inside the door, Dane and Beasley following. They took the stairs around the interior wall, Beasley stopping to stare at the carvings. As Dane climbed through to the rampart, he could hear Beasley snapping pictures, his heavy breathing echoing off the old stone.

Dane walked up next to Freed who was peering through his binoculars. The view across the river from the interior rampart wasn't any clearer, but they could see more of the country-side in the other directions.

"The walls!" Beasley was gasping for breath as he joined them. "There is so much on them. It's not like Angkor Wat or any of the other sites. This is different! Older. Yes! Definitely older."

"Take it easy," Dane said. "You have a heart attack here and it's a long haul out."

"But don't you see?" Beasley really wasn't talking to anyone. "There's only sculpture at those places. This has writing!" Beasley turned to Dane and grabbed his shoulders. "It's writing! An early form of Sanskrit."

"Can you read it?" Dane asked.

"I can make sense of some of it," Beasley said.

"Then read it," Dane ordered. He turned his attention back to Freed. The small black man lowered the glasses, a worried look on his face.

"That's it," Dane said in a low voice.

Freed shot him a look. "I guess we--" he paused as they all heard the sound of

rotor blades coming from the east. "Syn-Tech," Dane said. "How do you know that?" Freed asked, swinging his binoculars back to his eyes. "Sin Fen told us, remember." "Huey," Freed said, catching site of the aircraft. "About two miles away."

"I've got contact on FM!" Hudson yelled.

Ariana was sitting in a chair across from him, the Berretta loosely held, resting in her lap. She didn't react like Carpenter and Ingram, both of whom jumped up at the announcement. Mike Herrin had come forward earlier, but he didn't appear to hear. He was sitting in the corner of the communications area, eyes closed, rocking back and forth, humming to himself in a low voice.

"It's a helicopter," Hudson said, pressing the headset against one of his ears. He keyed his FM radio. "Bravo Two Nine, this is Angler. Bravo Two Nine, this is Angler. Over."

"Angler?" Ariana asked. "Is that your code name?" Hudson nodded. "How long have you been working for Syn-Tech?" she asked. "I only agreed to forward them the data from this mission," Hudson said. "Piggybacked on the GPS signal," she said, earning a surprised look from the

radio man.

"You knew about that?" Hudson's attention shifted back to the headset. "Roger, Bravo Two Nine. I can read you broken and distorted. Over." Hudson said. He held his hand over the mike. "I'm going to put the FM on the speaker."

He turned back to the radio and hit a switch. "Roger, Bravo Two Nine. We are awaiting your arrival. Our situation is critical and we require immediate assistance. Over."

A voice came out of the speaker, riding on top of a mixture of popping static. "This is Two Nine. I've never seen anything like this. Visibility is bad. We can . . . read the beacon although . . . fades out every once in a while. We . . . four . . . . your . . . coming . . . ."

Hudson keyed the mike. "Bravo Two Nine, say again. You are coming in broken and distorted. Over."

The speaker now issued forth screeching static. "This . . . . difficulty . . . ."

Hudson waited a few seconds. "Bravo Two Nine, this is Angler. Come in. Over."

There was an ear-shattering screech of static issuing out of the speaker.

"There it goes," Freed said as the helicopter banked over their head and swooped down into the valley. It did a run at the wall of fog, curved along it for about a half mile then did a circle over the river, gaining altitude all the time.

"Having second thoughts," Dane said. His hands were splayed over the stone wall. "They go in, they're dead."

Beasley and Freed glanced at each other.

"They're going in now," Dane said.

The chopper headed straight for the fog, still gaining altitude. Less than a quarter mile from the edge of the fog, a large circle of gold light appeared around the helicopter. It contracted rapidly, centering on the aircraft. There was a flash of light, then small pieces falling to the jungle below. Seconds later, the sound of the destruction, like a distant peel of thunder, rolled over their location.

"Jesus!" Beasley whispered.

"It means we made the right decision not to try to fly in or even to fly this close," Freed said.

"You think walking in is going to be any better?" Dane asked.

The screams of the helicopter pilot reverberated through the commo section, then there was an echoing silence.

Mike Herrin suddenly jumped up. "They've got to get us! We've got to get out of here! They're up there waiting for us. I can hear the helicopter."

He jumped on top of the table and reached up for the top hatch, hands gripping the opening lever. Ariana and Carpenter grabbed his legs, but he struck out with a vicious kick that hit Carpenter square in the face, sending her tumbling back, taking Ariana with her.

The hatch opened. Ariana could see past Herrin and that the swirling fog was allowing a dull light from the sun to penetrate.

"Mike!" she yelled, holding onto his legs. "Come back in!"

Ingram had taken Carpenter's place and had Herrin's other leg, holding him half inside the hatch. Ariana was looking up when a large shadow suddenly appeared in the space around Herrin's torso filling the hatch. She heard Herrin scream and felt his leg spasm in her arms. The scream ended as abruptly as it had begun, replaced by a very loud clicking sound, and then Herrin fell back inside the airplane; the bottom half of him at least. Ariana looked up from the twitching legs. There was surprisingly little blood oozing from the bisected torso.

"Oh, Jesus," she muttered. The sound was back, as if something was sliding over the top of the plane, but now she could see the massive scales through the open hatch as they slithered by. She pulled out the Berretta and aimed up.

"No!" Carpenter yelled, grabbing her arms. "Don't!"

Ariana staggered back as Carpenter swung the hatch shut. They could feel the entire plane moving now, rolling slightly to the left. The noise continued for another ten seconds then was gone and the plane was still.

Then the speaker came alive again, this time with the dots and dashes of Morse code. As Ariana covered the lower half of Herrin's body with a cloth, Hudson anxiously copied down the message.

D-O-N-O-T-U-S-E-V-O-I-C-E-O-N-R-A-D-I-OD-O-N-O-T-U-S-E-V-O-I-C-E-O-N-R-A-D-I-O

C-U-T-P-O-W-E-R-T-O-C-O-M-P-U-T-E-RO-R-D-I-ET-I-M-E-I-S-S-H-O-R-TC-U-T-P-O-W-E-R-T-O-C-O-M-P-U-T-E-RO-R-D-I-ET-I-M-E-I-S-S-H-O-R-T

"A little advice on how to do that would be helpful," Ariana said as she saw the letters. "Ask them how!" she ordered Hudson. Ingram and Carpenter were staring at what remained of Herrin, blood slowly seeping through the cloth.

"Do it!" Ariana snapped at Hudson. The radio man pulled out his knee key and began tapping out the question, sending three letters repeatedly:

H-O-WH-O-WH-O-WH-O-W

Ariana watched as Hudson's hand wrote out the letters to the reply:

T-R-YD-O-N-T-K-N-O-W-H-O-W W-I-L-L-T-R-Y-T-O-H-E-L-P O-N-O-U-T-S-I-D-E

"Ask for some identification," Ariana told Hudson.
W-H-O-A-R-E-Y-O-U
The dashes and dots came back immediately.
R-T-K-A-N-S-A-S
"I don't understand," Ariana tried to make sense of the letters.
"I do," Carpenter said.
The other three turned and looked at her.
"RT Kansas stands for Reconnaissance Team Kansas," Carpenter informed them. "That's the code name of a Special Forces team that went into this area in 1968."
"1968?" Ingram repeated.
"How the hell do you know this?" Ariana demanded.
"It's in the classified CIA file for this area, which goes by the code name Angkor Gate," Carpenter said.
"How do you know that?" Ingram demanded.
Ariana stared at the other woman. "You're CIA?"
Carpenter nodded. "Yes."
"Is anyone here who they're supposed to be?" Ariana asked.
"None of that matters right now," Carpenter said. "Our priority should be to get the hell out of here."
"How?" Ariana gestured up at the hatch. "You saw that thing. You know that I was telling the truth about the seven-headed snake. I don't know how or why it can be, but it is."
"Someone's trying to help us," Ingram said, pointing at Hudson's notepad with the Morse messages.
Ariana ran a hand through her long hair, feeling how dirty it was as she thought furiously. "Who's trying to help us? Who is RT Kansas and how can they still be here since 1968?"
"There were four men on RT Kansas," Carpenter said. "Three of them were listed as missing in action. The team leader's name was Sergeant Flaherty."
"Ask it that's Flaherty," Ariana ordered Hudson.

192

He tapped out the question.

There was a terse reply.

"Yes," Hudson said, not bothering to write it down.

"Flaherty was the one that got away?" Ariana asked.

"No. Flaherty was one of those listed as missing in action," Carpenter said.

"How can that be?" Ariana asked.

"I don't know," Carpenter said, "but maybe if we do what he wants, he can help us get out of here."

Ariana slapped a palm on top of the communications console. "All right. I'm tired of sitting around here and just reacting. Anyone have any bright ideas how to shut down Argus without getting fried in the process?" Ariana asked.

"We destroy the plane," Carpenter said.

"We happen to be inside the plane," Ingram said.

"We're going to have to leave one way or the other," Carpenter said.

"How do we destroy the plane?" Ariana asked.

"We blow up the fuel tanks," Carpenter said.

"Can't do," Ingram said. "Haven't you listened? The wings are gone, which means the fuel tanks are gone."

"Not all of them," Carpenter pointed down. "The center section fuel tank is below the main fuselage between the wings. It holds over ten thousand gallons of fuel, more than enough to blow this plane into tiny little pieces."

"But how do we ignite that tank?" Ariana asked.

"I can do it," Carpenter said.

Ariana turned to Hudson. "Tell Flaherty we're going to blow the plane. Tell him we're going to need help getting away once we have everything rigged."

"You do not have to worry about Syn-Tech," Sin Fen informed Paul Michelet.

Michelet pulled the seat belt across his lap and buckled it as the pilots added power to the turbine engines. "How do you know that?"

"I have communications with someone who knows," Sin Fen said.

"If my daughter wasn't involved in this, I'd--"

"Please do not threaten idly," Sin Fen said. "We can work together; you just have to do what I tell you to."

A truck raced up to the helicopter and screeched to a halt. Two men dressed in black fatigues stepped off, duffel bags on their shoulders. They strode up to the chopper

and threw the bags in, before taking seats themselves. Sin Fen glanced at Michelet who smiled coldly. "Insurance," the old man said. With a shudder the helicopter lifted off the tarmac. Sin Fen took off her headset so she didn't have to listen to Michelet any more.

She reached down and stroked Chelsea's ears. "Good dog." Chelsea turned her head and her golden eyes looked up at Sin Fen. "He'll be all right," Sin Fen said. "He'll be all right."

"We're getting strange readings, sir."

Captain Rogers looked over at his senior science officer. "Clarify," he snapped. The control room of the *Wyoming* was a far cry from the crowded, dark metal rooms of World War II submarines. Rogers sat in a leather chair, securely bolted to the floor, overseeing the rest of the occupants of the high tech facility. The room was lit by subdued lighting that allowed each crewmember to focus on their computer screens and equipment displays.

"Radioactivity is higher than normal. We're also getting some electromagnetic

interference." "Dangerous?" "Not at these levels." "Source?" "Something in the water ahead of us."

"Distance?"

"Eighty kilometers."

"All right. Our orders are to close on the boundary. Let's do it. Keep monitoring and let me know if there's any change."

CHAPTER THIRTEEN

"This is simply amazing!" Beasley was running his hands over the stone and the drawings etched on it. "No one's ever found anything like this. No one even suspected something like this existed. There's nothing like it at Angkor Wat. And this is older. Much older."

Dane listened to the historian babble while he watched Freed. The security man was scanning the area where the helicopter had crashed. The Canadians had also seen the helicopter destroyed and Dane could sense their unease about going into the valley.

"There are no survivors," Dane said.

Freed pulled the binoculars down. "How do you know that?"

"You are going to have to start believing what I say," Dane said, "or else what is the point in having me along?"

Freed stared at Dane. "I don't like this."

"That's good," Dane said.

"No, not that," Freed jerked his thumb at the fog. "I don't like having you along; I don't like that strange woman who showed up at the airfield; I don't like things going on that I don't understand."

"Join the crowd." Dane pointed across the river. "I think that should be our focus. My suggestion would be that you and the Canadians stay here and let me go in alone."

"I can't do that," Freed said.

"I didn't think so, but I'm not sure you're going to be able to get the Canadians to go with you."

"They'll move," Freed said in a tone that told Dane they probably would. They both turned at Beasley's exclamation.

"I'm beginning to see it now!" Beasley was still focused on the imagery on the stone wall, oblivious of all that was going on around him, the destruction of the helicopter already fading in his mind.

"See what?" Dane asked.

Beasley shook his head, his eyes wide in surprise. "It's outrageous."

"What is?"

Beasley staggered back. "What these writings and symbols suggest. If it were not right in front of, I wouldn't believe it was truly real."

"Tell us," Dane said in a measured voice, trying to calm the other man.

"OK. Let me think for a second." Beasley rubbed his forehead. "According to this, the kingdom of the Khmers was established here over five thousand years ago. It says the Khmers came here from somewhere else where they had ruled a massive kingdom for five thousand years before. But that can't be."

"Why not?" Freed asked.

Dane watched Beasley force himself not to explode at that question. "Because according to our accepted concept of history, human civilization didn't begin until only three thousand years ago! The Khmers could not have had an empire that predates that by seven thousand years." Beasley was fingering his beard. "But this says they did." Beasley pointed at a section. "Not only that but--" he paused.

"What?" Dane asked.

Comprehension came over Beasley's features and his voice changed, suddenly becoming more confident. "No, it's not impossible. It makes sense."

"What make sense?" Dane once more asked.

"The Khmer. Where they came from. Civilization." Beasley's word were clipped as he moved along the wall, reading further.

Dane forced himself to wait on the Professor. Finally Beasley came to a halt and turned to face both he and Freed.

"According to what is written here, the Khmer's empire before they came to Southeast Asia was a large island located in the sea beyond the land beyond the sea." Beasley went on quickly. "I read that to mean an island in the Atlantic, with the land beyond the sea being the Americas."

"But--" Dane began, but Beasley cut him off.

"It mentions a dark Shadow. Here it tells how the Khmer left their ancient homeland and traveled across the ocean to escape the

Shadow, but it followed them. How the warriors stood guard for generations against the Shadow."

"And?" Freed asked.

"I don't think there was a happy ending," Dane said as Beasley read further.

"There some talk of battling the--uh--" Beasley paused.

"The what?" Freed demanded.

Beasley gave Dane a smile. "The monsters. The *Naga* and others." He pointed to the eastern wall. "There it talks about the time further back. Before the Khmer came here. When the island, their home, was destroyed by what they call the 'fire from the dark Shadow' about five thousand years ago and the people were scattered across the Earth.

"But the way they describe the island. Rings of land and water surrounding a central hill on which stood a temple and the palace of the rulers. There's only one other place I've heard of that was described like this. That fits the ancient legends exactly!

"The island was Atlantis!" Beasley said. "It had to be." Beasley closed his eyes and recited. "'Atlantis was the kingdom of Poseidon. When Poseidon fell in love with a mortal woman, named Cleito, he built a palace in the center of the land and surrounded it with rings of water to protect her.

"Cleito gave birth to five sets of twins, all boys, who were the first rulers of Atlantis. Atlas was the name of the first king of Atlantis. They built a large temple to worship Poseidon and cut a canal through the rings of land to facilitate trade.'" Beasley opened his eyes. "There's more but I figure you don't want to hear it right now. All from Plato, written in 360 BC.

"Think about Angkor Thom and Angkor Wat," Beasley said. "The moats the Khmer put around the city. I'd say the Khmer were trying to imitate what was done at Atlantis except they didn't have the ocean. They had to make their own water supply and insure that it would always be there."

Dane was listening to Beasley but he was more concerned about what was across the stream. If that radio call had been real and Flaherty was really out there then--Dane started. If Flaherty had sent that message just a few days ago . . .

"Let me have the PRC-77," Dane said to Freed cutting off Beasley's excited rambling.

"Why?"

"If that message you played for me was legit, then my team is still in there and they have commo," Dane said.

Freed pulled his backpack off. Dane took it and lifted up the top flap. He saw the faded green paint on the top of the radio. He turned the frequency knob, the clicking noise almost comforting, reminding him of missions long ago, dialing up frequencies in the dark by feel. He screwed in the whip antenna, then turned the radio on. He dialed up the emergency FM frequency for that last mission, then took the handset.

"Big Red, this is Dane. Over."

Dane waited for five seconds, then pressed the transmit button again. "Big Red, this is Dane. Over."

Still nothing.

"Big Red, this is Dane. If you can hear me, break squelch twice. Over."

"Oh shit," Freed hissed, grabbing Dane's arm and pointing to the west. A large golden circle was forming directly opposite them in the mist, a mile away.

The radio crackled with two squelch's, then a quick burst of Morse code. Dane's mind was still working on the code, interpreting the letters, making them into words, as he raised the mike again. "Big Red, this is--" Dane paused as the letters came together in his head:

N-O-V-O-I-C-E

He dove down as a lightning bolt of gold flashed out of the center of the circle, heading directly toward their location. Freed grabbed Beasley and pulled the portly scientist down behind the cover of the stone rampart. The bolt struck with a thunderous crack. Dane heard stone shatter and felt himself peppered with fragments. He rolled onto his back and looked up. A large chunk of the rampart had been blown out, the stone splintered.

"You OK?" Freed asked, slowly getting to his feet.

"Yeah," Dane said. Beasley was staring at the hole in the wall.

"No voice," Dane said. "That's what the Morse was."

"Figure it out a little faster next time," Freed said.

198

"You all right?" A voice echoed up to them from below, McKenzie calling out.

"We're OK," Freed yelled back.

"What the hell was that?" McKenzie demanded.

"I don't know. Get back to your security position," Freed ordered.

"Security?" McKenzie was incredulous. "Against thunderbolts out of the mist?"

"Get back," Freed hissed.

Shaking his head, the Canadian did as ordered.

"Do you have a Morse key?" Dane asked.

"Nope."

"Damn," Dane muttered.

The radio came alive again with dashes and dots crackling out of the speaker. Dane pulled a small pad out of his breast pocket and rapidly copied them down. When he recognized that the message was repeating itself, he stopped copying and began translating.

D-A-N-EB-I-G-R-E-DD-O-N-T-S-E-N-D-V-O-I-C-EG-O-T-O-G-R-I-D7-8-2-9-4-3 W-I-L-L-T-R-Y-T-O-C-O-V-E-R-Y-O-U

Dane looked up from the pad and through the newly blasted hole in the rampart at the mist. Flaherty was out there. Alive.

Freed had his map out, checking. "That coordinate is north of where the plane is down. About ten klicks."

Dane stood. Without a Morse key he couldn't 'talk' to Flaherty and it was obvious his former team leader wasn't going to be sending much more than the terse message they'd just received. There was no way he could check on the MILSTARS issue like this. He looked at the map.

The grid was direct center of what looked to be a large, depression shaped like a rough rectangle, about seven kilometers wide by twelve long. The dark green marking covering the entire area indicated thick jungle. Of course, a notation on the bottom of the map informed the reader that the data represented was not verified. Dane noted that the area inside the depression held no contour lines and no detail, as if the map makers had simply made a best guess. He remembered Beasley's comment on the plane about the blank areas on ancient maps. It appeared there were still blanks on modern ones too.

Dane looked up. "It's out there," he pointed to the right front.

"We go to the plane first," Freed said.

Dan shook his head. "No."

"Listen, this is my mission--" Freed began.

"Fine," Dane said. "You go to the plane and take the Canadians with you. I'm going to that grid coordinate. Flaherty said he'd cover us if we went to the coordinate he gave."

"What kind of cover can he give?" Freed demanded.

"I don't know," Dane admitted, "but I'll take anything. You go to the plane, I don't think you'll get any help."

"We're wasting time standing around here jawing," Freed said. He led the way down the interior stairs, Dane and Beasley following. "Let's move out," Freed ordered the Canadians.

"What happened to that chopper?" McKenzie asked, the other three men standing behind him, fingering their weapons uncertainly.

"That's why we couldn't fly in," Freed said. "That fog does something strange to electromagnetic devices."

"That was no fog that knocked that chopper down," McKenzie said. "That was no fog that about blasted you guys to little pieces."

"Let's move," Freed ordered.

"I don't--"

"You move now," Freed said, "or you can walk home. The only way you're getting on the helicopter to get back to Thailand is if you stay with me and I'm going in there."

"Sounds familiar," Dane said.

Freed ignored him. "Move out."

Dane didn't move. "To where?"

Freed hesitated. "How about we go to the plane, then north to the grid?"

Dane shook his head. "We don't want to spend any more time than we have to in there. Ed must have a reason he wants us to go to that grid and he's already inside. He must know about the plane, too. I trust him and I think we should do what he says. I'm going to the grid."

Dane could see Freed look past him to the shattered rampart of the watchtower. "All right. But only if we then go to the plane."

Dane saw no need to respond to that. Even with Flaherty 'covering' for them, whatever that meant, he wasn't overly optimistic about making it to the grid coordinate.

The Canadians spread out and led the way down the ridge into the river valley, Freed, Dane and Beasley following them.

Dane felt the same feeling of fear and distress rise up inside of him, but he could control it better now after years of entering destroyed buildings and disaster areas. He focused his mind on the immediate task of climbing down the hill.

"You came well supplied," Ariana remarked as Carpenter lay out a length of blue detonating cord. The two of them were in the center of the console area. Directly below their feet, according the plane's plans, lay the center fuel tank. They'd left Ingram in the communications area watching over Hudson, waiting to see if they received any more messages from Flaherty in response to their request for help once they left the plane.

"Always prepared, just like the Boy Scouts," Carpenter said as she pulled a blasting cap out of the lining of her carry-on bag.

"Why were you sent to spy on us?" Ariana asked.

"Because of this area," Carpenter said. "The CIA has been paying close attention to it for a long time."

"Why?"

"Because--" Carpenter paused and pointed up. "Why the hell do you think? There's some weird ass stuff happening here and it's been happening for a long time and we're trying to figure it out."

"Why didn't you warn me then?"

Carpenter paused in her work and looked up at the other woman. "Your father was given enough information to know this was a strange and dangerous place. He was told about the other planes that went down and the people lost. I guess he just figured it was worth it to send the survey." Carpenter picked up the blasting cap. "Hold this."

Ariana took the cap. She knew what Carpenter said was true. Her dad had known and he'd sent them anyway. The payoff. Always the payoff.

Carpenter crimped the metal casing on the end of the blasting cap, attaching it to the detonating cord. Ariana watched the woman's fingers moving deftly and knew they had done the same thing many times before.

"What is this place we're in?" Ariana asked.

"Got me," Carpenter sat back and wiped the sweat off her forehead. "I got tagged for this just before this mission. From my briefing, nobody knows. That's why we're here. Guinea pigs let loose in the maze. Everyone's waiting to see what happens to us. I'd say it's more than just us, though. Your father had to have launched a rescue mission and since they haven't been knocking on the door yet, I'd say that big snake got them or something else. Same with the Syn-Tech chopper. Same with whatever rescue mission my Agency launches, if they launch one at all. I didn't get a warm and fuzzy feeling from the guy who briefed me that he really gave a rat's ass about me. He wanted to know what was in here, Angkor Gate he called it. I don't think he was too concerned about whatever price had to be paid to get that information."

"Jesus," Ariana muttered.

"Yeah, baby, we've both been screwed," Carpenter said. She held the det cord and cap in her hands. "We're ready to blast."

Ariana turned toward the front of the plane. "Let's see if we have any news on how we're supposed to get out of here."

When she entered the commo section, Ingram held out a sheet of paper. "We just got this in."

Ariana read it.

G-O-T-O-G-R-I-D

7-8-2-9-4-3 G-O-T-O-G-R-I-D7-8-2-9-4-3

Ariana pulled a map off the counter and slapped it onto the table. "All right, this is what we've got." She stared at the area that the grid designated, then looked up at Ingram, Hudson and Carpenter. "It's about five klicks north of here."

"I can't make it," Hudson said immediately.

Ariana shrugged. "Fine. We'll leave you."

"You can't--" Hudson began, but stopped at the glare she gave him.

"We will help you get there, but don't you dare tell me what I can and can't do you son-of-a-bitch."

"But how do we know there's something there to get to?" Ingram asked.

"As this point I don't think we have much choice," Ariana said. "Let's get ready."

"Ariana!" Carpenter's voice echoed from the back of the plane. "You've got to see this."

Ariana ran to the center console section, avoiding the gold line that had killed Daley. Carpenter was looking into the mainframe of Argus.

"What's going on?"

"Look," Carpenter said. "Something's happening."

Ariana stared as a piece of Argus's hardware disappeared inside the golden glow surrounding it.

"What the hell is going on?" Ariana asked.

"Twelve hours," Carpenter said. "I think we might be too late."

"Let's get moving!"

"It was using the MILSTARS satellites," Jimmy confirmed, studying the latest imagery, "but the points of convergence are not based on that."

"But the power was being carried via MILSTARS," Conners argued. They were in her office now, the walls covered with imagery, reams of computer printouts covering every available surface and the floor. "What's carrying it now?"

Jimmy threw down a computer printout and slumped down into a chair, ignoring the paper underneath him. "I think it outgrew the need to use MILSTARS. Many of these lines run across European and Russian satellites. This thing, whatever it is, is using anything up there it can get a hold of. I think it's on the verge of not needing the satellites any more. Of being able to sustain itself."

"Damn," Conners muttered. "I guess we'd better update Foreman."

The chopper flared to a hover above the blasted clearing. The two men in black hooked thick ropes into the roof of the helicopter bay, then threw the free ends out into the downblast. Bags slung over their shoulders, they stepped out into the air and rappelled down to the ground.

Sin Fen watched quietly, her mind on other matters. The chopper moved away slightly and she could look down and see the men pull chain saws out of the duffel bags and begin clearing away branches and other debris that would interfere with their landing.

Sin Fen felt Chelsea stir next to her, but she kept her hands tight on the dog's collar. She closed her eyes and reached outward. Dane was close to the Angkor Gate. Very close. And soon he would be in.

CHAPTER FOURTEEN

After getting off the satellite phone with Conners, Foreman stared at the electronic map at the front of the operations center and watched the various moving symbols that represented the military forces being marshaled by the Pentagon. The *Wyoming* was closing on the Bermuda Triangle Gate and other aircraft and ships were vectoring on the vortices where activity was strongest. Part of the Seventh Fleet was circling around the southern tip of Vietnam to go on-station in the Gulf of Thailand.

But there was no plan yet. Everyone was still reeling from the failure of Thunder Dart's mission to stop the propagation. They'd thrown the most technologically advanced equipment the country owned against this threat and been beaten. The pilot of the Thunder Dart had been recovered but the 2.2 billion dollar aircraft had been swatted like a fly.

But it wasn't just the United States. Foreman had been in contact with both his Russian and Japanese counterparts. The Russians had used a hunter-killer satellite to take out one of their own communications satellites that had been taken over by the propagation. The result had been one hunter-killer satellite blown apart by the golden glow. The Japanese Navy had sent their most modern destroyer into their closest Gate, into the heart of the Devil's Sea, and it had not been heard from again.

Foreman looked at his commo board. The light indicating a link to Sin Fen was dark. She'd relayed to him Beasley's interpretation of the carvings in the watchtower that she had sensed from Dane's mind.

As he watched, another light flickered on and a tone sounded. Foreman leaned forward and threw a switch.

"Foreman here."

The President wasted no time on greetings. "What next, Mister Foreman? So far we've lost Bright Star, Thunder Dart, and one of our MILSTARS satellites."

Foreman didn't say anything.

"My scientific people confirm the radiation and electromagnetic spread," the President continued. "I've been in contact with the Russian President and he confirms some of what you told me. They are investigating both at Chernobyl and Lake Baikal but they don't know much more. I've also gotten reports from the NSA that the Russians lost one of their satellites trying to deal with this. I need some more options."

"My man is getting ready to go into the Angkor Gate," Foreman said.

"Goddamnit!" the President exploded. "According to these readouts I'm getting, we're going to have people dying around these Gates in less than twelve hours."

"I have nothing further to tell you than I've already told you, sir," Foreman said. "The minute I learn something from inside Angkor Gate I will immediately contact you."

"That's not good enough."

"I will get back to you, sir," Foreman said. He didn't add that he feared they were too late.

The phone went dead.

"It's all set," Carpenter said. She held up a small green plastic tube. "This is the fuse. We'll have five minutes." A length of blue cord ran from the fuse down into the floorpanels where Carpenter had wired it to two pounds of C-4 explosive placed against the top bulkhead of the center fuel tank.

Ariana nodded. "OK." She had the 9mm pistol in her hand and a small backpack slung over her shoulder. Ingram was holding on to Hudson's right arm, helping him stand. They were all next to the emergency door over the right wing, or where the right wing had been, Ariana reminded herself.

"We pop the door," Ariana instructed, "then go down the emergency slide which will inflate." She looked at the faces that surrounded her. Carpenter's was impassive. Ingram looked afraid but determined. Hudson's was just afraid.

"Let's do it." Ariana grabbed the emergency level and shoved it. With a loud sucking noise the door swung open. There was a loud hiss, then the yellow emergency slide popped out and rapidly inflated.

Ariana took a quick look. It was daylight but only a feeble gray light penetrated the mist. She could see splintered tree trunks underneath the plane and the beginnings of thick jungle just ten feet from the side of the plane. Beyond twenty feet, she saw nothing.

"Go!" she yelled at Hudson and Ingram. The two men flopped onto the slide and disappeared out of sight. Ariana turned to Carpenter. "Do it."

Carpenter pulled the fuse, checked it and gave a thumbs up. The black woman was by Ariana and down the slide. Ariana took one last look around the interior of the plane, at the bodies covered in sheets and jackets and at that moment she realized her father would have been more mindful of the expensive computers and other equipment she was about to destroy. She stepped onto the slide.

Dane felt the cold water flow around his legs and paused. The mist on the far bank was thicker than he remembered. His eyes could penetrate only a few feet in but it wasn't his eyes that were warning him. Like the steady beat of a heart, a warning pulsed in his brain, telling him to be aware, to be afraid, but this time, unlike thirty years ago, it also drew him on, into the mist.

He glanced over his shoulder. Freed, Beasley and the four Canadians were right behind him. Dane waded forward. He reached the far bank and climbed up without a backward glance and was enveloped in the fog.

The helicopter settled gingerly onto the blasted foliage. Sin Fen stepped off as the engines began to power down. She walked to the edge of the clearing and faced the jungle, to the west, but her eyes were closed. Chelsea was next to her, tail wagging, tongue hanging out.

She reached out for Dane. She felt him, his essence, but it was flickering and she knew it was moving into the Gate. She sensed the water he had just passed through and could pick up images from his mind--he had talked to Flaherty on the radio.

She concentrated one message to send to him:
Listen to the voices of the Gods

Chelsea began barking, nose pointed to the east. Sin Fen turned in that direction. A Huey helicopter came in low and fast, flaring to a landing next to the chopper that they had come in.

Six men jumped off, weapons at the ready. They were white men, dressed in tiger stripe fatigues, with a hard look about them that spoke of much death and pain. She saw them walk up to Michelet, who pointed in her direction.

They came toward her, Michelet right behind. She picked up the threat from all of them, but it was hard to separate out individual thoughts.

"Do not do something foolish," Sin Fen warned.

"You're Foreman's bitch," Michelet said. "He set all this up."

"He gave you enough information to back out," Sin Fen said. "You are the one that put your daughter and her crew in harm's way."

Michelet shook his head. "He's a manipulative liar."

Sin Fen laughed. "Ah, that is ironic."

She caught movement out of the corner of her eye. One of the tiger stripe men brought something up in his hand and a small piece of metal flashed toward her. Sin Fen looked down at the small metal dart caught on her vest. She focused at the man holding the stun gun. He staggered back, dropping the gun without triggering it, his hands going to his temples.

Another one of the men fired his stun gun, the dart hitting her in the back. He was quicker, pulling the trigger as she turned.

Sin Fen went rigid from the electric current coursing through her, then the world went black and she collapsed. Chelsea whined and ran into the jungle.

The leader of the men stood over Sin Fen's body and looked at Michelet questionably. Michelet pointed to the ravine on the northern edge of the camp. "Tie her up and throw her in there. Let the animals finish her."

The leader gestured to two of his men. They pulled a piece of nylon rope out and began tying Sin Fen up.

"Syn-Tech?" Michelet asked the leader of the men.

"Being taken care of, sir. I coordinated with the Cambod's to take care of that problem."

"How much did that coordination cost me?" Michelet asked.

"Two hundred thousand."

Michelet walked to the center of the LZ, in between the two helicopters and looked to the west. His stood hands on hips. "No one screws with me and gets away with it. No one."

The leader of the mercenaries stared at him without comment.

CHAPTER FIFTEEN

"Move!" Ariana yelled, grabbing Hudson's arm and pulling him across the tangled vegetation. She glanced over her shoulder at the plane. The tail was lost in the fog but she could see the rotodome and the golden beam shooting from it into the sky.

Carpenter grabbed Hudson's other arm. Together they hauled him across a large splintered tree trunk and then they were on the ground. Ariana turned and looked back over the wood. The plane had almost disappeared in the mist, about fifty meters away.

"Duck," Carpenter said.

Ariana tucked her head down behind the cover of the tree trunk. There was the sharp crack of an explosion, followed by a thunderous secondary explosion. Ariana could hear shrapnel fly by overhead and slash into the vegetation. With a loud thump, a twenty foot section of fuselage landed less than forty feet away. Ariana stood and looked. The plane was gone. She checked her map and pointed into the mist shrouded jungle.

"That way."

Dane paused as he heard the sound of a explosion. The mist muffled the sound as if it were occurring underwater, followed by a second, deeper explosion a second later.

"What the hell was that?" Beasley demanded.

Freed and the Canadians were also turned in the direction the sound had come from.

"The plane's gone," Dane said.

"What!" Freed stepped in front of Dane. "How do you know?"

"I just know," Dane said.

"But--"

"There are some survivors."

"How do you know?"

Dane didn't bother answering.

"But the equipment," Freed said. "The images they caught."

Dane pushed Freed out of the way. "We have to keep moving. We can't stand still."

"Why?"

Dane just shook his head. He reached out with his mind for Sin Fen, but there was no answer. He felt her absence, like a blank spot in his mind.

Dane moved into the jungle. The sound of the stream behind them faded. The mist was thick, but Dane could sense lighter areas, and using that sense he picked his path. He knew Flaherty was ahead of them somewhere, in the vicinity of the area they had been directed to. He couldn't 'hear' Flaherty like he had been able to contact Sin Fen, but he could feel the presence of his old friend, like a distant torch on the edge of his consciousness. And the way that torch was flickering told Dane that the explosion had been the *Lady Gayle* being destroyed and that the people who had survived the crash were heading in the same direction. He also sensed that if he stayed to the lighter areas they would be safe, that the creatures of the mist would not find them. Somehow Flaherty was helping them, keeping them safe from the dangers inside the Gate. For a little while at least.

Dane paused, hearing the breathing and muted sound of weapons and equipment jangling behind him. He peered ahead. He felt the fear, just as he had the first time he had been in the Angkor Gate, but he could control it, just like he had been able to on cross-border missions before that last one. He didn't know what was behind the threat he faced, but he knew there was a threat and he had a good idea of the nature of it from his previous experience. And Flaherty was out there.

Dane moved on, the others following.

"It's changed," Jimmy said.

"The pattern?" Conners asked. She felt a pulse of adrenaline flow through her tired veins. It had been a while since Thunder Dart had taken out the MILSTARS satellite, but perhaps it had taken that long for the effect to be felt.

"No, the source." Jimmy swung his laptop around so she could see. "There was a momentary flicker, like the power got interrupted, and now it's back but the flow is different. Close, but different." Jimmy tapped the screen. "See how these lines have shifted?"

Actually, Conners couldn't, but she nodded anyway.

"That means the source of the radiation and electromagnetic fluxes has moved. Not much. Maybe about seven or eight kilometers."

"Will it change the rate of propagation?"

"No."

"The strength?"

"No."

"Great." Conners picked up the phone. "I'll inform Foreman."

The AH-1 Cobra gunship had Cambodian Air Force markings painted on the

side. It was a relic from the Vietnam War, appropriated from the Vietnamese Army when it had invaded Cambodia years ago and kept flying by cannibalization of other AH-1s that had been shot down or abandoned when the Vietnamese pulled out.

The Syn-Tech camp consisted of four tents surrounding a small open field on which sat a Russian Hind-D helicopter.

The AH-1 came in low and fast, the 7.62mm minigun in the nose firing as soon as it cleared the tree line. 2.5 inch rockets followed, blasting the Hind into tiny pieces. The pilot of the Cobra came to a hover and continued firing, chasing the survivors into the cover of the jungle and thoroughly destroying the camp.

Michelet's revenge was complete.

Ariana could hear movement around them, but nothing that sounded as large as the snake that had killed Herrin. They were moving steadily downhill. Ariana kept them on track by picking a tree as far as she could see into the fog and heading toward, then picking another one. Her compass was spinning wildly but according to the map, downhill was the way to go.

Ariana pushed aside a large hanging growth and paused as the hair on the back of her neck stood up. "Jesus!" she heard Ingram exclaim.

A large plane was set vertically into the ground, tail first, looming like a large cross over the path they following except that the wings were swept back, almost touching the ground themselves. The nose of the plane disappeared into the mist, about a hundred and forty feet above them. The edge of the massive tail disappeared into the jungle floor. The flat gray paint was marred with lines of rust showing through and plants had woven their way around the metal skin. It was obvious the plane had been there for a while.

"It's a B-52 bomber," Carpenter said.

"How the hell did it get like that?" Ingram wondered out loud.

"Same way we landed with no wings and lived to talk about it," Ariana said.

"The engines are gone," Carpenter said. Ariana looked up. Where the engines had been on the wings, the metal had been neatly cut. She looked down. No sign of the engines below the wings. Whatever had cut the engines off had also taken them.

"The bomb bay is open," Carpenter noted.

Ariana shook her head. "Let's keep going."

"I'm not going any further," Hudson said. "We're screwed. We're really screwed. This isn't the way out of this place. This is the way in."

"In to what?" Ingram asked.

"I don't know and I don't want to know." Hudson pointed up at the plane. "That's a warning. I'm not going in there. I say let's go the other way and get out of here."

"You don't have a say," Ariana reminded him.

"The hell I don't," Hudson yelled. "I get a say about where *I* go. And I'm not going any further. I'll just wait right here until you come back."

"We might not be coming back this way," Ingram said.

Ariana stared at Hudson for a long moment. She could still hear movement in the jungle around them. "All right." She turned to the others. "Let's go."

"You can't--" Ingram began Ariana chopped her hand through the air.

"Like he said, it is his decision. I'm not responsible for him. When he took SynTech's money that ceased. And he killed Mansor by allowing him to go out there when he had a SATCOM dish the entire time. I don't give a damn about him any more" She turned. "Let's move."

They walked forward and passed underneath one 85 foot wing, Ariana and Carpenter facing forward, Ingram looking over his shoulder until Hudson and the B-52 disappeared from sight.

"It's a damn graveyard!" McKenzie hissed. The Canadian's face was pale, his eyes wide as he took in what lay across their route of march.

Dane didn't say anything. His mind was racing beyond, sensing how close Flaherty was. And where his old teammate was, he knew there would be answers.

But even Freed appeared shaken. They were at the mouth of a narrow ravine. A small creek ran down the center of the draw, passing them, heading toward the large stream they had crossed earlier. But what caught the attention of Freed and the other's were the skeletons littering the draw, a veritable carpet of shattered white bone.

"This has to be hundreds of people," McKenzie said. "And look at the weapons."

There were numerous AK-47s scattered among the bones, the black of the metal contrasting vividly against the white bones.

"A battalion," Freed said.

"A battalion?" McKenzie repeated.

"A Khmer Rouge battalion disappeared in this area and was never heard of again," Freed amplified his statement.

"What wiped them out?" McKenzie wondered. He bent down and picked up an AK-47. With his other hand he picked up a fistful of expended brass. "They fought, fought hard." McKenzie looked around, as if expecting something to come out of the mist and trees.

"We can't do anything here," Dane said. "Let's keep going."

"I ain't going through there!" McKenzie protested. "Something killed all these men! Look at this!" The Canadian picked up a skull. The left side of it was cleanly sliced off. "What the hell did this?" He pointed to their left front. A line of skeletons were against the rock wall of the draw, as if they had been literally blasted into the stone. "What did that?"

"Let's go," Dane said quietly.

"Bullshit!" McKenzie was adamant. "I'm not going through there."

Dane shrugged and started walking. Bones crunched under his boots. There was no way to avoid stepping on them.

"Hold on!" Freed called out.

Dane paused but didn't turn.

"You don't come with us, you're on your own," Freed yelled to McKenzie. "No pay and no ride out of Cambodia."

McKenzie laughed. "Dead men can't spend money and don't need rides." He turned, the other Canadians right behind him, and they headed back in the direction they had come from.

"You coming?" Dane asked Freed. "Or was the plane and its data more important than the people?"

"I'm coming." Freed tapped the one mute spectator to all this on his shoulder. "Coming Doctor Beasley?"

Beasley watched the Canadians disappear in the mist, then his shoulders slumped, the decision made for him. "All right."

Mitch Hudson had watched the others fade into the mist before he slid his small backpack off. He was lying underneath the right wing of the B-52, the metal over his head like the massive flying buttress of a medieval church. Propping his injured leg up on a log, he opened the flap to the pack and pulled out a small black box. He was unlatching the top to the box when he heard something crashing through the undergrowth to his left. He paused, eyes darting fearfully in that direction.

Still watching the jungle, he flipped the lid open. He grabbed the coil of thin wire that lay on top and threw it out, away from himself. It extended for twenty feet and lay on top of the broken foliage. The small high frequency radio was his last resort, something he had made sure Syn-Tech agreed to before he committed to work for them. The Syn-Tech base camp at Angkor Wat was to monitor the set frequency, 24 hours a day. And they were to send help when Hudson called. The one piece of information that Hudson had focused on that Syn-Tech had gotten from the CIA was that high frequency radios seemed to work inside this strange area.

He knew that the chopper he had called in with the SATCOM beacon had been destroyed, but he was sure Syn-Tech knew that also and would approach with more caution, landing outside of the Angkor Gate and sending someone in for him on foot. Before he turned the radio on, he felt the outside of his shirt pocket, his fingers tracing the outline of a computer disk. It held all the data from *Lady Gayle* prior to the crash and it was his ticket out. He wasn't foolish enough to believe that Syn-Tech would send another rescue team just for him, but he knew they would for the disk.

He twisted the on-knob. The small screen glowed. The lithium battery would only give him fifteen minutes of air time, but he didn't anticipate needing that much. A minute to contact Syn-Tech, then the rest could be spent guiding them into here.

Hudson picked up the small headset and slipped it on his head, putting the small boom mike just in front of his lips.

"Big Daddy, this is Angler. Over."

There was just the hiss of static in his earpiece.

"Goddamn," Hudson muttered. He hunched forward over the radio set. "Big Daddy, this is Angler. I have the data. Over."

The static grew louder, but there was no intelligible reply. Hudson's major concern was that Syn-Tech had shut down listening. He knew the radio was working and he felt reasonably confident the HF was getting through.

"Big Daddy, this is Angler. I have the data. I need recovery. Over."

Foreman leaned forward in his chair. There was a lot of static, but there was no doubt there was a voice, someone trying to transmit on the high frequency band.

"Big .....,this....gler. ...."

"Can you get a fix on that?" Foreman asked his communications expert.

"No, sir. It's very weak and dispersed."

"Anything from Syn-Tech?"

"No, sir."

Foreman checked a commo board. Sin Fen had been quiet for too long. Foreman looked to the side as the printer spewed out a sheet of imagery from Conners. The pattern was still growing. There was a dark swirl in the mist above the Angkor Gate, with lines branching out, reaching to the other gates. It looked like a massive tornado was centered above the Gate, high in the atmosphere. The storm was getting ready to break.

Hudson thought he heard something. He pressed his hands against the small earpieces, muffling any outside noise.

"Say again. Over."

Then he realized the noise wasn't coming from the headset. He sat up bolt upright. He knew there was someone or something behind him. He just knew, just as he knew he was a dead man. Ripping off the headset, Hudson spun around. There was nothing. His chest heaved in relief, then the breath froze in his throat as a half-dozen green elliptical spheres, like oversized footballs three feet long, drifted down from above, surrounding him completely. He looked further up and could see more of them issuing forth from the open bomb bay door of the B-52.

Hudson's hand gripped the mike tightly. "Big Daddy, this is Angler. Big Daddy this is Angler."

He could now see that there were two bands of black crisscrossing the front of each sphere and the bands seemed to be moving, were glistening with a liquid blackness, reflecting the gloomy light back at him

"Big Daddy, this is Angler. I have the data. Big Daddy, this is Angler. I have the data." Hudson closed his eyes and chanted the words like a mantra.

Foreman was studying the imagery when the static-ridden voice calling for Big Daddy broke for two seconds, then a heart stopping screech sounded as clearly as if the man issuing it forth was in the control room with them. Every operator paused in what they were doing and looked up at the speakers bolted to the front of the room.

Then there was only the solid hiss of static.

Foreman raised his voice. "Get back to work!" He threw the imagery down on the desktop.

Hudson had the radio clutched to his chest. One of the green ellipses had just churned through the trunk of a tree less than ten feet from him, sending splinters flying into him and causing him to scream. He reached up and felt his right side where blood was flowing.

"Oh, God. Oh, God," he whispered as he backed up until he smacked into the flat metal of the wing.

The creatures formed a semi-circle in front of him, then began closing the distance.

At that moment, a blue beam shot of the jungle mist and hit him straight on, knocking the air out of his lungs. He felt the metal of the wing slide along his back as the blue beam encompassed his body and picked him up off the ground. He looked down and could see the ellipses reacting, coming up for him, when he was rapidly pulled forward toward the source of the light, passing over them.

McKenzie paused, the other three Canadians bunching up behind him.

"You're lost, aren't you?" Teague, the next senior man whispered hoarsely.

"It's that way," McKenzie pointed, but the wavering fingertip belied the surety of his words.

"Oh, man, I knew we shouldn't have taken this gig," Teague said. "There's no such thing as easy money in this part of the world. Everyone's got a angle. We could have just--" he paused as something crashed through the jungle to their right. The muzzles of four M-16s swung in that direction. Then there was something to the left and all four men spun about in that direction.

The woods around them exploded in moving forms. McKenzie fired on full automatic into something that bounded forth on four legs toward him, the bullets slamming it back. The only impression he had were rows and rows of gleaming teeth.

One of the men screamed as his body exploded in a gush of blood and viscera. The tip of a green ellipse, black teeth churning, came out of his chest.

McKenzie backed up, slamming a fresh magazine into his weapon. Teague was at his side, firing at an ellipse, the bullets bouncing off.

Another creature came bounding in, body of a lion, snake's head, scorpion stinger for tail, jumping through the air and landing on the fourth Canadian, claws ripping him open, the stinger darting forward and sinking into his face, right between the eyes. The snake's head rose up and hissed as the stinger dug through bone and entered the man's brain. The body jerked spasmodically.

"Oh, God," McKenzie moaned, seeing the man's fate.

Teague shook him out of his shock by firing a magazine on full automatic across his front.

McKenzie pulled the trigger but his finger froze at the last second as a golden beam sliced out of the fog and hit him and Teague, enveloping the both of them, pressing them together.

They were lifted off the ground, above the creatures, and then drawn into the mist.

Dane paused, hearing the distant sound of firing that abruptly cut off. He sensed inside his head, more than heard the screams which were too far away to carry. He glanced at Freed who made no comment, then at Beasley. The fat professor's pale face was bathed in sweat.

"We'll make it," Dane said. As he turned away from the other man he paused. Dane stood perfectly still, his eyes closed. Slowly his head swiveled back in the direction they had come.

"Chelsea," Dane whispered, not even aware he had also spoken out loud.

"What's wrong?" Freed asked.

Dane ignored him. He focused on the mental images. There was still nothing from Sin Fen but now he knew why. What he saw was distorted and fuzzy, but he could understand it. The view was through a series of lines and splotches that Dane knew were branches and leaves. And the perspective was low, less than a foot or two above the ground. But he could hazily discern two helicopters and black suited men walking about a blasted clearing. For just a second the entire image focused tight and he could see very clearly Sin Fen lying on the ground, trussed up tightly, her eyes closed, her face slack.

"Damn," Dane hissed.

"What?" Freed repeated.

Dane pulled out his pistol and pointed it straight between Freed's eyes. "Your boss is screwing everything up. He's taken down my partner."

Freed didn't even blink. "Your partner? The weird woman? You didn't even know her before she showed up. She had Agency written all over her."

"So?" Dane stared at Freed. "Don't you get it? We've left your corporate fighting far behind. This is much bigger than all that. I should just kill you right now," Dane said, but he paused as the mental image changed again. Chelsea was moving, running away from the base camp, heading toward the west. Coming to Dane.

No! Dane projected the command as forcefully as he could.

Chelsea halted, her head swinging about, searching for her master. The jungle surrounded her, full of strange noises and scents. She didn't like this place.

Chelsea's tail rocketed back and forth. She whined.

Easy, girl. Easy.

Dane was aware of Freed moving back, out of the aim of his pistol. Dane lowered the gun.

Rescue, Chelsea. Rescue.

Chelsea whined once more. She didn't know where the voice was coming from. It was her master but it didn't sound quite right. Her golden eyes peered into the shadows of the jungle, searching.

Then a picture came into her brain. Something she had just seen. The nice woman lying on the ground. Chelsea understood that was who her master wanted her to rescue. But she sensed he was in danger also. Her head swung back the way she had come and then to the west, indecisive.

Go!

There was no defying the command. With a low growl, Chelsea turned back the way she had come.

Dane returned to reality and the muzzle of a gun. His pistol was down at his side, but Freed's wasn't.

"What the hell are you trying to do?" Freed demanded.

"I don't need you," Dane said. "If you need me, come along. If you don't, go after the Canadians."

Freed's eyes shifted in the direction the automatic fire had come from. He lowered the pistol.

"Don't get in my way." Dane added. "And when we get back, Michelet will pay."

"We'll deal with that when we get back," Freed said.

Dane continued moving, then stopped once more, but this time because of the large forms that were now becoming visible ahead in the mist. Beasley stepped up next to him and then a few steps further.

The professor finally stopped in stunned silence. "My God!" he exclaimed in a low voice, taking in the massive stones that marked a line directly across their path. Each stone was over eighty feet in height and shaped in a vaguely human form, with long faces taking up over a third of the height. It was hard to see them clearly because a thick layer of vegetation had grown around them. It was clear, despite the trees and creepers that covered the stone, that each was exactly the same size and that where there wasn't carving, the stone was cut as smoothly as if by a scalpel, although the surface was pitted with age and weather.

"It makes Stonehenge look like a kid's block set," Beasley said as Dane and Freed joined him. "How the hell did they move those things? They've got to weigh seventy or eighty tons each. Those are forty feet taller than the biggest statues on Easter Island." Beasley pulled out a small video camera from his backpack and took a panoramic shot of the rank of megaliths in front of them, standing almost shoulder to shoulder.

Dane pointed at a narrow opening between two of the megaliths bases. "We go through there."

"What's on the other side?" Freed asked.

Dane knew the answer to that. "Angkor Kol Ker."

CHAPTER SIXTEEN

"The navy and air force are detouring ships and planes around the Bermuda Triangle," Foreman said into the satellite phone mike.

"This thing keeps growing like it is," Patricia Conner's voice was tight with an undercurrent of forced control, "they're going to have a hard time keeping this under wraps. The Bermuda Triangle Gate hits the coast of Florida in six hours."

Foreman rubbed his head. He didn't know who this woman was, but he had been living with the nightmare of the Gates for over fifty years all by himself. "The Japanese are getting ready to go public. They're forcing their fishing fleet away from the expanding Devil's Sea Gate, but it's a huge logistical problem. The fishermen want an explanation." Foreman gave a bitter laugh. "The irony is that even if they go public they still don't have an explanation."

"Looking at my map and the propagation charts," Conners came back with, "some of these Gates are going to be killing people soon. The radiation levels are high enough."

Foreman let out a deep breath. "I know, but there's nothing--" he paused as another light flickered on his console. "I'll have to get back to you," he said.

"We've got activity in the Angkor Gate!" Conners yelled before he could cut the connection. "A surge of radioactivity on the eastern side!"

"Hold on," Foreman said as he flipped open a new circuit.

"Talk," he ordered.

A voice echoed out of the speaker and Foreman recognized the pitch as the distinct one coming from a submerged submarine transmitting on ULF, ultra-lowfrequency through water.

"This is Captain Rogers from the *Wyoming*. We have a situation here."

Rogers ignored Commander Sills' look at his last radio transmission. A 'situation' was understating current events. Alarms were sounding and the crew was racing to battle stations.

"I will hook you into our ops center," Rogers said. "I'm a little busy to give you a blow by blow right now." Rogers reached down and flipped a switch.

"Come hard right at flank speed," Rogers ordered his helmsman.

"Aye-aye, sir. Hard right at flank."

Rogers looked at Sills. "Sit-rep?"

Rogers was watching a gauge. "External radiation climbing."

Rogers glanced down at the radiation badge clipped to his shirt front. "Power, chief!" he yelled a the petty officer in charge of driving the sub.

"We're at max speed, sir."

"Status?" he asked Sills.

"External radiation still climbing, sir. Way beyond safety limits."

"Damn!" Rogers looked back at Sills. The executive officer was shaking his head. "It's through red, sir."

Rogers closed his eyes. He reached down and peeled back the tape on his badge. The line underneath was red. Everyone in the control room was staring at him. Rogers picked up the mike connecting him to Foreman. "We're red. From stem to stern. One hundred percent casualties. We just aren't dead yet, but we will be."

Foreman listened to Rogers' report. There was nothing he could say. He was startled when a voice came out of the speaker; he had forgotten he'd kept to the NSA open.

"That's going to happen on land soon," Conners said.

"I know." Foreman glanced at some of the messages his operators had picked up. "The Japanese lost a scout plane ten minutes ago. Totally gone. God knows what's happening to the Russians. They've lost all communication with their monitoring element near Chernobyl."

"It's the beginning of the end, isn't it?" Conners said.

To that, Foreman also had nothing to add.

Chelsea could hear the helicopters, near the place she had left. She paused and sniffed. There was much that was new to her in this strange place, many strange scents, sights and sounds.

Despite her bulk, she could move quietly when needed. Snout low to the ground, she slipped through the jungle, approaching the noise and the scents of the humans and the place she had last seen the nice lady, searching for the scent she remembered.

There were three paths among the four massive statues that barred the way. Ariana stared at the trio of tunnels through the stone.

"Which one?" Ingram asked.

"I don't like this," Carpenter muttered.

The statues on either flank merged with the stone walls of the draw. The arms of the statues touched, so that the openings were eighteen feet high by four wide, underneath the large hands. The opening disappeared into darkness. Each was draped with foliage, further restricting the view.

"I say the center one," Ingram said.

"I don't know," Ariana said. She felt very uneasy. She could see the eyes in the statues, almost sixty feet above her head, bright red painted stone, barely visible through the swirling mist.

All three heads turned as the sound of a tree trunk breaking, split the air. Ariana recognized the slithering noise that followed. And it was coming closer.

"Oh, shit," Ingram exclaimed. He turned and ran for the center tunnel. Ariana and Carpenter followed as the sound grew louder and more trees gave way.

Ingram was into the tunnel when he suddenly stumbled in front of them, down to his knees. He gave a short yell, looking over his shoulder. That was when the ceiling came down. The stone block completely filled the passageway and obliterated Ingram; the only indication of his death, the red blood seeping out from under the finely cut stone.

Ariana and Carpenter stepped back as the blood came toward their feet. Ariana shook herself out of her shock and grabbed Carpenter's arm. "Let's go."

They ran back to the front of the statues. The sound was much closer, somewhere close by in the mist. "Left or right?" Ariana asked Carpenter.

"What makes you think either of them will work?" Carpenter asked.

"We go through or we wait for that," Ariana pointed in the direction of the slithering noise. They could now hear the hissing.

"Left," Carpenter said. "People tend to go right when lost in the woods so if there's a choice, it should be left."

Ariana wasn't quite sure of the reasoning but there was no time. Together they ran around the base of the statue and into the opening. They paused, looked at each other, and then together ran forward through the tunnel.

"Sweet Jesus!" Beasley exclaimed.

They were standing on the edge of the high ridge that extended left and right as far as they could see into the fog. The ground in front sloped down and, in that direction, there was no mist for the first time since they'd entered the Angkor Gate. Two kilometers straight ahead, burning bright, a golden beam rose from the apex of a steep mountain about five hundred meters above their heads and into the heavens where the sky was dark and swirling. But they could see that the "mountain" was manmade, a massive, steep pyramid of intricately carved stone, now covered with a thick layer of vegetation. And at the base of the mountain were the remains of a walled city, the stone crumbling under the weight of the years and jungle that had overgrown it. Outside of the walls, a wide moat stretched from there to the base of the ridge that they were on. It was hard to tell if there was water in the moat, as it had been reclaimed by the jungle.

"What the hell is that?" Freed asked.

"Angkor Kol Ker," Dane said.

"This is the greatest discovery--" Beasley began, but Freed cut him off.

"No, I meant that golden beam, you idiot."

"I believe that is what is destroying our world," Dane said, feeling the images that Sin Fen had given him of the Gates. He started down the slope.

Ariana slumped to the ground, momentarily exhausted not so much from the run through the tunnel, but from the sudden drop-off in adrenaline now that they had made it through without being crushed. She had sprinted the entire way, her shoulders hunched, anticipating the stone above their heads to come sliding down, but nothing had happened.

"Look at that," Carpenter whispered next to her.

Ariana looked up. She saw the golden beam coming out of the pyramid and the ancient city around it. Ariana struggled to her feet, shaking off the exhaustion. "Let's go."

"There's nothing we can do for those men?" The President's voice had lost its earlier edge. It had been Foreman's experience that reality had a way of doing that. He leaned back in his seat, listening to those in the White House Situation Room discuss the latest development with the *Wyoming*.

"We not only can't save those men," General Tilson, the Chairman of the Joint Chiefs of Staff said, "but we can't even recover the submarine itself. It's so hot that any boarding crew would also receive a fatal dosage of radiation."

"How long do they have?" The President asked.

"About four hours before they all start getting sick," General Tilson said. "Every man on board will be dead inside of twenty-four hours."

"What are you going to do about it?"

"The commanding officer on the *Wyoming*, Captain Rogers, has decided to stay on station and continue performing their last assigned duty, which was to monitor the Bermuda Triangle Gate and be prepared for any contingency. There's really nothing else for him to do."

The President's voice became firmer. "Gentlemen, I've been asking for options, but I've yet to get any. Before many more people get affected, we have got to do something!"

A silence filled the speaker and Foreman still didn't move in his glass cubicle. He looked down at the console. Still no connection with Sin Fen.

"The source of this is in this Angkor Gate, isn't it?" the President asked.

Foreman finally spoke. "It started there," he acknowledged. "There seems to be other sources opened now at other Gates."

"But this was the beginning?" the President pressed.

"Yes, sir."

"Then why don't we just blast it?" the President asked. "Wipe this Angkor place off the map?"

Foreman could hear the startled consternation that suggestion caused in the war room. Bancroft's voice was the loudest. "Sir, this place happens to be in the middle of another country. We just can't blast it off the map! Think of the international fall out."

"Think of what we're facing here!" the President returned. "This thing gets any worse there won't be any international anything to worry about."

"Sir," Foreman said. "I agree that we have to destroy this source, but the problem is two-fold on a practical level. First we don't know exactly where inside the Angkor Gate the source is and we're now talking about an area over two hundred square kilometers. It's blocked all our imaging techniques.

"The second problem is how to destroy the source once found. You now know the history of these Gates and how they affect people, aircraft and ships. And you know what happened to the Thunder Dart. Anything that we try sending into the Angkor Gate will be destroyed. Michelet lost his plane; a chopper was just blasted trying to fly in there. We can't see in and even if we could, I don't know how we would take any action."

"So we sit and wait until it consumes us?" the President's voice went up a few levels.

"Sir, I'm trying to find the source," Foreman said.

"Try harder."

CHAPTER SEVENTEEN

Water washed over the top of Dane's boot, soaking it and going up to his waist as he stepped into the moat. He looked at the slime covered water. The ground underneath his boot was smoothly cut stone. He could see that the moat extended for four hundred meters before ending at the crumbled wall that surrounded the city. Numerous trees and plants had taken root in the moat, making it part of the jungle, but Dane wondered what it must have looked like when the city was newly built and the moat full of clear water.

The air crackled and swirled overhead, dark streaks in the midst of the greyish-yellow clouds that blocked the sun. Jagged bolts of lightning lit up the sky in all directions.

He splashed forward, Freed and Beasley following closely.

To the south, wading through the same water, Ariana and Carpenter also saw the city walls. They no longer sensed forms around them and both felt more at ease now that they could see and weren't surrounded by the mist. But the golden beam coming out of the center tower of the dead city and the ominous sky overhead produced its own share of anxiety.

Carpenter looked over her shoulder, back toward the massive ridge that surrounded the city. "Think the snake has a way through?"

"I hope not," Ariana answered.

"What do you think is in the city?" Carpenter asked.

"I don't know," Ariana snapped.

"I do something to you?" Carpenter asked.

Ariana halted in surprise and looked at the other woman. "No."

"Well, you sure act like it," Carpenter said. She wiped a hand across her forehead and flicked away the sweat. "I'm just a minion, doing what I was told to do. I didn't screw up your mission and I sure as hell helped you get this far. If you're pissed at your father, pissed at Syn-Tech, pissed at God-knows-what, that's fine, but we're all we got, so let's try to treat each other a little better, OK?"

Ariana slowly nodded. Carpenter reached out and gripped Ariana's forearm and squeezed. Ariana wrapped her fingers around Carpenter's, feeling the muscles rippling under her fingers.

"Let's find out what's going on," Carpenter released her grip.

Chelsea eased under a bush, her nostrils flared wide. She edged forward to Sin Fen's unconscious body, battered and bruised from the fall down the ravine. Chelsea dipped her head and ran her rough tongue along Sin Fen's cheek. There was no response. Chelsea whined, wishing for her master.

She leaned forward, this time pushing her soft muzzle against the woman.

There was a hole in the stone wall. The blocks, each about four feet square, were blasted apart, as if a large hammer had come down on them. Dane climbed up some of the rubble and began working his way over it. Freed followed, giving Beasley a hand.

Dane felt his skin tingle as he crossed the center of the wall and entered Angkor Kol Ker. He paused, letting the other two catch up.

"Feel that?" Freed asked.

"Yes." Dane stood perfectly still. "This is the heart of it."

Dane looked left and right. A broad road ran along the inside of the wall. Directly ahead streets ran between stone buildings which the jungle had battered but not completely obliterated. And above them, a kilometer away, the golden beam reached into the dark sky from the tip of the Prang.

As Dane climbed down the rubble, he heard something to his left. He spun in that direction, weapon coming up, even though he sensed no threat. The muzzle centered on two women, one black, one white.

"Ariana!" Freed ran forward.

Dane lowered the weapon as Freed reached the women. He followed with Beasley at his side. Freed rapidly did the introductions.

Ariana took them in with a sharp glance. "How do we get out?"

Dane almost smiled. She was wasting no time getting to the heart of the matter.

Freed pointed back in the direction they had come. "That way."

229

Dane shook his head. "We haven't accomplished what we came for."

"I have," Freed said.

Dane swept his hand toward the moat. "You're welcome to go back."

Freed paused. "We wouldn't have a chance without you."

Dane turned in the opposite direction. "That's what we're here for."

Ariana followed his gaze. "A similar beam came out of our plane, but we blew it up."

"Do you know what it is?" Dane asked, even though he already knew the answer.

"I don't know what any of this is," Ariana said.

Dane focused for a moment on the other woman. "You are with Foreman also?"

he asked Carpenter.

"How did you know that?"

Dane gave a short laugh. "Seems like his reach is everywhere. He's had many years to prepare for this."

Carpenter shrugged. "You obviously know more than I do."

"What are we doing?" Freed asked in exasperation. "Let's get out while we can."

Dane shook his head. "If we don't stop that--" he pointed at the beam--"there will be nothing for us to 'get out' to."

"How do we stop it?" Freed demanded.

But Dane wasn't listening. There was a crackling noise to the right. A small black circle had appeared in the air, about a foot in diameter and four feet off the ground. The circle grew elliptically, extending down to the stone street.

"Hold!" Dane ordered as Freed brought his M-16 to bear.

A man with a large red mustache stepped through the black and the circle disappeared.

"Ed," Dane whispered.

"Dane," the man acknowledged.

Dane stared in disbelief. His team leader looked the same as he had the day Dane had last seen him, over thirty years ago, his face drawn with fatigue and stress, but his hair was still bright red, his body still straight and hard with youth.

"How--" Dane began, but Flaherty stepped up to him and gripped his arm.

"There's not much time. We have to stop them."

"Stop who?" Dane asked. The others had crowded around, watching the reunion silently.

Flaherty pointed at the golden beam. "The ones who control that."

"But--" Dane stepped back, his system overwhelmed. "But who are you? You can't be--"

"It's me," Flaherty assured him. "I know it's hard for you to accept but it is me."

"Where were you?" Dane asked. "It's been over thirty years."

A shadow passed over Flaherty's face. "Thirty years?" He shook his head slowly. "I knew it was a while, but thirty years?" He fixed on Dane's eyes. "Linda?"

Dane blinked, the question assuring him it was his old teammate more than anything else the man could have said. "She's married, Ed. A long time. She has grandkids."

Flaherty nodded, the words sinking in. "It's all right. It's the way it should be. I can't go back any way. Never could. Never can."

"But how--" Dane couldn't get the words out.

"I don't know," Flaherty said. His face showed his own confusion. "I went sideways. That's the best way they explained it to me. They saved me from the Shadow and took me a step sideways, which is where they were. Where they've always been."

"Who is *they*?" Freed demanded.

Flaherty held up his hands. "The Ones Before. That's what they were called by the people of this city long ago. I don't know exactly who or what they are, but they sent me here to help you stop the others."

"The others?" Dane repeated. He tried reaching into the other man's mind but there was a wall there he couldn't penetrate.

"Those of the Shadow," Flaherty said. "They want to take our world. They need it. We have to stop them."

"Jesus Christ!" Freed began. "I don't know--"

"Shut up, Freed," Ariana snapped. "How do we stop the Shadow?"

"The beam," Flaherty looked at Ariana. "You didn't stop it at the plane soon enough. The Shadow were able to cannibalize your plane and the computer on board and move what they needed here, to the Prang. They can only use what they take here, on this side. They can't come through yet, not without protection inside their machines. Neither can the Ones Before who saved me. They also use what they can and they used me. They saved me."

The words were coming out in a tumble. Dane reached forward and grasped his team leaders arm. "Easy, Ed. Easy. We'll help."

"Animals--if that's what you want to call them--some of them, from the other side, they can come through. But water seems to stop them. But water doesn't stop the machines the others use. Or the beams."

Dane was trying to follow what his old friend was saying.

Tears welled up in Flaherty's eyes. "I can't come back, Dane. They saved me, but I can't come back. They're controlling this space around me, but they can't do it for long, and then I have to go back." He leaned forward. "You have to stop the Shadow. You have to."

"How?" Ariana repeated.

"Stop the golden beam. Now. Before it's too late. You only have ten minutes before the final connections are made and it can't be stopped. All the Gates will be connected and then they'll open wide."

"What can we do in ten minutes?" Dane asked.

Flaherty put a hand to his forehead, as if he were in pain. "Destroy the Prang. The Shadow can stop anything you send in here that uses electromagnetic energy. They can see that, use it, like we see light. And radiation. That's what they really use and what they really need. They want our planet. This place and the others like it are the launching points for their invasion into our world. You can't let them get any further."

Dane looked past Flaherty at the massive Prang. Ten minutes wasn't enough time to get back out. And if even if they got out, how could they destroy it not using weapons from the outside.

Dane closed his eyes. He cleared his mind, opening it. He saw it, and he knew that the image had been sent to him. From whom he didn't know, but it was the Voice of the Gods as Sin Fen had told him.

Dane focused his mind and sent a sharp mental spear to the east.

Chelsea felt her master. He was with her. She looked around, head turning in all directions. But where was he?

But the command was as if he were whispering in her ear. She leaned down and sunk her teeth into Sin Fen's shoulder. The woman started, eyes slowly opening out of her unconsciousness.

Sin Fen shook her head, feeling pain, nausea. And on top of that an insistent voice.

Dane? she mentally asked.

We must act quickly! Dane's voice was in her head, echoing through her brain. Chelsea was already tearing at the rope that was wrapped around Sin Fen as Dane sent her his message, showing her what must be done.

"Hey!" Someone was shaking Dane on the shoulder. He opened his eyes and

looked into Ariana's deep blue ones. "We've got to do something. Now!" She was pointing back, across the moat. With a loud cacophony of hisses, seven snake heads on one body slithered into

view, pausing at the edge of the moat. "It won't cross the water," Flaherty said. "Great," Carpenter spoke for the first time, "but how the hell do we get out of

here?" "Maybe we don't," Dane said. "But we've got to stop the beam." "The Ones Before can assist you in getting out once you destroy the Prang,"

Flaherty said. "How do we do that?" Freed asked. "I'm getting us some help," Dane said.

Sin Fen pushed the remains of the rope off of herself and stood. She rubbed Chelsea's head, long fingers scratching her ears. "Good girl."

Chelsea bowed her head, pushing up against the fingers.

"No time for more, big dog," Sin Fen said. She began climbing her way out of the ravine pulling a knife out of the top of her boot as she did.

"Sir, we're only twenty miles off shore of Florida," Commander Sills told him. "This thing keeps growing like it is, we're going to run out of water."

"Hell," Rogers said, "it does that again, a lot of civilians in southern Florida are going to be like us."

He felt warm. He had no idea what someone who'd taken a fatal dose of radiation was supposed to feel. The last thing he wanted was for his crew to suffer. He planned on staying on station as long as his crew could remain operational, but once the sickness grew too acute, he would take the *Wyoming* down and end it quickly for all. And keep his contaminated submarine from hurting anyone else.

Sin Fen crested the edge of the ravine. A black suited mercenary turned at the sound of her arrival. The alarm died in his throat as she flicked the razor sharp knife into his neck. She had his submachinegun in hand before he hit the ground.

She walked into the camp, firing before anyone was even aware she was there. The other five mercenaries died in less than ten seconds, never knowing what had happened.

She caught Paul Michelet trying to climb into the passenger seat of one of the Huey's. She halted his escape by the expedient means of firing through the cockpit plexiglass and stitching a neat pattern of bullet holes in the pilot's chest.

"Please!" Michelet held up his hands, turning away from the chopper toward her.

Sin Fen fired, a quick pull of her finger, only one bullet coming out of the muzzle, smashing into Michelet's right leg just above the knee and knocking him to the ground.

"Shut up," she said as he screamed.

She grabbed her sat-phone which was lying on top of several packs and punched in.

"Yes?" Foreman was aware that his hands were gripping the edge of his seat, the knuckles white.

"Dane is at Angkor Kol Ker," Sin Fen's voice was level and controlled. "The Prang in the center of the city is the main source of the propagation. The main Gate."

"What can we do?"

"We have to destroy it."

"Yes." Foreman agreed. "But we can't send in aircraft. We can't even fire a

cruise missile in. Nothing we have will work in the Gate." "Dane has a plan." "Tell me."

234

Beasley was staring at the ruins around them, taping them with his camera. Carpenter was seated on a large stone, exhaustion showing in her features. Ariana was watching Dane, waiting. As was Freed. Flaherty looked tired also, his features drawn, as Dane had remembered them after cross-border missions. He knew the clock was running, that they only had minutes left, but the bulk of the Prang defied them, the golden beam shimmering with power.

Flaherty caught his glance. "Just like back in Kansas, eh, partner?"

Dane nodded. He lowered his voice so only Flaherty could hear. "You don't know what happened to you?"

Flaherty shook his head. "I don't know where I am when I'm not here, only that it isn't here. I know it doesn't make sense, but it's so confusing. There's another side. Really 'over the fence' if you want to call it that. Some other dimension where these 'others' exist. And they're fighting over there, the Ones Before and the Shadow--that's what they were called long ago but I don't even know what they call themselves. I only hear their voices. Inside my head.

"And here," Flaherty gestured broadly, "is where they cross over into our side and continue their fight. And Earth is just like another place to be conquered and used. And the ones who sent me don't want the Shadow to succeed in doing that. It's been going on a long time."

"Why can't the Ones Before stop it?"

"They have limited access to Earth. As do the Shadow. But the Shadow's power is stronger here. From what I gather, the Shadow have better technology and the upper hand in the war. The Ones Before have been fighting a purely defensive battle for a long time. A very long time.

"They fought here on Earth before, in the past," Flaherty added.

"Atlantis," Dane said.

Flaherty nodded. "It was destroyed completely. Some people escaped."

"These others," Dane said. "Are they human?"

"I've never seen them," Flaherty said once more, but Dane sensed a curtain coming down in his friend's mind, blocking his mental access, an act that disturbed Dane.

Dane pointed across at the *Naga* which was now coiled on the far side of the moat, seven heads all staring back with malevolent eyes. "And that? And the other creatures? The things that attacked us?"

"Part of life on the other side." Flaherty shook his head. "Hell, I don't know man. I don't know a lot of things."

Dane was about to ask another question when he paused. Sin Fen.

Dane closed his eyes. The plan was in progress. He had work to do.

Patricia Conners listened to the plan relayed to her by Foreman. "I can't do that," was her summation.

"Why not?" Foreman asked.

"I can't see where you want to go," she protested. "And the only way I can communicate with the KH-12 satellite is by radio and we know that the Gate will disrupt that."

"Just do what I told you to," Foreman said. "The rest will be taken care of."

"But remember what happened to Thunder Dart and Bright Eye," Conners objected.

"Just do it!" Foreman's voice was sharp.

"All right." Conners grabbed her cap off the top of the computer.

"Oh, man," Jimmy muttered as she sat down at her computer. "You gonna do it?"

"We don't seem to have any other options."

"But how are they going to--"

Conners held up her hand as the other one hit a command on the keyboard. "Ours is not to wonder why."

One hundred and fifty miles directly above the Angkor Gate, the maneuvering

thrusters on the KH-12 satellite came to life at Patricia Conners' relayed command. But instead of moving laterally, the satellite slowly rotated over.

"There's not much time," Flaherty said. "I'm going to have to go back now." He stepped back from Dane. "Can you stop it?"

236

Dane blinked. "Yes."

Flaherty took another step back. "They can't keep me here any longer. It will get dangerous for you." He looked to his right. A ray broke off from the main beam and began coalescing into a golden sphere off to the side of the top of the Prang.

"Oh, shit," Freed was on his feet.

"How do we get out?" Carpenter yelled at Flaherty as he took another step back, a black hole forming behind him.

"You'll know," Flaherty said. He raised his hand. Dane could swear he saw tears running down his team leader's cheeks. Then Flaherty was gone.

Dane turned his gaze back to the sky.

The main thrusters fired and the KH-12 performed a maneuver that had never been envisioned by its creators as it headed straight down, the Earth's gravity adding to the power from the rockets.

"Something's happening!" Commander Sills yelled, his voice echoing through the operations center. "We're picking up something on sonar. Solid contact. Six kilometers away."

"What is it?" Captain Rogers demanded.

"It seems to be another submarine but the reading is very strange!"

Dane was no longer standing in Angkor Kol Ker. He was above, far above, looking down, seeing the planet from a high altitude. And it was coming closer. He reached, feeling control, able to shift his position as he felt a warmth on his face, the beginning of the atmosphere.

Ariana stared at Dane, his eyes totally unfocused. Then she looked up at the Prang. The golden ball was now solid, about five feet in diameter.

"Get him down from there!" she screamed as the ball streaked toward their position. With Freed and Carpenter helping, they grabbed Dane and rolled him behind several large stones. The ball hit with a loud explosion, sending shards of stone flying through the air.

There was a yelp of pain. Beasley was still standing where he had been, videocamera in one hand, the other pressed against his ample stomach, blood flowing through his fingers. Beasley slowly staggered back against the city's wall and slid to a sitting position.

"Damn," Freed muttered as he ran over to the professor, pulling a compress out of the aid kit on his combat vest.

"Look!" Carpenter drew Ariana's attention away from the first aid efforts.

Another golden ball was forming, this one twice the size of the first one.

"What the hell!" Conners exclaimed. She jiggled the control stick for the KH-12 but there was no response. But her computer told her that the satellite was firing thrusters and maneuvering. "I've got no control," she announced.

"Then who does?" Jimmy asked, looking over her shoulder, noting the indicators.

"I have no idea."

Dane could now see the outline of southeast Asia below him. It grew larger at a tremendous pace, the shoreline expanding out of his view, only dark green below. He forced himself to slow down, not knowing how he was able to do it, but he could focus now, and he could see the faintest traces of a rectangle in the green below. And there, just off to his right, was the golden beam.

Dane adjusted, moving toward the beam, until he was going down, just parallel to it.

"Oh, man," Freed said. The golden ball was now solid. He knew this one would take them all out. "Dane!" Freed shook the other man but there was no response.

Dane could now see Angkor Kol Ker below him. The golden beam just to his right. The KH-12 was inert mass now. All systems had been shut down and there was nothing to attract the attention of the power of the Shadow.

Dane gave it one last nudge.

The KH-12 weighed 18 tons, over 36,000 pounds. The solar panels had sheared off early on in the descent through the atmosphere, but their loss scarcely diminished the craft's weight. It smashed into the top of the Prang at a speed of over 4,000 miles an hour. The mass times velocity equaled an explosion equivalent of the bomb Michelet had dropped to clear the landing zone.

Dane snapped his eyes open, He heard yelling around him, then the thunderous crack of an explosion. A fireball had replaced the Prang and out of it flew large chunks of stone. Dane rolled over on his side, next to the others who were huddling behind several blocks.

"What the hell was that?" Freed yelled, as the sound of stones hitting the ground sounded all around them.

Dane peered up through the dust and debris. The Prang, and the golden beam, were gone.

"It's stopping!" Jimmy was staring at his screen in disbelief. "It's stopping!"

"What about the other sources?" Conners asked.

Jimmy shook his head. "They're stopping too. We did it!"

"What did we do?" Conners muttered to herself.

Foreman was watching the data forwarded from the NSA. He understood it, but he didn't allow himself to let go and feel the relief yet. The propagation through space had stopped but the Gates still existed. Isolated now, but that only brought them back to where they had been at the start.

"We've got a second contact!" Sills relayed to Captain Rogers. "Right behind the first one. Big. Damn big."

"What is it?"

"Too big to be a sub. Jesus, it's six times bigger than a Typhoon."

Rogers knew a Typhoon was the largest submarine in the world, the pride of the Russian ballistic missile fleet and displacing over 26,500 tons when submerged. Almost two football fields long and almost fifty feet wide, a Typhoon was twice the size of his own submarine. But the thought of something six times bigger than that staggered him.

"Arm all weapon systems," he ordered. "Bring us in closer."

Rogers glanced around the operations center. The boat's chaplain was moving through, quietly talking to men, giving last rites.

"Now would be a good time for that way out your friend talked about," Ariana said, her hands still working on stemming the flow of blood from Beasley's stomach wound. The ground under their feet buckled, staggering everyone the group, sending them searching for handholds.

"Oh, shit," Freed muttered as the earthquake stopped for a moment. He pointed out from the wall.

The stone floor under the moat had split and cracked, the water pouring through, draining out. On the far side, the *Naga* was rising up, leaning forward, following the disappearing water with seven sets of eyes. It slithered into the moat.

Freed settled the stock of his M-16 into his shoulder and aimed.

"There!" Dane yelled, pointed to the right where Flaherty had appeared and disappeared. Another black hole was opening. Circular, about eight feet in diameter, it shivered a foot above the once more heaving ground.

Dane reached down and grabbed one of Beasley's arms. "Let's go!"

"In there?" Freed still had his weapon pointed at the *Naga* which was now halfway across, less than two hundred meters away and moving quickly.

"You want to stay?" Dane asked as Carpenter grabbed the other arm and Ariana kept the pressure on the wound. They moved toward the black hole.

Freed fired an entire magazine on full automatic at the *Naga*. The only effect it seemed to have was to increase the serpent's speed. "Oh, shit!" Freed yelled. "Move people, move." He backed up, slamming another magazine home.

Dane reached the hole. Together, he and Carpenter lifted Beasley and thrust him through. Dane waved his hand, like a gentleman offering a lady the door, and Carpenter jumped through, Ariana following. He turned to Freed who was firing again.

The *Naga* was less than forty feet away, rising up, heads darting. "Come on!" Dane yelled as he jumped.

His body felt strange as he passed into the circle, like going into a thick, jellylike field, and being pressed through. Then with a snap he was in open air again. He landed on a metal grating, stumbling into Ariana who was just standing back up.

Freed's face appeared, then the rest of his body.

"Jesus--" Freed began when the words turned into a scream as one of the snake heads came through the hole, the jaw snapping shut on

Freed's left arm. Freed's eyes were wide open, the scream ending in a breathless gasp.

Dane grabbed Freed's right arm as the creature began drawing Freed back through the hole.

Suddenly the black circle cycled shut, slicing through the snake head just behind the eyes, the cleanly severed head falling onto the metal grating.

"Get it off of me!"

Dane looked about. They were in a narrow compartment with metal walls and numerous pipes running along the ceiling. He saw a fire ax clipped to wall and grabbed it. Sliding the handle between the jaws, he levered them open, the fangs releasing Freed's mangled arm, blood spurting from a severed artery. Dane whipped his belt off and wrapped it around the limb, just above the spurting red. He cinched it down and the bleeding slowed to a trickle.

Freed lay back against the metal wall, his face pale. "Where are we?"

Dane looked about, more slowly this time. He noted the name stenciled on the handle of the ax he had used. "We're on the *Scorpion.*"

The hatch into the compartment suddenly opened and a sailor stuck his head. He blinked at the scene in front of him. "Who the hell are you?"

"I've got to talk to the Captain!" Dane said.

CHAPTER EIGHTEEN

"Sonar has identified the first object, sir," Commander Sills reported. "It's the *USS Scorpion.*"

Rogers stared at his executive office in disbelief. Every submariner knew the story of the *Scorpion*, lost in deep water in 1968. He shook off his shock. "And the second?"

"Not a clue, sir, but it's chasing down the *Scorpion*."

"Move to engage the second."

"Aye-aye, sir."

The *Wyoming's* crew was dying but they had enough for one last battle. The sub raced toward the *Scorpion* which was moving very slowly, They didn't have a clue as to what the second, large object could be, but Captain Rogers was determined to protect the *Scorpion* at all costs. He had no idea how a submarine reported crushed in the depths of the ocean over thirty years ago could have suddenly appeared, but if there was the slightest chance any of the crew were alive, he felt the sacrifice his own crew had already made would be worth it.

The forward torpedo tubes were armed and Rogers fired as soon as they were within range.

"The Gates are shrinking," Foreman reported.

"I can feel it changing," Sin Fen spoke into the satellite phone. Chelsea was at her side, snout raised in the air, also sensing the difference.

"Do you have contact with Dane?" Foreman asked.

Sin Fen reached out to the west, but there was nothing. "He's not there. Or he's not alive."

"Damnit, we need him. He stopped this but I don't think we've seen the end of it. We need to know what happened and we need him."

Then Sin Fen caught the faintest of touches, like a hair against her skin. "He's alive."

"Where?"

Sin Fen focused. She briefly saw what Dane saw. "He's on the *Scorpion* in the Bermuda Triangle!"

"The *Scorpion* is still moving, sir," Sills reported

"What's the readings?" Rogers asked.

"Radiation is down. The Gate is closing in on itself, but both the *Scorpion* and the large contact are still inside."

"Range to *Scorpion*?" Rogers asked.

"Two kilometers and closing."

"Can we talk to them?"

Sills ran a hand though his hair. "In '68 their radios were much different than what we use. They--"

"Can we talk to them?"

"I'll try, sir."

"You'll be all right," Dane told Freed as he started to follow the sailor forward. He checked the improvised tourniquet he had put on the man's arm. "I'll get the ship's doctor."

The sailor was still staring, not so much at them, but at the huge severed snake's head that was oozing black blood. "Who are you?"

"Take me to your captain," Dane placed a hand on the man's shoulder and pressed with his mind into the other's.

"Aye-aye, sir."

The sailor turned and went through the hatch, Dane following. The next compartment was the galley and they passed a couple of sailors, then they were in the sub's control room.

Men were working furiously, commands were being yelled.

A man in his mid-30s stood in the center, next to the periscope. He had the eagle of a Navy Captain on his collar. He saw Dane and paused in mid-command.

"Who the hell are you?"

"Sir, there's no time," Dane said. "We have to get out of here!"

"What is going on?" Captain Bateman. "My reactor went off-line and we've lost all contact with our surface--"

"Sir!" a man called out. "I have radio contact with a submarine calling itself the *USS Wyoming*."

"There is no *USS Wyoming*," Captain Bateman. "Put it on the speaker."

243

There was a crackle, then a voice came out of the speaker. "This is Captain Rogers of the *USS Wyoming*. You must take a heading of 270 degrees immediately at the fastest speed possible. You are in grave danger."

"Identify yourself," Captain Bateman demanded. "I've never heard of your ship."

"We don't have time," Rogers replied. "It is 1999. You've been missing for 30 years and if you don't start moving you are going to be missing again!"

Bateman turned toward Dane and stared at him in shock.

"It's true," Dane said. "You've been gone for thirty years."

"It can't be," Bateman shook his head. "It's 1968."

"You entered a Gate," Dane said. "You know that. You were working for Foreman and you entered something very strange." Dane stepped forward and grabbed Bateman on the shoulders. "Captain, you have to save your ship. A heading of 270 degrees. Now!"

Bateman shook his head, but he yelled to the helmsman. "Two-Seven-Zero degrees. Flank speed."

"Torpedoes are tracking," Sills was looking a computer screen that relayed the firing data. "Torpedoes at impact."

Rogers waited as his ship closed on the *Scorpion*. He knew how long it would take for the sound of the explosion to travel through the water. The seconds passed by. He raised an eyebrow at Sills.

"We're passed time, sir. They all must have missed."

"How the hell could we have missed something six times bigger than a Typhoon?" Rogers demanded.

"What happened to us?" Bateman demanded.

Dane was the focus of every man in the control room.

"I don't know," Dane answered. "We have to get out of here and then we can try to figure it out."

"Object is less than a klick away."

"How far to the *Scorpion*?"

"Eight hundred meters. The *Scorpion* is underway. Heading, 270 degrees."

"Slow to one third," Rogers ordered. "Bring us about, hard to port." Rogers was watching the symbol representing the *Scorpion* on his screen and picturing the relative positions of his sub and the other one in his mind.

"Contact is closing on *Scorpion* again."

"Sir!" the radio man held up a handset.

Rogers took it. "Yes?"

"This is Foreman. You must save the *Scorpion* at all costs. Is that clear?"

"Clear." Rogers handed the set back. "Great." He turned to Sills. "How long before the *Scorpion* is clear of the Bermuda Triangle Gate at the rate she's moving?"

Sills punched into his keyboard. "A minute and twenty seconds."

"And until the large contact closes on her?" Sills had that number ready. "Forty-five seconds." "Put us between the two." "Aye-aye, sir." "How long will that take? "Thirty seconds." Rogers glanced to his side. "Chaplain, I'm afraid you need to pray faster."

CHAPTER NINETEEN

The *Wyoming* slid between the *Scorpion* and the large contact it had on its screens. The contact was a gigantic sphere, over a mile and a half wide, the surface a dull black, but obviously made of some sort of metal. In the front center, a huge doorway spiraled open, over a hundred meters wide.

The sphere was on course for the *Scorpion,* but the *Wyoming* was directly in the way. The sphere slowed as the *Wyoming* slid into the opening.

"The *Scorpion* is appearing on SOSUS," Foreman was listening in to the report from Naval Headquarters. "It's clear of the Gate! Surfacing!"

Foreman picked up the phone. "Conners, what's the latest on the Bermuda Triangle Gate?"

"It's still shrinking," she reported. "At an even faster rate."

"Angkor Gate?" he asked.

"It's down to a small area, about six kilometers wide and getting smaller."

Captain Bateman shoved the hatch aside and climbed, Dane right behind him. Dane blinked in the bright sunlight. He looked about. To the rear of the *Scorpion* he could see the mist, but it was getting further away with every passing second, the storm closing in on itself.

Carpenter, Beasley, Freed and Ariana joined him. They looked in the same direction.

"Are we safe?" Freed asked.

Dane nodded. "For now."

Foreman's elation was dampened by the next report from naval headquarters. "The *Wyoming* is gone, sir."

EPILOGUE

"The last time we met, you were pointing a gun at me," Foreman said.

Dane stared at the old man on the other side of the conference table noting the changes the years had etched. Foreman had aged well, except that his once-thick snow-white hair was thinner than Dane remembered. "You were lying to me then," Dane continued, reaching down to his left and rubbing Chelsea's left ear. The golden retriever cocked her head and pressed against his hand.

"Withholding information," Foreman clarified. "Lying is too strong a word to be used for the situation."

They were seated in a conference room inside CIA headquarters at Langley. Sin Fen sat next to Foreman. Foreman would be leaving shortly for a high level meeting in Washington with the president and the National Security Council to discuss what had just occurred both in the Angkor Gate in Cambodia and the other Gates.

The shocking sudden reappearance of the submarine *Scorpion*-- listed as lost in US Navy logs in 1968--was being kept under wraps, but Dane knew it could not last much longer. They could not explain the fact that not a man in the crew seemed to have aged a day in thirty years. Nor could the crew explain it. As far as they were concerned, just minutes had passed between the time they last radioed Foreman in 1968 that the reactor was going off-line as they entered the Bermuda Triangle to the moment Dane appeared on the ship's bridge two days ago.

"Why do you still need me?" Dane asked.

"Because that mission you started on thirty years ago never ended," Foreman said. "Because you stopped the invasion through the Angkor Gate."

"For the moment," Sin Fen added.

Foreman nodded. "That's why I need you."

Dane glanced at Sin Fen. Her mind was a black wall to him. Then back at Foreman. There, he could tell more, but not as much as he would have liked. He knew the old man was telling the truth, but he also sensed there was so much Foreman didn't know or was holding back. Based on his experiences with the CIA man, Dane knew it was likely a combination of both.

"I put everything in my report," Dane said.

"Also," Foreman continued as if he had not heard, "we lost the *Wyoming*, inside the Bermuda Triangle Gate."

"Other submarines have been lost in the Gates," Dane said.

Foreman steepled his fingers. "Not one with twenty-four Trident ICBMs on board. With each missile carrying eight Mk 4 nuclear warheads rated at a hunred kilotons each. That's 192 nuclear warheads. And our

friends on the other side, whoever or whatever they are--the Shadow as your man Flaherty called them--seem to have a penchant for radioactive things. We defeated *their* weapons in this first assault, but we might not do so good against our weapons that they've captured."

"Great," Dane said. "We get the *Scorpion* back, the Shadow get the *Wyoming* and its nukes."

"We got you," Foreman said. "You have some sort of power, some sort of attachment to these Gates. You made it in the Angkor Gate and out again. Two times. That's once more than anyone else has ever done."

Dane simply stared at the CIA representative. He felt as if he were in a whirlpool being sucked in against his will into a dark and dangerous center. And to be honest, he wasn't sure how hard he should swim against the power drawing him in, if he was even capable of resisting.

Foreman slid several photos across the table. "The top one is the Angkor Kol Ker Gate. Then the Bermuda Triangle and other Gates around the world."

Dane looked at the first photo. It was a satellite image of Cambodia. There was a solid black triangle in the center, about six miles long on each side. It was located in the north-central part of the country, in deep, nearly impenetrable jungle.

"Each Gate is now shaped the same and stable at that size," Foreman said. "That solid black is something new and we don't know what it means. It's never been reported as long as we have recorded history. No form of imaging can penetrate it. Ground surveillance from those visually watching the Gates over land say the fog has coalesced into solid black. Remote sensors sent on remotely piloted vehicles, whether sent via ground, air or sea, simply go into the black and cease transmitting. And they never come back out, even if they are programmed to return.

"The Russians--and this is classified as is everything else we discuss--sent a team into one of the Gates on their territory near Tunguska two days ago. The team hasn't come back and is presumed dead.

"I'm afraid that although we stopped the propagation it went on long enough to allow this thing, whatever it is, to gain a solid foothold on our planet at each of the Gate sites. That's something that never happened before."

"That we know of," Sin Fen added.

"It means they're waiting," Dane said.

"They?" Foreman asked.

"The Shadow."

"For what?" Sin Fen asked.

"To attack again," Dane said.

ATLANTIS